W9-CJN-424

# Also by Pete Hamill

### Novels

*A Killing for Christ*
*The Gift*
*Dirty Laundry*
*Flesh and Blood*
*The Deadly Piece*
*The Guns of Heaven*
*Loving Women*
*Snow in August*
*Forever*
*North River*

### Short Story Collections

*The Invisible City*
*Tokyo Sketches*

### Journalism

*Irrational Ravings*
*Tools as Art*
*Piecework*
*News Is a Verb*

### Memoirs

*A Drinking Life*
*Downtown: My Manhattan*

### Biography

*Diego Rivera*
*Why Sinatra Matters*

# TABLOID
# CITY

A NOVEL

# PETE
# HAMILL

**LITTLE, BROWN AND COMPANY**

# LARGE PRINT EDITION

Little, Brown and Company
Hachette Book Group
237 Park Avenue, New York, NY 10017
www.hachettebookgroup.com

First Edition: May 2011

Little, Brown and Company is a division of Hachette Book Group, Inc.
The Little, Brown name and logo are trademarks of
Hachette Book Group, Inc.

The author is grateful for permission to reprint the excerpt from
"The Tunnel," from *Complete Poems of Hart Crane* by
Hart Crane, edited by Marc Simon.
Copyright 1933, 1958, 1966 by Liveright Publishing Corporation.
Copyright © 1986 by Marc Simon. Used by permission of Liveright
Publishing Corporation.

Library of Congress Cataloging-in-Publication Data
Hamill, Pete.
    Tabloid city : a novel / Pete Hamill. — 1st ed.
        p. cm.
    ISBN 978-0-316-02075-6 (hc) / 978-0-316-17808-2 (large
print)
    1. New York (N.Y.) — Fiction.    I. Title.
    PS3558.A423T33 2011
    813'.54 — dc22                                      2010026166

10  9  8  7  6  5  4  3  2  1

RRD-C

Printed in the United States of America

*in memory of*

José "Chegui" Torres
1936–2009

Champion. Writer. Singer.
Dancer. Laugher. Brother.

*para siempre, 'mano*

...You shall search them all.
Someday by heart you'll learn each famous sight
And watch the curtain rise in hell's despite;
You'll find the garden in the third act dead,
Finger your knees—and wish yourself in bed
With tabloid crime-sheets perched in easy sight.
                          —Hart Crane, "The Tunnel,"
                                    from *The Bridge*


I have no one to speak to, no one to consult,
no one to support me, and I feel depressed and
lonely. I do not know what to do...
                          —Umar Farouk Abdulmutallab,
                                    the "underwear bomber"

# NIGHT

*12:02 a.m. Sam Briscoe. City room of New York World, 100 West Street.*

HERE COMES BRISCOE, seventy-one years old, five foot eleven, 182 pounds. He turns a corner into the city room of the last afternoon newspaper in New York. He is the editor in chief. His overcoat is arched across his left shoulder and he is carrying his jacket. The cuffs of his shirt-sleeves are crisply folded twice, below the elbows. His necktie hangs loose, without a knot, making two vertical dark red slashes inside the vertical bands of his bright red suspenders. He moves swiftly, from long habit, as if eluding ambush by reporters and editors who might approach him for raises, days off, or loans. Or these days, for news about buyouts and layoffs. His crew cut is steel

3

gray, his lean furrowed face tightly shaven. The dark pouches under both eyes show that he has worked for many years at night. In the vast, almost empty room, there are twenty-six desks, four reporters, and three copy editors, all occasionally glancing at four mounted television screens tuned to New York 1 and CNN, Fox and MSNBC. A fifth screen is dark. Briscoe doesn't look at any of them. He goes directly to a man named Matt Logan, seated at the news desk in the center of the long wide room. Other desks butt against each other, forming a kind of stockade. All are empty.

–We got the wood yet? Briscoe says.

Logan smiles and runs a hand through his thick white hair and gazes past Briscoe at the desks. Briscoe thinks: We live in the capital of emptiness. Logan is fifty-one and in some way the thick white hair makes him seem younger. Crowning the shaven face, the ungullied skin.

–The kid's still writing, Logan says, gesturing to his left. Maybe you could remind him this is a daily.

Briscoe grunts at one of the oldest lines in the newspaper business. Thinking: It's still true. He sees the Fonseca kid squinting at his computer screen, seeing nothing else, only the people he has interviewed hours earlier, far from the city room. Briscoe leans over Logan's shoulder, glances up at the big green four-sided copper clock hanging from the ceiling, a clock salvaged from Pulitzer's *World.* Thinking: Still plenty of time.

—What else do we have? he says, dropping coat and jacket over a blank computer monitor. The early editions of the morning papers are scattered on the desk, the *Times,* the *Post,* the *News.* Logan clicks on a page that shows four possible versions of the wood. The page 1 headline. Briscoe thinks: I'm so old. He remembers seeing page 1 letters actually cut from wood in the old composing room of the *Post,* six blocks down West Street. The muffled sound of Linotype machines hammering away from the composing room. Most of the operators deaf-mutes, signaling to each other by hand. Paul Sann trimming stories on the stone counters beyond the Linotype machines, his editor's hands using calipers to pluck lines of lead from the bottom of stories. Everybody smoking, crushing butts on the floor. Hot type. Shouts. Sandwiches from the Greek's. All gone forever.

One possible front page says JOBS RISING? With a subhead: *Mayor Says Future Bright.* New unemployment numbers are due in the morning. The AP story will lead what they now call the Doom Page, always page 5, the hard stuff about the financial mess, with a sidebar trying to make the recession human. Names. Faces. Losers. Pain. If they

5

have jobs, it's a recession. If they don't have jobs, it's a depression. Foreign news is on page 8, usually from AP and Reuters, no overseas bureaus anymore, plus features bought from a new Web service that has correspondents all over the planet. OBAMA MOURNS AFGHAN DEATHS. Plus a thumbsucker out of the one-man Washington bureau. The problem is that most readers don't give a rat's ass. Not about Iraq, not about Afghanistan, only about whether they can still feed their kids next week, or the week after. Two more suicide bombings in Baghdad. Another bombing in Pakistan. A girls' school. More stats counting the dead, without names or faces. It has been months since foreign news was used as wood.

—What else ya got? Briscoe says.

Logan picks up a ringing phone, whispers to the caller, but keeps clicking on the various page 1 displays. BLOOMIE'S LAMENT. All about more city job cuts, the need for a fair share of the stimulus package, the crackdown on parking permits for well-connected pols, the assholes in Albany grabbing what is not nailed down. And closing libraries while heading for the limousines. News should be new. This is all old. With this stuff, Briscoe thinks, we might even achieve negative sales. Logan gets off the phone.

—Where was I? he says. Oh, yeah. The Fonseca

kid got the mother. Her son was admitted to Stuyvesant two years ago. Now he's shot dead in the street.

Logan makes some moves on the keyboard, and then Briscoe sees six photographs of a distraught thin black woman pointing at a framed letter.

–That's the mother, Logan says. The letter is from Stuyvesant. When he was accepted.

She is staring into the camera, her face a ruin, holding a framed photograph of a smiling boy in a blazer. The woman is about thirty-five, going on eighty.

–The quality sucks, Briscoe says.

–Yeah. We don't have a photographer tonight so Fonseca shot it with a cell phone. Anyway, that's the vic in the other picture. The dead kid. In his first year in Stuyvesant, after winning a medal for debating.

Logan points to a young man's body on a sidewalk, facedown, chalk marks around him.

–Then he's dead, late this afternoon. Shot five times.

–Why?

–The usual shit, Logan says. Drugs. Or someone got dissed. So say the cops. Who ever really knows? But there's a Doom Page angle too. The mother lost her job six weeks ago. They're gonna throw her out of the house, and the cops think maybe the kid started dealing drugs to save the house.

—Put that in the lede. If it's true.

—I already told Fonseca.

Briscoe glances out the window, where he can see Stuyvesant High School in the distance, across the footbridge over the West Side Highway toward the river's edge. The school where all the bright kids go, a lot of them now Asian. The lights are dim, the kids slumbering at home before Friday's classes, the school corridors inhabited by lonesome watchmen. Briscoe sees the running lights on a solitary black tanker too, moving slowly north to Albany on the dark river. Delivering pork to the pols, maybe. Which way to the river Styx, Mac? Most of the river is dead now. That pilot who landed his plane in the river? Ten years ago, he'd have smashed into a freighter. Now it's nothing but sailboats and ferries. Briscoe exhales slightly. Another dead kid. How many had there been since he started in 1960? Five thousand dead New York kids? Twenty thousand? More than have died in Iraq, for sure. Maybe even more than Nam.

—Anyway, it could be wood, Logan says. Depends on the story.

—It always does, Briscoe says, in a hopeless tone.

He turns and sees Helen Loomis three empty

desks to the right of Fonseca. Briscoe has known her since each of them had brown hair. She was shy then too, and what some fools called homely, long-jawed, gray-eyed, bony. Down at the old *Post.* She sat each night with her back to the river, smoking and typing, taking notes from street reporters and interviewing cops on the phone, her dark pageboy bobbing in a private rhythm. She was flanked by good people, true professionals, but most of them knew that she was the best god-damned rewrite man any of them would ever know. Later, the language cops tried to change the title to "rewrite person." It didn't work. The rhythm was wrong. Too many syllables. Even Helen Loomis described herself, with an ironic smile, as a rewrite man. In her crisp, quick way, she could write anything in the newspaper. Finding the music in the pile of notes from beat reporters, the clips from the morning papers, files from the Associated Press, and yellowing clips from the library. She was the master of the second-day lede, so essential to an afternoon paper, and she often found it buried in the thirteenth graf of the *Times* story, or in the jump of the tale in the *Herald-Tribune.* Or, more often, in her own sense of the story itself. When her questions were not answered, and the reporter had gone home, she made some calls herself. To a cop. A relative. Someone in a corner bar she found in the phone company's immense old street index. Her shyness never stopped her, even when she was calling someone at ten after three in the morning. She was always courteous, she always apologized for the hour, but she worked for an afternoon paper. That is, she worked according to a clock that began ticking at midnight and finished at eight. Now, fuck, everything has changed, even the hours.

Briscoe waves at Helen Loomis. She doesn't see him. Doesn't respond. She is wearing small reading glasses, her body tense behind the computer, peering at the screen, nibbling at the inside of her right cheek. Her helmet of white hair doesn't move in the old bobbing style. Briscoe long ago realized that she hadn't looked loose, or in rhythm, since cigarettes were banned from all the newsrooms in the city. But she comes in every night, always on time, always carrying a black coffee and a cheese Danish, always ready to work. And once an hour, she moves to get her coat and goes down to smoke in the howling river winds.

In addition to a few breaking stories, she writes the "Police Blotter" now, made up of two- or three-graf stories of crimes and misdemeanors that don't deserve to be blown out. Cheap murders, usually at bad addresses. Assaults. Rapes. In the city room, they used to call the column "Vics and Dicks." A young female reporter out of Columbia objected, and it was renamed "Bad Guys" for the reporters and "Police Blotter" for the readers. There was, alas, no music in these tales, no way for Helen Loomis to turn them into haiku or a blues riff. Most of the dickheads now were robbing techno-junk: cell phones, iPods, digital recorders. A digital camera was a big score.

Briscoe knows in his heart that it wasn't the end of cigarettes that took the music out of her. Not really. With Helen, it was the final triumph of loneliness. Young Helen Loomis was only one of many great reporters he'd known who were drawn to the rowdy newspaper trade because of the aching solitude in their own lives. Their own pain was dwarfed by the more drastic pain of strangers. As bad as your own life might be, there were all kinds of people out there in the city who were in much worse shape. Their stories filled the newspapers. And for a few hours, the lives of reporters and rewrite men. Until the clock ticked past all deadlines. And the profane, laughing city room emptied. Helen Loomis was now a straggler at a late-night party that was already over. When the deadline was gone, she had nothing left but cigarettes and loneliness. The music of her prose was gone forever.

Or, hell, he thinks: Maybe it was just the cigarettes.

Now he glances around the room again.

—Let me know when the Fonseca kid finishes, he says to Logan.

And carrying coat and jacket he walks to his dark office at the far end of the city room. Thinking: The kid, that Bobby Fonseca, has loneliness in his eyes too. Except when he's writing. Briscoe unlocks the door. Flicks on the lights. Hangs his garments on a gnarled coat tree he carried away when P. J. Clarke's was remodeled. On his desk, there is a wire rack holding folders. One is marked "Newspapers." Full of dismal news clippings or printouts about shrinking circulation and shrinking ad revenues and shrinking page sizes and rumors of extinction. Layoffs, buyouts, furloughs. The papers themselves were a subset of the main story of Doom, everything that had followed the obliteration of Lehman Brothers that day in September 2008. In the newspapers, everybody was hurting. The *Times*. The Tribune Company. McClatchy. The *Boston Globe*. Gannett. The *San Francisco Chronicle*. Briscoe didn't know if anybody really cared, except the people who made the newspapers, the people he loved more than any others. In his mind's eye he sees the three young techies working on the *World* website in their small uptown office. Culling stories from the newspaper, from the AP and Reuters. Lots of raving blog messages from readers. This just in. Breaking news. Nobody in the city room bothered to read the site. Not even Briscoe. But one man certainly did. The man they all called the F.P., the Fucking Publisher.

Another folder is marked "Love." Filled with absurdity and betrayals and homicides. Wives killing husbands. Husbands killing wives. Mistresses killing men and men killing lovers. The endless ancient tale. Almost always at night. After two in the morning. When Cain whacked Abel, it was almost surely two-thirty in the morning. Just as surely, it had to involve a dame. If I live long enough, Briscoe thinks, I'll write a book about it. At home, he has two entire file cabinets heavy with folders that are also marked "Love." Enough for twenty books. If I live, he thinks, I might even write one of them.

Romantic love isn't part of the deal much anymore. Now the clips are full of assholes coming home loaded, going for the gun, killing the wife, the three kids, themselves. Iraq War vets. Or gas station attendants. Or men who can't pay the subprime mortgage. Guys whose wives weighed 108 when they got married and are now 308. Or God guys, listening to the Lord's whispered commands in the men's rooms of saloons or the front rooms of churches. They don't often strike in New York. Usually it's in what is laughingly called the heartland. Where there is always a handy gun. When these great Americans are finished with their bloody farewells, some cop stands before the house of the freshly dead and says: "They had issues." Like what? Global warming? Nuclear proliferation? The stimulus package?

Fuck. Stop. His mind is always wandering now, he thinks, like water in a stream that pauses in tiny coves and eddies.


*12:08 a.m. Josh Thompson. Madison Avenue and 92nd Street.*


He needs thicker gloves. Goddamned New York City is cold, and now it's raining. Spattering the poncho that covers him. The rims of the wheels are very cold, steel ice, his gloves already soaked, so that he can't feel the tips of his fingers. He must feel or he can't control the goddamned chair. Need a blanket too, Josh Thompson thinks. Need a lot of things.

He pauses at a corner, flexes and unflexes both hands. Warm me, blood. Make me feel. He remembers a fireplace in his father's house in

Norman, when the Oklahoma winds blew for days, his mother long gone, his father dressed in an old army coat, all of the old man thawing, except the heart. Dead now. The frozen heart gave out and he died cursing God and the Democrats.

Okay. He can feel now. Move on. Toward downtown, where the truck driver said he could find a cheap place to stay. Decent fella. Name of Vic. All gray hair and scraggy-ass beard, but big and strong. At the mall parking lot in Virginia, Vic pushed back the passenger seat and lifted me and the wheelchair at the same time, turned us a little to the side so I could see the country go by. I held on tight to the thing under the poncho. The MAC-10. Loaded. The short barrel wedged under my ass now.

Later, it gets dark and the truck driver stops talking about his daughter in college and starts talking about Nam. Some place called Bon Song. Or Bong Son. Where he got shot in the left arm and three of his buddies got killed. A pass home for Vic. Nothing for his buddies except graves. Wanted to know about Iraq. Josh Thompson didn't say much. Fuck it, the truck driver said. You can still have a life. And Josh said, Yeah. And closed his eyes and faked sleep. Opened his eyes later, saw houses with lights still burning, more malls and truck stops and trucks, all going

15

somewhere, closed them again, then woke up at the entrance to an amazing bridge. Into New York, and Vic dropped him off, said he couldn't go into the city, had to take another bridge onto Long Island, already late.

—I'm really sorry, soldier, Vic said.

—No, man, you been more than kind.

Vic lifted him and the chair down from the cab, then pointed and said, Down there, soldier. They got cheap hotels. All the way down.

Josh Thompson moves now, past dark bags of trash, pushing the wheels harder, careful not to dislodge the gun shoved under his crotch. Nobody on the wet streets. Traffic grinding along to his left, heading in the opposite direction. Stores closed. No place to buy gloves. Or a blanket.

He thinks: How much bread I got left?

And answers himself: Enough.

Enough to get what I need.

**12:12 a.m. Helen Loomis. City room of New York World.**

She is finished now with another episode of the daily serial she still calls "Vics and Dicks." The clock tells her that she must wait another eleven minutes for a cigarette. Then another two hours before heading home. Her eyes glance at the *Post* as she turns the pages but she reads almost nothing. She removes the reading glasses, folds them, gazes around the deserted city room. The year she turned sixty-five her normal vision actually got better. She needed glasses to read, but the glasses for seeing signs and streets and taxis were folded in the drawer at home. Now in the city room she sees only ghosts. Kempton, pulling on a pipe, referring to some sleazy Brooklyn pol while quoting Plotinus. Gene Grove and Al Aronowitz and Normand Poirier and Don Forst, all of them cracking wise, and Ben Greene pulling plugs on the switchboard. I have so little interest in heaven, she thinks. I've lived in it.

She often wonders if Sam sees the same ghosts. He was there too, twenty pounds lighter with brown hair and a Camel bobbing in his lips. He no longer smokes but seems more drained than ever. Sometimes he must look around the city room the way I do, she thinks, and remember other rooms in other buildings, the reporters cursing and laughing, making sexist remarks, and racist jokes, and wisecracks about everybody on the planet, including each other, and, of course, the opposition. Jokes about the *Times*. And the *Daily*

*News.* And the *Journal-American.* I hear them still, she thinks. I see them before they needed glasses. There are the photographers, Louis Liotta, Arty Pomerantz, Barney Stein, Tony Calvacca. Each of them rowdy and sardonic and very goddamned good at what they did. They are rushing to show us copies of photographs that will never make the paper. Still wet from the developer. Look at this one! Bodies in Bath Beach with heads torn open by gangster bullets. A woman with wide dead eyes and a severed breast. A shot of blonde busty Jayne Mansfield's black hairy crotch, pantyless and winking, as she sits smiling on a steamer trunk on the deck of an ocean liner.

Helen sees them. All gone now, their names mere whispers in the emptiness. Unknown to the young. Foot soldiers in the tabloid wars. Too many are dead now. But even the living are MIA. Living in gated communities in Florida or Arizona. Now the photographers use digital cameras and send their images from computers out of the trunks of cars or from press rooms at political rallies or the press pens above the fields at the ballparks. They never make it to the city room. There are credit lines in the paper now that she can't match to a face. Now they cover baseball games in new stadiums, but I'm not going. She thinks of the game they cover as scumball. It's not the game her father loved. Not the game she loved too. The game of Furillo and Robinson, Snider and Reese and Mantle. And Willie Mays. Jesus Christ. Willie Mays... Now it's scumball, full of steroids and treachery, played by millionaires for millionaires. Played without joy. And we sit here in an emptied world of reporters who almost never come in, using gadgets for stories, sometimes sitting at home, watching events on television, and Googling to cover their asses.

When I was young, there was a comic strip about a guy named Barney Google. He had a horse named... what the hell was the name? Firehouse? Fast Track? Sam would know. He might be the only guy in Manhattan who would know. I'd better Google Barney Google. Now.

She needs to pull on her coat and go down to the street for a Marlboro Light. But first she reads again the newest edition of "Vics and Dicks." The daily catalog of felonious New Yorkers. Two grafs each. Not a name or a sentence likely to attain immortality.

In Queens, some fat balding unemployed thirty-eight-year-old lout knocked down a seventy-nine-year-old woman at 17-39 Seagirt Boulevard. Grabbed her purse. Shoved her to the sidewalk.

Ran. His face immortalized on an overhead video camera. A real tough guy. Meanwhile, out in Bushwick, two employed hookers got in a knife fight on Jefferson Street. One of them was working the wrong turf and a pimp told her to leave and she wouldn't and the pimp's hooker started shouting and the knives came out and they both ended up in the emergency ward at Queens General. Slash wounds on arms, hands, and faces. And, of course, under arrest. The pimp home sleeping, or smoking dope.

Up on Fifth Avenue, near 30th Street, a forty-seven-year-old master criminal named Rodriguez, recently laid off at Pathmark, tried to pry open a bodega door with a broom handle. A pedestrian said, "Hey, man," and the guy walked away. Ten minutes later, he was back, with the broom. He didn't notice the cop now stationed across the street. He started prying again, and, of course, was locked up. Another unemployed dumbbell tiptoed into a dark room, full of exhausted people, in Lenox Hill Hospital. He started lifting a pocketbook from a sedated patient. Another woman shouted. He knocked her down, breaking her elbow, and ran into the waiting embrace of a cop.

On and on. "Vics and Dicks." Now it should be "Tales of the Recession."

Christ, I need a cigarette.

Now.

Helen Loomis pulls on the down coat, fastens the hood, gives Matt Logan a wave, taps her wristwatch, and heads for the elevator.

*12:15 a.m. Malik Shahid, aka Malik Watson. Eighth Street and Sixth Avenue. Outside Barnes & Noble.*

Lean, his full black beard buried in the collar of a black cloth jacket, he is gazing at the books in the store window without seeing them. Trying to stay dry. He is looking for someone, anyone he can score off. Too early. Too much traffic on the streets. Too many whores and whoremasters. High heels in the rain. He even tried begging on Christopher Street. Holding an empty coffee cup from a diner named Manatus. Saying the word "change." Humiliated. They went by, the whores and whoremasters. All my age. One old lady dropped a quarter in the cup.

A fucking quarter.

I need a hundred dollars, at least.

Gotta get it tonight. Gotta get it for Glorious Burress. My woman. Gotta get it for the child. To pay a doctor tomorrow. Me, with no I.D. Me, with no credit cards. Me, who doesn't fucking exist

21

in this world. Gotta get money, even if I gotta take it.

The rain comes. On some narrow street of shops and stoops in areaways, he sees a guy coming toward him. Skinny motherfucker. Sees him trip on a curb, then right himself.

Malik's heart quickens. The guy comes closer. His jacket soaked. Malik thinks: Head lock, shove him into that doorway. Punch hard. Head. Or neck. Then balls. Reach into the pockets. Grab the bills. One more in the head. Then walk away easy. Into the subway. To Brooklyn. To the Lots. To Glorious.

But then: a police car appears. Slow. Cop sure to be looking. Malik walks as if without care or interest, hands in his pockets. The drunk goes the other way, humming some tune, fumbling for keys in his coat. The police car eases by.

Shit.

Malik thinks: I know you are testing me, O holy one.

But I need you. Not for me. For my woman. For the baby. For a clean warm room in a hospital. Oh please. Now.

And wanders on.

**12:20 a.m. Sam Briscoe.** New York World, *his office.*

Briscoe is shadowy in the muted light of the cowled green desk lamp. On the blotter, his secretary, Janet Barnett, has left her usual two pale blue folders. One is marked "Bitching." Bulging with printouts of e-mail messages, handwritten letters from pissed-off readers. Why is A-Rod still a Yankee? Fire his ass. Why does my grandson, now nine, have to save AIG when he grows up? Why no editorial about Obama wasting our money on the faith-based initiative? Take the BMWs away from the preachers! The other is marked "Important." He stares at that one, blowing out air like a relief pitcher with men on base.

He glances at the television set, on a shelf beside the bookcase. The remote lies before him on the desk, but he does not use it to turn on the set. He rises out of the expensive chair he bought with his own money to support his back. He stretches, sees the typewriter on the shelf to the right of the television set. The old Hermes 3000. The one he carried to Vietnam and Belfast and Beirut. The one he still keeps oiled. The one for which he buys new ribbons every four months from a hidden typewriter store on West 27th Street. A holy relic.

He lifts the "Important" folder.

On top, a single typed page tells him: *Mr. Elwood says you should come to his office at 8:30 ayem Friday. He says it's urgent.*

He pictures young Richard Elwood. The F.P. He sees the narrow face that came from his father, the sharp chin, sees him in expensively sloppy clothes, the four-hundred-dollar black jeans, and carefully cut casual black hair. And sees his mother's wide-set peering eyes. Briscoe starts talking to himself without speaking a word. I know what the kid is going to tell me. But why at eight-thirty in the morning? Do I work until seven-thirty and then take a cab to 50th Street? Or do I go home now? Christ, I've lived too long. I'm being summoned to the palace by a twenty-eight-year-old. The dauphin. A kid who spent two summers here as an intern, couldn't get a fact straight. And earned his place at the top of the masthead because his mother died.

In the silence of his office, Briscoe glances at the framed photograph of Elizabeth Elwood, high on the top shelf, beside the framed account from the 1955 *Times* of the end of the Third Avenue El. There's a photograph there of Briscoe with his daughter, Nicole, standing by the Eiffel Tower when the girl was sixteen. Nicole is now forty and lives three blocks from that tower with her hedge-fund-managing French husband. Briscoe sighs. He looks again at Elizabeth Elwood. How old was *she* in that photo? Sixty? Thin, with high cheekbones, elegantly defiant white hair, those wide-spaced intelligent eyes, an ironical flick in the smile. Taken around the time her husband died. Harry Elwood. A genius at investment banking, when no bankers aspired to run gambling joints.

In 1981, Elizabeth persuaded Harry to buy the title to the long-vanished *New York World*. It was Joseph Pulitzer's great New York paper, a smart, hard-charging broadsheet that lived beyond his death in 1911 until the Great Depression killed it. Elizabeth Elwood wanted to revive the *World* as an upscale tabloid. To be published in the afternoon, out of competition with the *Post* and the *News,* who owned the morning. To be published right here, in the building where the *World-Telegram* once lived. She would run her *World* the way Dorothy Schiff ran the *New York Post,* and Katharine Graham the *Washington Post.* Her husband agreed, probably with a sigh heavier than the ones that Briscoe has been sighing tonight. Then she tracked Briscoe to Paris, where he was happily writing a column at the *Paris Herald,* and called him from New York.

—I'm starting a paper, she said.

—What?

—I want you to be the editor, and teach me the business.

He barely knew her. Glancing encounters, at parties, or public events.

—You're out of your mind, you know, he said.

Two days later she was in Paris, on a day of spring rain, sitting across from him at a table inside the Deux Magots. Three hours later, at the end of lunch, he agreed to edit the new version of the old *World*.

Long ago. In a different century. A different world.

A world of paper itself, and ink, and trucks, and bundles dropped at newsstands.

A world that is now shrinking. Under assault from digitalized artillery. The future? Yeah. The goddamned future. Probably starting at breakfast with the F.P. Somewhere, his mother weeps.

Briscoe looks at the second message. A printed e-mail. From Cynthia Harding. *Sam: I know you can't be at table tonight, but call me tomorrow and I'll give you a fill. Much love, C.*

Cynthia. He hadn't seen her in the past six days, but how long now had he been with her? Images jumble in his mind. Going with her to Brooke

26

Astor's place the first time and to Jamaica another time and how he fell in love with her, and she with him, or so she said. When he wanted to marry her, she said no, not now. When she wanted to marry Sam, he said no, not now. She joked once that they lived apart together. Sometimes other women for me. Other men for her. And then together. As she said, forever. After tonight's party, she'll sleep late. Tonight's a small dinner to raise funds for the public library. Once again, she was saluting the memory of Brooke Astor, whose name, Cynthia always said, must survive her long, blurred good-bye and the ugly legal mess that followed. She never mentions hard times when asking for money from rich friends and acquaintances. Nor how it will be difficult to keep the library going at full strength. She doesn't have to. For a second, Briscoe is in her bed in Paris, in the suite at the Plaza Athénée, hears her low voice. Remembers that she took the photograph of Nicole that stands now on the shelf in this room. He folds the printed e-mail and slides it into his back pocket. As a reminder. I'll call her tomorrow, he thinks. After meeting with the F.P. He gazes out at the city room. Young Fonseca is standing beside Matt Logan. With any luck, the kid has the wood.

## 12:21 a.m. Cynthia Harding. Patchin Place, Greenwich Village.

She is wearing a long black simple Chanel gown, leaning back in a Billy Baldwin slipper chair in the small room beside the dining room. Thinking: Why don't you all just leave? Please. I've been awake since six in the morning. Please, just go... The light is muted, seeping from the electrified flanges of old gas lamps. The sliding doors are closed. She can hear the clatter of dishes beyond the doors, as the remains of dinner are carted away, down the hidden back stairway that leads to the basement kitchen. Two large French windows open to the dark garden. The glass panes now streaky with rain. A gaunt bony man in his fifties is talking. Two older, heavier men are together on a small couch. They remind Cynthia of those two theater producers from Dublin, the ones they called Sodom and Begorrah. The room itself reminds her of Dublin. What did Sam once call it? A tabloid version of Merrion Square.

Sodom is smoking a cigar, flicking ashes into a ceramic dish. They are a couple, from an immense white-shoe law firm.

—Of course, I always liked Cummings's poetry, after I learned to read it out *loud*, says the gaunt man. Cynthia thinks of him as a bone-colored Giacometti or an exclamation point under mild sedation. At once laconic and blasé. His name is Carson, retired after many years at an old-line publishing company, a big supporter of the library. He goes on about Cummings in a dry voice.

–But I much preferred his paintings, he says. If he'd painted more, he'd be known today as one of America's greatest painters ever.

Sodom: I didn't know he painted.

Begorrah: Nor did I.

–Oh, yes, says Carson. After the Great War, he went to Paris, painted up a storm.

–I'll be damned, says Sodom.

–That's a Cummings, Cynthia says, gesturing casually at a portrait between the windows.

The painting shows a brooding young man, in a mildly cubist style, the colors glowing. Sodom stands up, wheezing and squinting, laying the cigar in the ashtray. All eyes turn to the painting, and Cynthia remembers buying it through a dealer in the year she took her first apartment in this building. Nineteen eighty-one. Before she bought the entire building and made it her last home. What was his name, that dealer? She remembers his ferrety face, his oily manner, but no name. My mind rusts. How in the name of God did I get to be sixty?

—Just marvelous, Sodom says. In her head, Cynthia hears a song. "Too Marvelous for Words." Sinatra singing it on a late-night jukebox. Or Sam, in the shower upstairs.

—Yes, Carson says. He has been in this room at several earlier dinners for the library. Before the collapse of everything. Has seen the painting before. Has looked it up.

—It was painted in nineteen twenty-eight, he says.

—*Marvelous.*

The word bounces musically in Cynthia's mind.

—Did he paint it here in Patchin Place? Sodom says.

—Paris, I think, Carson says. Cynthia nods in a vacant affirmative way. Yes. Paris.

—What would he have become if he'd stayed *there?* Sodom says.

—A corpse, Begorrah says. Hitler would have had him gassed, for using Semitic punctuation!

The partners chuckle in a dark way.

Goddamn you, Sam. Why couldn't you be here tonight? For an hour, anyway. On the way to the paper. And answers herself: Maybe he heard that the boss was coming, formerly known as Little Dickie Elwood. They couldn't call *him* Little Richard. His mother was a wonderful person. So was his father, Harry. And young Dickie, Dickie at nine or ten, was a nice boy. Not now. Bosshood is a curse. And Sam's boss was the youngest person at table tonight. Called to dinner at the invitation of someone at the library. A check sent this afternoon by messenger, so he could avoid touching it in front of strangers. A lesson from his parents. No show, please. Polite and modest in his matching paisley cummerbund and tie. Until asked about newspapers. Then he fell into bosschat, all about the digital age and why newspapers were doomed, not now but eventually, and a century of their content could be carried in a single laptop. Or better, on various electronic readers. Content provided by Google or somebody. He owns the *New York World,* for God's sake. Which is made of words on paper. Better that Sam wasn't here. He might have thrown him out the window.

Dickie departed early, pleading a morning meeting. So did that hedge-fund swindler, Myles Compton, or was it Compton Myles? How did he get on the list? Sitting in laconic reserve, with performed smiles, poking at the food. He delivered an early check too.

—Well, Carson says, rising from his seat like a long unfolding Swiss army knife. He must be six-four. I'd better go, he says. If my heart bursts here, the ambulance could never get through the gate.

31

Laughter.

–Thank you, Mr. Carson, Cynthia says, rising to shake his bony hand. Hoping the others would follow. The top of her head is level with his shoulder.

–Can I give you fellows a ride? Carson says.

–Well, yes, as a matter of fact, yes, says Sodom, eagerly tamping out his cigar. He and his mate stand up now, glancing around for the door. All the others rise too. Cynthia Harding is relieved. The smoke rising from the murdered cigar makes Cynthia think of other good-nights, other cigars. Her second husband smoked cigars at breakfast. That's why he became the last husband. Sam was a cigarette guy then.

She leads the way down the stairs to the basement. From behind the door to the kitchen, Latin music plays softly from a radio. Dishes clatter. The coats of the guests are on a rack near the door that leads up a few steps to the street. Overcoats are donned, hats clamped on heads. Each wears gloves. Cynthia thinks they look like musicians from some aging society band of the early 1960s. A nostalgia act even then. The door opens and they all leave. The cold damp night air enters, rain seeping from the dark sky, promising worse, maybe even snow. They exchange hugs and good-nights. The door closes behind them.

Cynthia Harding places the flat of her back against the papered wall at the foot of the stairs. She exhales deeply. Breathes in. Exhales again. Thinking: I want to squat down here on the floor. I'm so tired I want to bawl. There were so many things to go over, from the napkins to the coffee. Mary Lou helped as always. As always, I chose the flowers myself. Like Mrs. Dalloway.

Then she gathers energy and goes into the kitchen. The chatter stops. The radio is switched off. The two younger waiters are doubling as dishwashers, a skill not taught at acting school. The air is liquid. Odors of the meal. One Mexican dishwasher is eating. At the far end, standing before the gleaming double-doored stainless steel Bosch refrigerator, is their boss. Thirty-one, maybe, handsome in a George Hamilton way, as if practicing for a career on the Food Channel. He devised five menus, and Cynthia chose one. The billi-bi soup, thick with mussels, with zwieback-like toast made from artichoke flour. Roast of veal, in fines herbes sauce. Braised Bibb lettuce. No salad, because of time. Spanish melon with lime and ginger.

Brooke Astor would have been proud of the meal. Even though the veal was a shade over-cooked. Cynthia moves into the room, begins shaking hands.

33

–Thank you, everybody, Cynthia says, and smiles. You were all just wonderful.

–It was marvelous to be here, the boss says. She hears a fragment of the song. He smiles a practiced half-crooked smile, showing perfect white teeth. She imagines his body, gym cut, hairless. If he's gay, he gives no obvious signals.

–Yes, thank you, Mrs. Harding, a slim young aproned woman says. Your guests were fabulous. It was like having ten different Charlie Rose shows at the same time. So cool.

Out of sight, the chef already has the envelopes with the fee and the tips. Mary Lou took care of that too.

–Thank you, he whispers. Thank you.

Then Mary Lou Watson appears at the door. A lean black woman in her fifties. Cynthia's secretary. Her intelligent eyes look tired and unhappy. She knows that she must lock up when everything is finished and the catering crowd heads into the rainy darkness.

–Mary Lou will let you out when you're done, Cynthia says to the chef, then smiles and takes Mary Lou by the elbow, through the door into the hallway.

–Can't you stay over? Cynthia says. It's so damned late and so damned cold and it's starting to rain and you've got to go all the way to Brooklyn. The guest room—

—No, she says, smiling wanly. My husband's expecting me. The car service'll be fine. They come five minutes after I call.

—Well, good night, dear. And many, many thanks. Again. And for everything.

—G'night.

Cynthia trudges up the stairs. She doesn't look into the sitting room or the dining room. She remembers her nervousness addressing the guests, evoking the spirit of Brooke Astor. How Brooke had done so much for the New York Public Library, in good times and bad. How she believed with all of her immense heart in books, available to all, and believed in preserving documents and manuscripts and supporting research. Cynthia Harding didn't mention the awful final days, when Alzheimer's had erased her mind, while ghouls were looting her grave before she was in it. Everybody knew. They all read the papers. She didn't mention meeting Brooke at the home of Louis Auchincloss all those years ago, dear Louis, decent, brave, witty Louis. And how she and Brooke became friends. Lunching once a month, sometimes once a week, at the Four Seasons and the Knickerbocker Club and Mortimer's. Brooke was always impeccably dressed in a tailored suit from Oscar de la Renta or Bill Blass, a lovely, rakish hat, and, of course, white gloves.

Cynthia did tell the guests that Brooke's great lesson was a simple one: you could be rich, and a decent citizen too. Using a modest tone to avoid sounding as if she were claiming decency for herself. Brooke was gone, she told them, but lives on at the library and many other places too. Thousands and thousands of people who never knew her name were now enjoying the bounty of Brooke Astor. In this dreadful time, libraries were more important than ever. Then the man from the library talked quickly, with precision and wit, about how to make donations, and it was over. They had raised at least one hundred thousand dollars. About half the amount of a year ago. But even young Dickie came up with a decent check.

Now she turns on the staircase, passing the portrait of a young woman by Yasuo Kuniyoshi, and another by Robert Henri, of a Spanish dancer. At the landing is that landscape from Mexico, as solid as Cézanne, as moody as Corot. Painted by Lew Forrest. She wonders: Is Lew Forrest still alive? Over there at the Chelsea? She had read a brief obit a few years ago about the death of his wife, Gabrielle. Sent a card. Gabrielle was a smart, sharp woman. French. Even when Gabrielle was old and sick, alone each night in a hospice, Cynthia saw her as the lovely woman that Forrest painted when they both were young. The woman he loved for the rest of his life. Gabrielle looked down upon him from the wall of his studio at the Chelsea when Cynthia visited. She was not for sale. Must call tomorrow. If Lew Forrest is dead, I missed the news. The deskman at the Chelsea would know. There's a portrait of Gabrielle in the lobby too. Right to the side of a Larry Rivers. Or there was. And a lovely portrait of a young Mexican woman too. I must call Lew Forrest.

On the top floor she enters the bedroom, with the dark studio beyond, her desk covered with papers, closes the door behind her, and slumps in exhaustion. A lamp glows beside the bed. The covers have been turned. She begins to undress. Laying each item on a winged chair. Books are stacked on the night table, beside the bed, a small blue jar beside them. She glances at her lean nude body in the full-length mirror. Her graying pubic hair brings a smile, but she thinks: Not bad for sixty. The same weight I carried when I was thirty. It all depends upon the lighting. But Nora Ephron is right. I have to do something about my neck...

She pulls a terrycloth robe around her, knots the belt, moves into the bathroom, and starts running a bath. She adjusts the faucets until the water is hot, but not scalding. The mirror over the sink clouds with steam. She thinks: Sam has been in this tub with me. So have a few other guys. But Sam most of all. The tub is long and narrow, long enough to stretch out, feet planted beside the taps, a hand shower there too, a Jacuzzi. All instruments of pleasure. How many times have I come in this tub? Alone, or with another? Stop. This is not a catalogue raisonné. She squeezes her breasts. Places the robe on a hook. Then slides into the water.

The heat of the water forces her into the present. She feels years peel away. Decades. She closes her eyes and soaps herself, using a thick white ridged bar that she found in Paris. Soaping armpits. Soaping toes. Feeling her bones melting away.

**12:35 a.m. Lew Forrest. Room 802, Chelsea Hotel, West 23rd Street, Manhattan.**

He awakes but his eyes remain closed. There is a trace of brightness in his vision so he knows he has been dreaming of Paris. Again. A walk along the river. In May. With Gabrielle, for sure, or hell, maybe alone. Birds in the budding trees. Boats. A small canvas on the easel. Yes, a clichéd dream of

Paris. But he doesn't open his eyes. A line from Gauguin comes forward: I shut my eyes in order to see.

Opening his eyes doesn't matter anyway. Not anymore. The doctors have told him that he has 15 percent vision in his left eye, 5 percent in the other. Probably from the goddamned diabetes. All that wine. Too much whiskey. Sixty years' worth. Häagen-Dazs too, after I stopped drinking. Packing on the pounds. He sees Gabrielle laughing, in her ironical French way. He thinks: Oh, Christ, I miss you, baby. I miss Paris too.

He listens now, hears a lone bus groaning across 23rd Street, some drunks arguing. And Camus breathing. The greatest of all dogs, for sure. Named by Gabrielle right here in this studio. She confessed two years later that she had slept with Albert Camus himself, before she knew who he was. Before she met me. And here is Camus in the studio, black, handsome, with a Lab's deep intelligence and grace. Forrest thinks: I can see him, with my eyes shut tight. He is old now, like me. Thirteen. Ninety-one for a human. Forrest can smell Camus, because it's true what they say: You lose your eyes and then you see with your nose and your ears. The dog smells old. When he needs to go down to the street he gives off a sweeter smell, like fermented farts. His good heart never changes.

Forrest opens his eyes, and Camus is ten feet away, just past the easel and the bright splashy painting it holds. Forrest can't see him clearly but knows his hazel eyes are open, his tongue pink and loose between his teeth. Memory fills in blanks, in paintings, in life. The dog is waiting to take him on a walk. Forrest used to walk Camus. Now the dog walks him.

Soon, Camus.

Soon.

Forrest is stretched out on the ancient recliner. His hands feel the flaking imitation-leather arms of the chair. The same texture as my lower legs. A new painting is a few feet beyond his toes, all slashing reds and blacks and mauves, secure on the easel he bought after returning to New York from Paris in 1968, when he was a very different kind of painter. He doesn't know what time it is now, since there are no clocks in the studio, and Forrest hasn't worn a watch since 1961, when he read a remark by Picasso saying that civilization began to end with the invention of the wristwatch. He thinks: I couldn't read a wristwatch now, anyway. Can't see my prick, I can't see a watch. There's a telephone controlled by the switchboard in the lobby, but Forrest usually tells Jerry at the desk to block his calls. There is no television set here either. Forrest gave it to the young girl from *ARTnews,* down on the third floor. Lucy something. Jenkins? Hawkins? He could barely see the screen anymore, and listening to it was driving him mad. The verbal drivel. The slovenly language.

Sometimes that packaged noise made him want to rant on a street corner, like the old socialists on Pitkin Avenue, back in Brownsville. Rant in English. Rant in Yiddish. About the capitalist swine. The injured poor. The need for revolution. It was easier to give away the television set.

He ranted to that girl from *ARTnews,* who wrote an article last year about his twilight years. She laughed at the rant, his ravings about greed and gutless bloat, like Lew Forrest was the first guy ever to say such things. Then he politely asked her to keep that stuff out of the article, and she said, Sure, Mr. Forrest. Then she swerved and asked him what was the best decision he ever made. He said, Joining the army in 1943, on my eighteenth birthday. Taking the subway downtown from Music and Art and walking into the recruiting office on Whitehall Street.

—Why? Lucy said, in a surprised way.

—'Cause I lived through the war, and got the G.I. Bill, and the bill got me Paris. And my life.

He didn't tell her about the Bulge and she didn't ask. He figured kids her age didn't know much about the old wars. And certainly never heard of the battles. Forrest didn't mention that there wasn't another person on the planet who knew about the German round that went through his right thigh and saved his life. When the medics took him away from the battle, he was happy. The Germans had given him a ticket out of the fucking war. Only Lew Forrest knew any of that.

The G.I. Bill was waiting, and the bill was everything. Not just for Lew Forrest. For millions of them. He wanted to tell her, that Lucy kid, that the bill let him say to himself that he was never going back to fucking Brownsville. The Brownsville in Brooklyn, not the one in Texas. Never going back to Saratoga and Livonia, where the wiseguys from Murder, Inc. stood outside Midnight Rose's in their fedoras and pinkie rings, smirking at the working schmucks hurrying home from the few Depression jobs. Forrest made his vows in that hospital. He was never going back to the sour odors seeping from the cellar of their tenement. Or to his father's silence, as he headed out each morning to cut fur, or at least try to. Or to his mother cursing Hitler, his kid brother Stanley studying and studying for the test for Brooklyn Tech. Forrest hated all that. Lew Forrest, the American son, was learning how to say to the world: Kiss my *yiddishe* ass. And fuck living like this. I'm going to fucking *Paris.*

He dreams of it still, that Paris. He still smells the oil and turpentine in the halls of the school. He still hears Ben Webster on the radio in the bistro on his corner. And Ellington. And Lady Day. He heard her sing "As Time Goes By" before he ever got to see *Casablanca*. He remembers the bony bodies of the women he slept with, because nobody that year was fat, and they were all desperate for a free meal in starving Paris. Or just the feel of a warm young man's body. He made drawings of all of them. All pared down by hunger, like creatures out of Egon Schiele. But he never said any of this to the girl from *ARTnews*. He did tell her about his friend Buchwald.

–You mean *Art* Buchwald?

–Yeah, I met him at the V.A. where we were both picking up checks. He'd been a marine in the Pacific, then a student on the bill at USC. In Paris, he was broker than I was. I paid our checks in a few bistros.

–He just died, Lucy said. I mean, like a couple of years ago?

–Yes, Lew Forrest said. He was one funny son of a bitch, Mr. Buchwald. And he was from Queens, you know, from Hollis, I think, and so we got along right from the get-go. We spoke the same language. He loved asking me about the boys from Murder, Inc. and was astonished that I had

43

*seen* Lepke and Gurrah, two of the worst of them. In the flesh! For Art, Brownsville was like a fabulous Jewish kingdom, the hoodlums all members of the Round Table. He had a sad side too, a mother in a nuthouse, a father who turned him and his sisters over to an orphanage. Good for your character, he said, and laughed. But there was hurt in his eyes that never really went away. No wonder.

–Then at some point he got a job at the *Paris Herald*, reviewing restaurants. He started taking me along. The only time I ever ate at the Tour d'Argent was with Art. And at Maxim's too! He said, Welcome to journalism.

Lucy laughed with the shock of recognition, probably inspired by her own, fresher memories of free food at gallery openings and benefits for museums. And Forrest thought: Yes, Buchwald is dead, along with the whole lost patrol of laughing, drinking playboys of the western world who made Paris their own.

Now I'm on the way to join them, Forrest thought. I take all these goddamned pills from different-sized containers so I don't mix them up. Metformin. Amaryl. Zocor. Benicar. For blood sugar and cholesterol and blood pressure and some other fucking thing. To ward off conditions we never heard of in Paris. And absolutely never heard of in the Bulge. What was it Buchwald told him that time when he was sick and Forrest called him in Washington? Remember one thing about being old, Buchwald said: Before you go to bed, never take a laxative and a sleeping pill at the same time.

They both laughed so hard Forrest thought they were at a table on the terrace of the Deux Magots. With the French all looking at them, because the French never laughed as hard as New Yorkers. Nobody did.

Forrest now thinks: Better get up. Swallow the fucking pills. Get taken for my walk by Camus.

He moves to the side of the recliner, twists, stands. So does the dog. Waiting with infinite patience. The routine as coded in Camus's brain as it is in his master's. For a long moment, Forrest stares at the painting on the easel. Remembering that first magical visit to the Louvre, and seeing Géricault's *Raft of the Medusa,* and saying out loud: *I want to do that.* And how he made a life out of that ambition. Working on drawing and color and composition until his hand always did what he told it to do. A mountain or an eyelash. Loving Picasso and Matisse, but saluting older gods too, and pledging his fealty. The visiting New York dealers looked at his work and shrugged. They wanted something new. Bold, they said. Or angry. They wanted a cousin of Kline or Pollock, not Géricault. Lew Forrest wanted to make the imagined world visible. And went hungry too often, even after meeting Gabrielle.

Forrest glances down the length of the studio, past his bed, to the lighted area before the back windows. On the wall, there are two portraits he painted long ago. One was of Consuelo. The girl from Oaxaca. Again his mind fills in what he cannot see. Moody and dark, with golden skin in the morning light, voluptuous black eyes, high cheekbones, a perfectly curving nose. Consuelo, from that year in Mexico: what? Eleven years ago? Twelve? More? *Ay,* Consuelo.

The other portrait was of Gabrielle Marquand. Every time Forrest looks now at the blur of the portrait, he remembers the details of his first sight of her: sitting on a low stool outside Cabrini's life class at the Académie, on a break, wrapped in a robe, with worn flannel slippers on her feet. She is smoking a Gauloise to ward off hunger. She sees nothing except what is behind her unfocused wide-set brown eyes. Her burnt-sienna hair is tied tightly in a bun. He is astonished at her beauty.

—Excuse me, he says, in Brownsville French.

She looks up, her eyes wary and instantly focused.

*−Oui?*

−I would like very much to draw you, mademoiselle. In private.

She shrugs, takes an amused, indifferent drag on the cigarette. He hopes the amusement is about his bad French.

−Five francs an hour.

That afternoon she came to his tiny room, still damp with the remainders of winter. And so it began. She would be his wife, until the day she died. The portrait of Consuelo did not go on the wall until Gabrielle was gone forever.

He shuffles now into the narrow bathroom, lifts a bottle of Evian from the small fridge, unscrews the cap, then shakes out his pills, places eight of them in his mouth, and washes them down. Camus comes up beside him, his nails clicking on the hardwood floor. The big Lab knows the meaning of all sounds in this closed world. The pills are a prelude. Forrest reaches for the blue leash on its hook behind the door.

−Let's go, my man.

He pauses to pull on sneakers, laces them, sighs, thinking: All of this is to make death easier, isn't it? The disappearance of all the people you love. The doctor visits. The pills. The scaly flesh. The faded eyesight. The vanished dick. For every man on earth, it must always start with the dick.

Erasing one huge reason to live. He laughs, and says out loud: *No wonder some people choose suicide.*

And thinks: For me, it's never been an option.

I want to see how the story turns out.

### 12:36 a.m. Glorious Burress. The Lots, Sunset Park, Brooklyn.

She shifts, turns in the twisted sheets of the queen-sized bed, always on her back, never finding a position that brings sleep. Her belly is bursting with the child. She wants to rise, to bang on the locked door that holds her as a prisoner. She wants to find Malik in the rainy night, Malik who put the baby in her. To find a hospital with dry sheets and nurses and doctors. Or even a police station. Any-place where the walls don't drip. Where water is hot. She wants to find her mother.

Glorious Burress can't look at this room, its pale bare walls, its flaking paint, the holes ripped away near the splintery floorboards to make gates for rats. With eyes shut, she thinks: Malik got the key. Malik, that locked me in. Malik and his Mus-lim shit. No surprise, she thinks. He wanted me to change my name, the name that my mother gave me. Wanted me to take some fucking Arab name. He even wanted me to wear a burqa. Imagine: in fucking Brooklyn! Malik wanted me to be a masked marvel, for fuck's sake! I shoulda run. Shoulda slipped away. Gone to my cousin's house in Paterson. Instead, I'm here. Hurting bad. On the top floor. No fire escape. Hurting. *Oooooooooh . . .*

She feels as if a cannonball is trying to burst out of her belly, ripping everything in its way. She grabs the filthy pillow, bare, no pillowcase, pulls it tight into her face, and screams again in pain. *Ooooooooooaaaahhhhhhh!* The pain ebbs. She throws the pillow into the darkness. Then reaches down with one hand. The floor is cold. She hears a scratching sound. She shouts: *Stop!* The rats stop.

The floor is cold as Malik's black-ass Muslim heart, she thinks. Him and his Allah. Him and his holy Quran. If you exist, Allah, get me the fuck out of here. Unlock the door, Allah. Send me a fucking car service, Allah. Right downstairs, here in the Lots. Get me in the car, Allah, and take me to a fucking hospital.

And tell Malik to come back. He tells me he's got some stuff to do, and will bring back milk and bread and maybe pizza. Come on, Allah. Find the fucker. Try the mosque. Maybe he's there praying to you. Telling you how great you are. Maybe he's with some Muslim wife, putting a baby in her too. Find him, Allah. Maybe he's in that Gitmo. Down in fucking Cuba. Nice and warm.

Oh, she says out loud. Ooh, that *hurt!*

Her voice sounds thin and frantic in the darkness.

She feels the cannonball is trying to kill her now. Trying to rip her, to stretch her pussy as wide as her shoulders, to slam out free into the bed. In a river of blood.

Momma, she says out loud, where you at? I'm fifteen, Momma. I'm fifteen and you're not here. I need you, Momma.

She stares at the place in the dark where the door is. She stares at the glassy window. She hears the scratching of the rats. She listens to the rain on the window glass. She puts one naked foot on the icy floor.

*Oooooouh! OoooooUH!*

**12:40 a.m. Myles Compton. Madison Avenue and 59th Street, Manhattan.**

He sits alone in the back of the limousine, gazing idly at the dark windows of the shops they pass. His face looks older than forty-one, his lean body wedged against the door. Under the dark

Borsalino fedora, his face is rigid with tension. His overcoat collar is pulled high on his neck, a tweed scarf crossed upon his shoulders. The limo is warm. Compton is cold.

One final stop on the farewell tour, he thinks, and then I'm gone.

Everything is ready. He's sure of that. Everything except the weather. This goddamned freezing rain. Weather report says no snow until tomorrow night. He has the EU passport and three untraceable credit cards in his new name. He has ten grand in euros and dollars. All the big money has been moved without a trace. The Learjet is waiting near Newburgh, the second in Toledo. Maybe the rain will delay them, but so far they're flying. Myles Compton feels bad about his guys, his friends, his associates, but now at least they can blame everything on him. For sure, the Bulgarian will blame me. If any Bulgarian can ever admit to being a sucker. His lawyers might tell him to say nothing. No matter. By the time they all meet in the grand jury room at Foley Square at ten o'clock tomorrow—shit, ten o'clock *today*—I'll be a citizen of the wind.

—It's the next corner, he says to the Asian driver.

—Sure thing, sir.

—I'll be about twenty minutes.

—Yes, sir. I'll be waiting right here.

—Don't smoke in the car, okay? I'm allergic.

—Yes, sir, the driver says.

He's from an outfit called Eagle Limo, which caters to Japanese and Korean businessmen, and it's the first time Compton has used the service. He has no account with them. He will pay cash. And when he called, for the first time he used his new name. Martin Canfield, he thinks. Martin Canfield. Say it again. Say it a lot. *Martin Canfield.* The Eagle car was waiting when he came out of the Oriental Garden downtown, after changing his tuxedo for a business suit in the men's-room stall. That was itself a relief. The jacket and trousers were bad enough, but he hated the bow tie, suspenders, cummerbund, and patent leather shoes. Now they were in the old Gap shopping bag on the floor of the limo, along with the bunched tuxedo. He sat in this costume through the dinner and speeches at Cynthia Harding's, the tux already stripped of its labels. Trying to look normal. Poking at the food, forcing himself to eat and look interested. Hearing nothing that was said about the library or the noble life of Brooke Astor. Thanking Cynthia as he left. Brushing her warm cheek. Thinking, for one stupid beat: I don't know how old she is, but I'd like to boff her. While she reads a book.

The driver pulls over at the corner. Compton steps out and hurries through the light rain to the first apartment awning. The night doorman nods in recognition and waves him toward the elevators. He glances back and the doorman has picked up a phone. Even a mistress must be warned. He steps out of the elevator on 17 and Sandra Gordon is standing at the open door. She is wearing the white nightgown he bought her in London, the one that heightens the rich blackness of her skin. She smiles in a tentative way.

—Come in, she says, in a husky voice. He moves past her in silence, and she locks the door behind him.

He slips off the scarf, removes coat and jacket without separating them. He lays them on a chair like an actor playing casual. Sandra stares at him in a pensive way, her arms loosely folded, a thumb tucked under her chin.

—You look terrible, she says, and touches his face.

—I don't feel great.

—What's this all about?

He loves the British abruptness of her Jamaican accent, the rhythm softened by the tropics. And the aroma of her ebony body as he steps forward and hugs her. Her muscles are tense. She knows.

He figures she must have known from the tone of his voice when he called from the Chinese restaurant.

—I have to leave right away, he says. For Miami, then maybe another stop.

—The *Times* website says the grand jury reports in the morning.

—My lawyer will handle that.

She stares at him.

—You're going on the lam, aren't you? she says, chuckling in a dry way. It better be to Saturn, Myles. 'Cause they'll find you.

—The lawyers can get a delay. We're preparing new evidence. That's what they say.

He inhales, then breathes out slowly, thinking: The lies are coming very easily now, aren't they? I never even told the lawyers. And Sandra doesn't believe a word.

Sandra turns her back and pads on bare feet to the narrow oaken table that serves as a bar. Compton knows every inch of this small apartment, which is hers and hers alone. Sandra isn't rich, but she isn't poor either. She takes down a big salary, plus bonuses, at that advertising agency in the Lipstick Building on Third Avenue. She was a vice president there for four years before he ever met her. She owns this apartment too, and pays the mortgage and the maintenance herself. A year ago, when he offered to come up with the maintenance for her, and maybe pay off the mortgage, her eyes went cold, with a hint of insulted anger, and she said, in an icy way: "No, thanks."

Her anger that night made him feel like an asshole, but filled him with respect for her. Now Compton sits down and she brings him a scotch and soda. He holds it, then ventures a sip. That's all, he thinks. A sip. No more.

—How was the party? she says.

—Fine, fine, he says. You were right. Cynthia Harding is a fine woman.

—You didn't mention me, I hope.

—My lips were sealed.

He glances at the bedroom where, so many times, she has taken him out of himself. The door is open. The bedding is rumpled. His right leg begins drumming hard, until he wills it into stillness. She surely must have been asleep when he called from that pay phone in the restaurant. He wants to take her to the bed, to make love one final time. And thinks, no: It's time to go.

—I won't see you again, will I? she says, still standing, looking down on him.

He slides the glass under the chair, then stands. And embraces her again.

—Of course you will.

And kisses her neck. His hands grip her small

breasts. He presses against her. Feels himself getting hard.

—You'd better go, she whispers.

When he returns to the wet street, the driver is standing in a doorway facing the car, smoking in the cold. On the sidewalk, some loose pages of the *Daily News* are soggy with rain. Compton sees a woman across the avenue, wearing a thick down coat and a fur hat, walking a small dog to a fire hydrant. The dog lifts its leg. There are many parked cars, but no passengers are visible in their shadowy interiors. The driver stomps his cigarette twice and opens the door. Compton slides in. The engine starts, and they move up Madison Avenue, the windshield wipers moving slowly. He leans back, feeling empty. The tale is almost over, he thinks, the final act in the long sad story of big money. Or my own life in the Big Casino. Hedging all bets. Bundling shit and proclaiming it platinum. Bringing in all sorts of private players and handing them the dice. I never should have handed them to the Bulgarian. He placed his bets. And lost. Big.

The lawyer said, Never *ever* do business with a Bulgarian.

—Why not?

—Google "Bulgaria," the lawyer said. More crimes per capita than any nation on the planet,

Myles. They got guys there make the old Mob look like Quakers!

But he went to see the Bulgarian anyway, in a plush two-room suite at the Stanhope, across Fifth Avenue from the Metropolitan Museum. Expected a thick-necked muscle guy, with shaved head, oozing menace. Instead found a sparrowy little man with rimless glasses, squinting at the paperwork like someone from the IRS. About sixty years old. Asking a few questions in accented English. *And the return is what? The main bank is where?* Myles heard a toilet flush beyond the door to the second room, but no goons appeared. The Bulgarian's face was all lines. Finally, he looked up from the papers, removed the glasses. He smiled in a thin way, said "Deal."

The Bulgarian's eyes were a pale blue, like hotel mouthwash. The eyes were not smiling. Myles knows now that he should have fled. Instead, he shook the Bulgarian's hand. "Deal."

In the limousine now, Myles thinks: Fuck it.

I'm through with it all.

Except I've got enough dough to last me the rest of my life.

At 81st Street, across from the Frank E. Campbell funeral parlor, Compton sees a small shadowy man hurrying along in a space between parked cars, heading downtown, as if being pursued. He's in a wheelchair. Covered with a poncho. In the streetlight, his face is chalk white. The light changes. The limousine moves north. The rain falls harder, mixed with grainy pebbles of ice. The driver shifts to the faster swish-swish, swish-swish of the windshield wipers.

### 1:05 a.m. Freddie Wheeler. North 8th Street, Williamsburg, Brooklyn.

Wheeler hunches over the keyboard, a small gnarled man in a denim shirt and pale blue briefs, black socks, no shoes or slippers. His screen is framed with small Post-its that seem like leaves of a designer's tree. The computer faces a wall covered with larger scraps of paper, a collage of more Post-its, invitations, index cards covered with scrawled notes, jammed into rain-damp plaster with pushpins or tacked up with Scotch tape. The only thing on the wall that's not paper is the clock. Wheeler glances at it. Another hour. Hickory dickory cock...

Wheeler is alone in this one-bedroom in Williamsburg. He can afford larger but he loves the sense of a cell in a monastery. The radiator is knocking, dwarfed by gray metal file cabinets, disorderly shelves of books on movies and music and theater, hundreds of them, and CDs and DVDs and some old LPs: they are Wheeler's true monastic walls. He has two land lines, and his cell phone lies open. So do two laptops. Waiting for bulletins. From the competition...Gawker. Jossip. Jim Romenesko...None of them have what I have... Wheeler's thick glasses are clamped on the bridge of his nose. Time to work. He lays out Post-its and index cards beside one computer. He types in the name of the column and the website: CelineWire. com. And the date.

He is always tense when he begins the column. But he is relieved that he no longer has to write about Lindsay Lohan Paris Hilton Britney Spears. Well, maybe Lindsay if she kills herself, becoming another celebrity martyr. All three as dead as hip-hop...Politics the thing now, and Media, full of the new Names, waiting for verbs...

But tonight, folks...

Tonight Freddie Wheeler is ecstatically happy. Tonight the subject is Briscoe...The old hack... Shitcanned me, when?...Two years ago now?...I got more hits on the site yesterday than he sold papers...Told me that night he needed the space, and the money, for news, like I don't write news... Said the old three-dot stuff is long over, deader than Walter Winchell...Take a look at me now, Briscoe...Take a look at the website tomorrow...

Like most people will...And you'll be the lead item...I promise...Take a fucking look.

Wheeler remains still before the keyboard. He flexes his fingers.

Thinking: I looked at him that morning and said, Okay, Briscoe, go fuck yourself...He laughed in that way he has...The laugh of a half a Hebe... That's what he is, Jewish father, Irish mother... Clear out your desk, he told me...And go see Fay, for your check...I slammed his door so hard the glass fell out of the window that let Briscoe watch everybody in the city room...They all stopped moving...Briscoe's zombies...Stopped typing, stopped talking on phones. Some stood up...Some old bitch screamed in anger and that Jew kid from sports, Spiegel or something, came over, and stood in front of me...You got a problem, man? he said...I said, Yeah, I got a problem: you and all the other losers in this shithouse...I started to go past Spiegel and heard Briscoe's voice shouting Hey, Mark!...But Spiegel grabbed my wrist and shouted past me into the city room: Call security!...And now everybody was crowded around and a guy from downstairs...the big black dude from the front door in the lobby, he was there...and Briscoe came out, and said: Just put him in the street, Harry...Calming everybody down...Smiling...

Shaking his head...Spiegel said, You better go while you can walk...

Wheeler laughed all the way to the elevators, thinking: It wasn't Walter Winchell I learned from, you assholes.

My master was Céline.

Céline...King of all the three-dotters... There, his photo right in front of me now on the wall, here in Williamsburg, plus those lines from *Rigadoon* I typed years ago on that yellowing index card..."Gossip is right at home! Nothing fazes it! Peremptory! On the nakedest summits, Everest or Nevada....Gossip is at home all over, wherever you go, it creeps in somehow"—Louis-Ferdinand Céline...He knew everybody was shit...presidents, generals, archbishops...Show me a hero and I'll show you a shit...My slogan too...They're all shit...And fifty years later, Americans finally know it...I confirm it for them every fucking day...Famous in September, forgotten by New Year's...Joining the mountain of enrubbled American shit...

Yeah...Welcome to the shitocracy, America! Meet all the fashionistas...the priests and the pols...the boys in the band...Editors go, I'm shocked, I'm shocked...and leave their offices for the Days Inn to fuck little summer interns with big tits...Everybody at every magazine, every book publisher, all editors, all fact-checkers, all citizens of the Republic of Shit...My beat!

Comfort me, Louis-Ferdinand...I know, I know, you were a collaborator with the Nazis...I know you hated everybody who was not like you, starting with my fellow Jews...But you didn't lie...Comfort me...I continue your work.

Wheeler starts typing. *We've learned that the end is near for the* Daily Loser, *ancient Sam Briscoe, editor...Not days...Hours.*

He smiles, glances at the clock, thinks: I had to blow a guy in the Elwood website room to get this... tonight I get laid as a plain old reward. Tonight, of all nights. Tonight, when Briscoe falls, and I win.

And resumes typing.

**1:15 a.m. Sandra Gordon. 120 East 70th Street, Manhattan.**

All lights are out. The bedroom door is closed, the heavy drapes drawn, sealing out the sounds of the city. Except for her breathing. The white gown is folded on a trunk at the foot of the bed. She thinks: I'll drop it at Goodwill on the weekend. No, I have to get it cleaned first. She is curled on her side in pajamas under the heavy blanket, legs drawn up, hugging the thick pillow. She does not sleep.

Just like that, she thinks. He's on the lam.

And laughs at herself.

Gone. And she knows he's not coming back. Not in a few days. Not ever.

The worst of it is, she thinks, I always knew this could happen.

What do they say back home? He's an *'at steppa*. Myles tells her Miami, it must be Siberia. Always wrapped in secrets. Turning his back to her when he took a call on the cell. Texting close to his chest on his BlackBerry like she was interested in the messages he was sending, which she wasn't. Now the fall is under way, for him, for thousands like him. Maybe more. It's all they talk about at the agency. Or the client meetings. The Great Fall.

My man Myles is falling too.

Who knows where.

The funny thing was, she didn't really know him. Didn't know his mother's name or if she was even alive. Or the name of his father. Or if he was ever married. Or had kids. Once, early on, she Googled him, and found the name of his firm but no bio, no list of degrees, no experience in other places. She knew his hair was his own but was never sure about his teeth. He said he was her age, which would have made him forty-one. But who knows? Not Sandra Gordon.

She did know some things, which is why she didn't care about biography and other details. He was clean. Start with that. He took a shower when he got up and before he left his office and before he said good night to her. She knew his body was flat-bellied and hairless and free of marks. No scars. No tattoos. He ran his fingers over her butt one night and asked where the fine scars came from and she told some lie about a fall in a playground when she was a little girl, and then he caressed the scars, and kissed them and then oiled them.

Oh, my.

She knows he did everything she wanted him to do in bed and didn't do what she did not want him to do. She knew he loved her neck, the lobes of her ears, the curve of her back, and the delicate biting she would do when he was in her mouth.

She knew he liked her black skin, blacker than a cave at midnight. He might even have loved it. He would stand behind her facing the bedroom mirror and place his hands on her belly or fondle her breasts and kiss her neck. Her blackness made his own skin whiter. And she could feel his rush of arousal, the exhaling, the quickening of breath.

Even in the second year with him, one trip to bed was never enough.

He did ask for the résumé-style details of her life, Jamaica and then Columbia and then Harvard Business School. He always said he was impressed. But he never matched that information with information about himself. They had places, uptown and down, where they met for lunch or dinner, but they were never places where photographers might show up. Early on, she asked him if this was because she was black and he said no, no, it's because I don't want my face around anywhere. Celebrity is a killer. He talked about a shipping guy named Ludwig, one of the richest guys of his day, and how nobody had ever seen his face in the *Wall Street Journal,* or *Forbes,* or the *Economist,* or the *Time* business section, and that allowed him to live and work more freely. Ludwig could never live in the world now, he said, with all these scurrying rodents holding camcorders, trying to get on YouTube. Or be crowned as "iReporters" on CNN or Fox. Staying out of certain places is better for both of us, Myles said. That makes sense, Sandra said. She even wanted to believe it.

One night he did ask her how she started writing copy for an agency and she told him that she wanted first to write stories. About what? he said, his brow furrowing. About Jamaica, she said, and my coming to New York, and, well, all sorts of things. His face looked puzzled, as if she had told him that she wanted once to start a colony on Mars. And what happened? he said. I had to eat, she said. And he smiled in a relieved way.

Sandra Gordon never mentioned this again, never told him that she wanted to write about the things that truly mattered, to make sense of them, to make sense of herself. Above all, to freeze on paper the way chance is almost everything in life. Or at least in Sandra's life. If my father had not abused me when I was eight, my madda would not have hit him in the head with a club and gathered me with her to set off to a kind of freedom. She might not have found work in the kitchen of those two gay guys in Montego Bay, in a house full of books that neither she nor Sandra could read. One of the guys, a very kind man, found the girl a tutor, and she started reading, and then there was a big party and they bought her a pink dress and new shoes and showed her how to carry a tray of appetizers and how to curtsy.

Sandra Gordon, aged nine, was a nervous wreck. But at the party, chance expanded its role. One of the guests was Cynthia Harding, who was there with the Briscoe guy, from the *World*. Her beloved Sam. In the library of the house in

Montego Bay, Cynthia talked to Sandra about how books were the true food of the big wide world, and when she went home to New York, she sent Sandra copies of two *Babar* books and *The Little Engine That Could*. Stories too young for me, maybe, but I was only reading for about five months, and they were *stories*. Made of pictures and those little squiggles called words. Years later Cynthia explained that she was touched by my joy in reading. That I reminded her of why reading mattered. After those first books, she returned to Montego Bay once a year to visit, sometimes with Sam, sometimes without, and she kept bringing books. And sending them from New York. Right up the scale. From *Little Women* to Dumas. To Stevenson and *My Friend Flicka*. And when Sandra turned seventeen, Stendhal.

I have them still. All of them. And the letters that came with them. Full of counsel. Full of encouragement. Full of the future.

The year Madda died, Cynthia came to the funeral in Montego Bay and brought young Sandra home with her to New York. Arranging her first passport and a student visa. Placing her in a special cramming school in New York. A school so good, she was accepted at Columbia. And a month later Cynthia arranged to have all her books, all those letters, shipped from Jamaica to New York.

They are here now, in the other room, the one Sandra Gordon calls the studio. Four shelves of treasure from Cynthia Harding. From Babar to Zola. The legacy of sheer chance. If Madda hadn't hit my father, if she hadn't found her way to Montego Bay, with me in hand, if Cynthia Harding had not come to that party, I'd have had a different life.

Cynthia became a permanent part of her private résumé. Her second mother. She encouraged Sandra's writing, but also supported her decision to go for an MBA, her passport to the real world. To have a choice. Over those years, Cynthia spoke to her about boys, about sex, about putting first things first. Reminding her never to accept the feeling that she could not live without a certain man. "If you can't live without him," Cynthia said, "you can never live *with* him." Telling her never, ever to surrender pride. Encouraging her to be free for all the days and nights of her life. To stay away from men who are too dumb, or too vain, or too hungry. To always be independent in matters of money. "Establish your career," Cynthia said, "before you join yourself to any man." These were all more sophisticated variations on what Madda had told Sandra in her own clipped, stoic Jamaican way. "Depend on no man."

And Cynthia reminded her, more than once, "As long as you can read, you'll never be lonely."

They discussed movies too, and painting, and clothes, with Sandra explaining computers to Cynthia, and unraveling hip-hop for her. When Sandra began earning money, rising swiftly in one agency and then hired away by another, with more money each year and more power, she began taking Cynthia to dinner in various places, from Harlem to Brooklyn, places that her American mother had never heard of. She now bought books for Cynthia too and they talked for hours around those tables or walking on summer streets. Just the two of them. Sam was still in Cynthia's life. Sam would always be there for Cynthia as Cynthia would be there for Sam. By her example, Cynthia taught Sandra there were many ways to love someone. That didn't save Sandra from making her own mistakes.

Now, with another man gone, Sandra Gordon turns in her bed. She thinks about Myles. And she wants to weep. And tells herself: *no*. Not over him. Whoever he is. She turns, gripping the pillow. And at last the tears fall.

When they stop, and she wipes her eyes with a bedsheet, she thinks: Tomorrow, I'll call Cynthia. As I always do.

And falls at last into sleep.

**1:31 a.m. Sam Briscoe. City room of New York World.**

He knows he looks tired, because he *is* tired, but at least now he has the Friday wood. A MOTHER WEEPS. Maudlin, yes, unless you look at the mother's eyes, full of waste and loss and the dark invincible suck of the ghetto. Maudlin, yes, unless you look closely at the photograph of the smiling young boy and the letter from Stuyvesant on the wall behind him. Maudlin, absolutely yes, unless you look at the second front-page photograph. Of the young corpse in the street. Citizens forever of the tabloid night.

Or if you read the story by the Fonseca kid, spare and hard, with all mush words sliced away. The kid was deft too, with the way he folded in the unseen story: the foreclosure sign out front, another symbol of things ending. The piece was so good, Briscoe gave Fonseca an early slide. By now, he's almost certainly in a saloon.

Now I can pack the briefcase, Briscoe thinks, and take my own early slide. Go home and try to sleep a few hours before heading uptown to meet the F.P.

First, a final look. On the computer he scrolls through the day's package. The Doom Page. A hard-news follow about torture tapes. A grand jury reporting on some Wall Street swindle, with some Bulgarian as one of a dozen victims. On the world spread, an AP report from Pakistan about the muscular rise of new battalions from the lunatic armies of God. One of them blew up a school full of little girls, guilty of the sin of learning to read. And, of course, fear for the security of nuclear bombs. People are starving and these pricks spend money on bombs. His eyes glaze, then he forces himself to focus. A global-warming piece from Australia, where drought was destroying food supplies and there was great fear of wildfires. They can cut that for space...A two-graf bus-plunge story from Peru, no Americans on board...In sports, Knicks lose. Nets lose. The fans in the arenas sure to skip purgatory. More rumors of steroids in baseball.

Briscoe sighs and glances at his desk. He sees the invitation from Cynthia Harding. Ah, shit. And goes to e-mail. He clicks on the address book, punches in her name, starts to write.

*Dearest C:*

*Sorry this is late. I've been too goddamned busy with my wife, Miss World. I hope it went well and that you raised a few kilos of dough for the library. These days, they need every dime. I'll call you*

71

*tomorrow (Friday) and we can try to catch up. Dim sum? I miss you.*

*Much love, para siempre, Sam*

He reads it over, exhales, then hits "Send," and shuts down the computer. He puts the folder marked "Newspapers" in his briefcase, along with others, maybe to prep for the morning meeting, dons jacket, coat, and a fedora lying on the floor behind his desk. He turns out the light. He locks his door and walks into the nearly deserted city room, saying his good-nights, and promising Matt Logan to call if there is any news in the morning.

–May the wind be always at your back, Logan says, and smiles. The old Irish farewell. The one Briscoe's mother always used when he went off to school. Or to the navy. The wind at his front includes the morning meeting.

He notices that Helen Loomis is already gone.

Then he walks down the long hall to the elevators. He passes the row of typewriters he had installed on low glass-cased tables during the first year of this brave new *World*. They had belonged to people he had worked with or admired: Murray Kempton and Jimmy Breslin, Peter Kihss and Abe Rosenthal, Paul Sann and Buddy Weiss, Gay Talese and Meyer Berger, Eddie Ellis, Joe Kahn, and Carl Pelleck, Jesse Abramson and Frank Graham and Jimmy Cannon. Bill Heinz was there too. Remingtons, Smith Coronas, and hell, someone had even produced an old Royal that once belonged to Damon Runyon, and that led to a portable used by Hearst's favorite assassin, Westbrook Pegler, who once worked in this building. And on the walls, there were great *World* front pages, and a section of cartoons by Willard Mullin and Bill Gallo, Leo O'Mealia and Johnny Pierotti and, of course, Rollin Kirby from the original *World*. All originals, right off Briscoe's wall at home. The kid reporters don't know much about any of them. If Briscoe sees a kid in the hall staring at a certain typewriter, he always tells the kid to check the clips. Or Google the guy. He hopes the ghosts will rise from the typewriters and touch the kids as they rush off to a good murder or a terrible fire or some gigantic calamity.

And thinks: If the news ahead of me this morning is bad, where will they all go? The typewriters, the cartoons, the framed front pages, the kids. And, shit: Where will I go?

Out on West Street, the wind is blowing hard and cold from the harbor as Briscoe looks for a cab heading uptown. No limos for the *New York World*. Almost no cabs either. Sparse traffic moves out of the Brooklyn-Battery Tunnel off to the left.

No taxis. He begins walking to stay warm. The wind is at his back. He can see the glow of Battery Park City. The sprawl of apartment buildings did not exist down here when he started at the old *Post*. There were banana boats at the piers and in August the cargo included immense mosquitoes—migrants from Honduras, all without visas—and the sound in the sweltering city room was punctuated by people slapping them dead while typing their stories. No air-conditioning. The windows open. Much laughter. Always laughter.

Then he sees a taxi with its roof light on, steps into the street and hails it. As he slides in, he gives the address, explaining it's in SoHo. The driver says nothing, and starts moving. Briscoe feels a dull ache in his lower back. Not pain. An ache. He looks at the driver's name in the plastic slot.

–You from Pakistan, driver? he says.

–Brooklyn, he says curtly.

–Originally Pakistan?

–Eh.

That could lead to more talk, maybe, but Briscoe thinks, Ah, hell, just get me home. The driver makes an abrupt turn off the highway, as if closing the conversation. Briscoe accepts his dismissal, leans back, aching now for the cabbies of his youth, and their soliloquies on life and death, men and women and baseball. Gone forever. Maybe that's causing the ache in his back too. The ache of losing too many things. And people. Then thinks: *Stop*. That's like nostalgia for the clap. He watches a knot of drunken kids lurching from a club with an unreadable sign. Up the block, three very young women are also tottering toward Sixth Avenue on high spiked shoes. To be up this late on a Thursday night, none of them must have day jobs. Or they're college kids spending their fathers' dwindling money. Which is the same thing. Do they know how to sign up for unemployment? How many of them? Gotta tell a reporter . . .

At the corner of West Broadway and Spring, he overtips the surly driver, because he always overtips cabbies, steps out, and walks east toward Greene Street. Two blocks. A counterfeit of exercise. Cold air for the aging brain. He sees more stragglers from the saloons. In twos or threes. He glances up Wooster Street and is sure he sees a man in a poncho glistening with rain. Maybe even a combat poncho. Seated in a wheelchair. A glance. A freeze frame. Then the man is gone. What the fuck? And thinks: Another member of the VFW. The Veterans of Foreign Woes. Or Foreign Whores. Roaming around SoHo like it was the Ia

75

Drang Valley. Or maybe just coming from a costume party. If he has a gun, someone might be in trouble.

Briscoe crosses Wooster and remembers walking here one spring night long ago with Cynthia Harding, the two of them joined by anticipation. She would stay the night. Or maybe a week. Everything seemed possible. Until later, when she turned to him.

–What do you want, Sam? What do you want out of this life?

–Nothing, he said.

She took this remark as a dismissal and a month later she married her second husband and moved to Switzerland for two years. Married the old guy with all the money. Cynthia thought Briscoe meant he didn't want her either. And maybe she was right. He felt then, and feels now, that he has no talent for marriage. For the compromises and little lies that made shared lives work. He had tried it once, and that was enough. He had no talent for the mutual invasions of privacy. Laughter was never enough. At least not then. And maybe not now. After that night when they crossed Wooster Street, he didn't see Cynthia until after her second husband's funeral.

By then he knew that Cynthia was the one woman he could not live without. Life, he had learned, was a series of mistakes, delusions, and stupid losses. Not just for him. For most people. It's fourth and two and you don't score. Down by three runs, you pop up with two out in the ninth and the bases loaded. He said out loud: *Stop with the fucking sports metaphors.* And thought: If the Fonseca kid ever said such things, I'd cut them off his tongue. But one thing is sure: All true wounds are self-inflicted. Aside from his daughter, Nicole, Cynthia was now the only woman in his life. Yes, their lives were separate and private. But who said the sentence that has been moving in his head? You are who you are when you're alone. Even when he was alone, he was with Cynthia.

He stops at his building, glances warily around the wet cobblestoned street, then opens the outside door into the bright small lobby. He checks the mailbox. Grabs some envelopes, most of them junk mail, 50% OFF! TWO SUITS FOR PRICE OF ONE. The same as the signs now in all SoHo windows. Except for the signs saying TO LET. A few bills. He turns the key in the elevator slot for his floor, pushes the button, starts rising. Uses another key for his own door. On the third floor. Only one above him.

On the wall of the vestibule is a framed poster from the Picasso retrospective at MoMA more than twenty years ago. He saw it twice with

Cynthia Harding. He unlocks the door to his loft, flicks on the light switch, locks the door behind him. And sees the framed photograph of Willie Mays playing stickball on St. Nicholas Place in 1951. The picture always makes him smile. Welcome home, it says. Say hey. Joy lives.

On the street end of the loft, a desk lamp glows upon his large computer table, which is littered with folders and paper. To the side, a stack of old newspapers rises two feet off the polished plank floor. A computer rests on its own small table, and beyond it is an HP color printer. Small green lights blink in welcome. Not tonight, boys. Gotta get some sleep.

He removes hat, coat, jacket, tie as he walks deeper into the loft, dropping each upon the couches and chairs of the living area, and goes into the bathroom. He thinks: Been here so many years now. Since they were just starting to use the word "SoHo." Wasn't even legal to live here. His loft had been an old metalworking shop and the bare polished wood floors were gouged where machinery had been torn out, probably for shipment to South America. They all laugh at him now, his few living friends from those years. Briscoe had combined the luck of the Irish and the chutzpah of the Jews. They know he bought the loft in 1974 for fifteen thousand dollars borrowed from a bank, where he knew the vice president from the Lion's Head, then wrote a fast thriller under another name to pay off the mortgage and do the work the place needed, and now it's worth almost four million. Or was. Before the Fall. He thinks: I gotta fucking laugh. Four million, and I never even considered selling. Even after Joyce died. My only wife. Even after I went to Europe. He rented the place to a director friend from the Public Theater who was getting divorced. A friend who wouldn't steal the books. He's dead too.

In the bathroom, Briscoe turns on the taps of the tub, testing the heat of the water with his left hand. He dons a robe from the 1957 Golden Gloves tournament, where his friend José won the middleweight championship. He pulls on slippers and goes out to the wider loft, looking for something to read in the tub, walking past the tall bookshelves that fill one long wall from floor to ceiling. They are organized like tenements. The French tenement. The Mexican tenement. The Irish tenement. The Jewish tenement. The three tenements of New York histories and old guidebooks, novels and diaries that tried to define the city, and always failed. Each of the tenements were about places he had lived, and people he knew, and they defined him too. His mother was Irish, his father Jewish, both immigrants who met here

79

in New York, and their own past seeped densely from the leathery New York tenement, whispering to him as he walked by. And the Jewish tenement. And the Irish tenement. Not tonight, Momma. Not tonight, Dad.

He stops in front of the Italian tenement. Should he listen to Calvino in the tub? Or Barzini? Should he take some sentences of Eco to bed with him, or Manzoni, or Moravia, or Pavese? Ah: Machiavelli. The argument for a republic. *Perchè no?* But then he would be up for hours of dispute and agreement with a man who has been dead for five centuries, and was smarter in death than Briscoe has ever been in life. He lifts down Pavese's diaries, opens at random. Many pages brightened with a yellow marker. Thinks: No.

Nobody.

Alone.

And goes back empty-handed to the tub, slips off his robe, shuts off the faucets, slides in, and closes his eyes. He always loves this moment, the loft full of a teeming silence, a dense watery solitude. He stretches out. Cynthia. The tub at Patchin Place. The one in Montego Bay that time. The Plaza Athénée in Paris. He erases the images, and begins to think of Rome. The yellow light, the ocher walls, the gurgling of fountains. Talking with Fellini one night about Batman.

In a city so old that the buildings themselves dwarf the fear of death. What's a single human life, Rome says, compared to millennia? To be there again, reading Catullus, in some year before Vietnam. And did he really see a man in a combat poncho on Wooster Street tonight? And was it Cynthia who said that she was delighted to know that a street in New York was named after Bertie Wooster?

A MOTHER WEEPS?

Ah, shit.

Briscoe wants to be in the golden city, studying Latin to ward off Alzheimer's, waiting for Virgil to take him home...

Now he realizes that the ache is gone from his lower back, sucked away by hot water and visions of Rome. He opens his eyes.

### 1:45 a.m. Ali Watson. Fort Greene, Brooklyn.

Two blocks from home, driving slowly in the Mazda, wary of the rain, he tries the cell phone again. Calling the house. Hears it ringing. He says out loud: Come on, Mary Lou. Pick it up, woman. Come on, baby. Three rings. Four. On the fifth, he hears her recorded voice. For the third time in the last hour. *You have reached the Watsons. We are not available. Please leave a*—. With his thumb, Ali Watson cuts off the call. He turns into a street with brownstones on both sides, where there is never a parking spot. Some of the cars never leave the block. The owners move them in the morning to the other side of the street, to avoid the ticket, but they are always here. Alternate-side-of-the-street squatting. He clicks the work number at Cynthia Harding's house. Thinking: Maybe they all stayed late. Drinking, eating, talking. Mary Lou forced to wait until the final bell. No. The Harding lady wouldn't do that. Mary Lou's been working there twenty-one years. Definitely not. Mary Lou never did learn to drive, but on party nights at Patchin Place, she always calls the car service for the ride home to Brooklyn, and the Harding lady always pays.

No answer. He tries the other number. After four rings, the answering machine starts. Again, Mary Lou's voice. *You have reached the office of Cynthia Harding. Please leave...*

He looks at his watch. One forty-eight.

Shit.

Something's fucking wrong.

He eases the Mazda up the rainy street and pulls into the space beside the fire hydrant outside his house. He stops, turns off the lights. The wet street is empty. Not even a man walking a dog.

The jobs are going and maybe the dumb kids will rise again. The stats say no. Crime keeps going down. But lesson number one from the sixties is still true: Never create guys with nothing to lose. Not here. Not Pakistan. Not Iraq. Not Afghanistan. But definitely not Brooklyn. Ali Watson leans across the front seat and gazes up at his house. No lights burning. Not from any of the three floors where he has lived with Mary Lou since he made sergeant. This was where they would live until they died. Ali and Mary Lou and Malik until he finished college and went on to his own life.

Then Malik comes to him like a jagged scribble in his mind, and Ali Watson's heart quickens.

Malik, Malik, my only son. Twenty-three years old, but not yet a man.

Gone now for months, he thinks, God knows where. Maybe Pakistan, for all the fuck I know. Or Yemen. To become one of those goddamned foreign fighters we always hear about when generals hold press conferences. Or an amateur jihadist, who'll come home on a U.S. passport. The kind of knucklehead we talk about at the weekly meetings of the task force. He knows just one thing about Malik. He's gone. The task force has him on the list, and know to call if they pick up a scent. Ali Watson had told them all about his son. Ali became a Muslim because of Malcolm, and Malik became a Muslim because of Ali, his father. Mary Lou never became a Muslim, shouting at Ali once, *They were the goddamned slavers who sold us to the English!* And she was right. She always is. After the '93 bombing of the World Trade Center, Ali gave it up. Good-bye, Islam. Fuck you, and Paradise too.

Malik was seven in '93. Bright, smiling, an obsessive fan of the Mets and the Knicks. When he was twelve, he discovered the shelf near the top of the bookcase on the second floor. The shelf with all of Ali's old books about Malcolm and Islam. Books no longer read. Books he should have thrown out. A year later the boy told his mother and father that he was now a Muslim. Mary Lou said, *Don't be ridiculous.* But he went his own way, with a few friends that he had converted. Or who had converted him. He went to a mosque not far from here, just as he went to Brooklyn Tech, six blocks in the other direction. Ali tried to talk to him about it, to put doubt in him, or common sense, but he looked at his father with that knowing smile people have when they believe they know the truth, and you don't. Not a smile. A sneer. And he started looking at his mother with dead, bitter eyes.

Malik prayed five times a day, shoes off, facing Mecca. Even when he was out among the crowds on DeKalb Avenue. He didn't smoke or drink, of course, and that was a good thing. But he became more evasive by the day, barely talking to Mary Lou, looking at Ali as if he were a traitor. Ali tried to talk about the Knicks and the Mets, but Malik made a snorting sound with his lips, and retreated into silence. He was living with a secret script. Ali slipped into the boy's mosque a few times, well to the rear, but never heard any talk of jihad or violence, only the usual stuff about submission and Allah. But as Malik grew up, taller and more muscular than his father, he became more rigid, more fanatical, right up to September 11. After that, he was even worse. He tried to grow out his beard, but the hair was thin and scraggly, a teenaged sketch. He wore a kufi on his head. He had been accepted by CUNY, but when he turned eighteen, he left home. Taking a place with his friend Jamal. A month later, Ali checked with CUNY and discovered that Malik had stopped going to classes. Ali used all of his skills and his craft, his police and FBI friends, his gangster contacts, to track Malik, but all he could find were rumors and maybes. He gave many details to the task force, just in case. There were a few reports. Malik, Jamal, and a few other Brooklyn friends had been seen in Jersey City, or in Miami, or preaching in Compton, out in L.A. If Malik had a cell phone, it was certainly under another name. And serious jihadists didn't have Facebook pages. Malik called home once and Mary Lou answered. She insisted he come home, he shouted at her in Arabic (or what she thought was Arabic) and hung up. He never called again.

Ali told much of this to Ray Kelly when, as police commissioner, Kelly asked him to join the Joint Terrorism Task Force. Ali begged off. "Imagine if you had a son that might be in the Irish Republican Army," he said. "Not *is*. But *might* be." Kelly smiled and nodded, the way any good police commissioner would, especially a mick. Then he said he needed Ali because he understood the Muslim mind, and the way it worked in New York among American Muslims.

—Besides, he said. You can keep an eye out for Malik.

So many years now since September 11, and Ali still did his best for Kelly, every day of the week or, more often, every night. Some asshole shakes Ajax on the steps of a post office in the Bronx, and off goes Ali Watson and his young partner, Malachy Devlin. Three assholes in Crown Heights are bullshitting in a bar about blowing up the Williamsburg Bridge, the tip comes in, off go Ali and Malachy, saying that if these guys succeeded they would win an architecture improvement award.

Malachy Devlin is a good cop, a good partner, a Fed, smart, cool. The other guys say they are a typical Morgan Freeman–Colin Farrell movie. Sometimes Ali feels that way too. But the partners are not close friends. The younger guy has a wife and a little kid. He likes regular hours, and then goes home. But they work hard on the trail of knuckleheads who might be terrorists. If the evidence is more than just bullshitting, they lock them up, search the dumps where they live, track down their former wives and abandoned sons wherever they might be, set one free and follow him around, and if they realize it's just another case of three assholes bullshitting in a bar, which ain't a felony, they let them go. They process tips, calls, anonymous notes, rumors, and the Feds' reporting once a month about "chatter." In all of this, there is little to be found about Malik.

And here is Ali Watson, on his own block, caressing the gun in his holster before getting out of the car. Afraid Malik has come to visit. Afraid he called Mary Lou, out of the blue. Afraid she let him in. Afraid she said something that he thought dissed Allah. The world is full of nutso shit. Maybe it's a lot simpler. Just some junkie on the prowl. Maybe.

Ali unlocks the gate under the stoop, pauses, hears nothing, then opens the two doors leading to the garden floor and the kitchen. He does not turn on a light, but he knows every inch of this house, and in each room there are small plug-ins that throw pinpoints of light across the floors. He moves to the rear windows, holds one curtain aside, gazes into the garden. Empty.

Don't be here, Malik. Please. Be in fucking Pakistan. Be in Afghanistan. Be in Jersey fucking City.

Silently, he moves through the house, up two flights of stairs, inhaling the familiar odors of home, of food and old books and couches, of the place where he lives with his woman, the home place. His gun is now in his right hand. He passes the room that once was Malik's, but the door is open and the shades half drawn. Nobody there. He lifts a leg over the one step that creaks and then is on the second landing. Waits.

Nothing.

In the top-floor bedroom he takes the flashlight from beside the bed, turns it on. The bed is crisply made. All clothes are hung in the closets. Books and a clock beside the bed on Mary Lou's side. The bathroom is as it always is: gleaming and clean. No scrawled message on the mirror or walls. Watson exhales. Warmer here. Heat rising. But no human presence. His mouth is dry now. Holding the flashlight, he turns and hurries downstairs.

There are no signs of alarm anywhere. No Arabic graffiti. No blood.

In the kitchen he takes a Diet Coke from the refrigerator, leaves the door open, stands in the cold shaft of light and swallows a long draft. He screws the cap back on the bottle, places it on the door shelf, closes the door, and stands there in the dark.

Malik, Malik.

And oh, my Mary Lou.

He exhales hard, then switches on the ceiling light.

*1:55 a.m. Bobby Fonseca. Nighttown restaurant, Stone Street, Manhattan.*

When he walks in, the place is almost empty. A pair of bulky guys are at the bar. Maybe off-duty firemen. Laughing with a blonde barmaid. Three Japanese guys are at one table in the front room, looking gloomy in suits and loosened ties. What time zones do their bosses live in? They look like gamblers waiting for results. From the Nikkei, for sure. One has a laptop on his knee, flicking, mumbling to the others. All news all the time. Irish music plays from the sound system, the volume down low. The Chieftains. There is still light in the kitchen. No sign of Leopold Bloom. Or Stephen Daedalus. The large framed photograph of Mr. Joyce looks pensive in the gloom of the empty second room.

But there's Victoria, her arms folded, shoulder leaning against an arch. Lost in thought. Jesus Christ, Fonseca thinks, she is so fucking beautiful.

He peels off his dripping raincoat, drapes it on the back of one chair, lays his wool hat on another, sits at a table. His scraping of a chair against the floor wakes Victoria. She comes to him, smiling broadly.

—Hey! she says.

Her eyes are bright. Her breasts masked with the top of a dark green apron bearing the name of the restaurant.

—Hey, Victoria.

—You eating? Ya got five minutes to order.

—First things first, I guess. Three scrambled eggs, crisp bacon, rye toast, and a beer.

She touches his shoulder, hurries to the kitchen.

Victoria Collins, he thinks. Why would anyone in Bayside call an Irish kid Victoria? The mother must have picked the name. Or maybe Victoria did. Was she really baptized Bridget? They graduated from J-school at the same time. Last year. Except she was at Columbia and

Fonseca at NYU. He got a shot at the *World*. She was still looking. Her father some kind of union boss. Operating Engineers? Won't let her be an unpaid intern. Isn't in favor of free blogging. So she's a waitress. Waiting. Maybe envious of me.

She returns.

—So whattaya working on for tomorrow? she says.

—A murder. Sad. A bright kid shot dead. A kid from Stuyvesant.

—Chinese?

—No, black. When I left the paper, it was the wood. Who knows by tomorrow? The night is young.

—It is, she says, then hurries to the kitchen.

He thinks: Forget the eggs. Let me lick your thighs.

Victoria Collins returns with eggs, toast, beer on a tray. She lays each item gently in front of Fonseca.

—Heard anything? he says.

—A friend called, says there might be an opening at the *Daily News*. I sent a follow-up to my résumé. They must have three of them on file.

Fonseca lifts some egg on his fork.

—Maybe call the editor, Victoria. You know, follow-up with a voice attached. Try to see him.

A pause. She stands there.

—Want to celebrate the wood? she says. Without a smile.

Fonseca stops eating.

—Sure.

—Eat fast, she says. We're almost closing.

She walks back toward the kitchen and turns into a back room. Fonseca crunches a piece of toast. He has been here five times in the past month, and she always laughed when he came on to her. Now ... *now?* Tonight?

The firemen start arguing with a third man. A short red-haired guy. A regular. Fonseca can hear the names Lee and Gallinari and knows they are arguing about the Knicks. God. Don't they know that life is short? He eats quickly. Too quickly. Belches. And sees Victoria Collins come out of the back room. The apron is gone but she is carrying a thick coat under one arm. She hands him a bill. He hands her his Visa card.

—Right back, she says.

The three Japanese guys are standing now. Fonseca hears a sentence from the bar: *You kiddin' me, Charlie? Nate is great!* He sips his beer. And then she is back with the green plastic wallet that holds the check and a pen.

He opens it, starts calculating.

—No tip, she says.

—But I—

—My turn.

A minute later, they are out on cobblestones in the rain. Her down jacket has a hood. His wool hat is pulled tight on his skull. They walk toward light but there are no cabs.

—Where do you live, anyway? Fonseca says.

—East Village. Avenue B and Twelfth Street. And hey, Fonseca, what do I call ya?

—Fonseca's fine.

—I like Fonseca. Three Latin syllables! But, hey, Fonseca: whatever ya do, don't call me Vicky.

Victoria Collins laughs.

—Okay, Collins. Whatever you say.

A taxi turns the corner. They start waving and shouting. The taxi stops and they get in. The backseat is wet, but so are they.

As they are crossing Houston Street, Fonseca feels the cell phone thumping in his trouser pocket.


**2:07 a.m. Helen Loomis. Second Avenue at 9th Street, Manhattan.**

She's been home for thirty minutes now, but after a shower, and four cigarettes, she can't sleep. The apartment is dark, as always, and she knows it is spotless. Two doors are closed between the bedroom and the windows that open onto Second Avenue but she can still hear the usual sounds of emergency from the street, as she does every night. First, there was the ambulance siren, then heavier screams from a fire engine. They fade away, heading downtown. Then a shout, followed by an answer, then another shout, like a dialogue between angry seals. A new version of Whitman's barbaric yawp.

Helen Loomis turns on her side, squashing a pillow over her head, then hears a second fire truck, wilder, more guttural, the ladder. She gets up, pulls on a robe, opens the door to the kitchen, then to the long room with its dining table and bookshelves, and on into the living room. She opens the drapes a few inches, peers out into the rain-lashed avenue.

Across the street, under an awning, she sees Federico the mambo dancer. It's his time, and he is dancing. She knows he is seventy-two, knows that his wife is dead, his two daughters living in Miami, one grandson serving in Afghanistan. He should be too old for this. But Federico surges with life. He wears a woven straw hat, a Mets jacket, polished boots with lifts. Wires feed into his ears from a machine strapped to his chest. The wires give him Tito Puente. They give him

Machito. They give him El Gran Combo and Cortijo and Rubén Blades and Eddie Palmieri. They give him the Palladium on Broadway in 1958. She knows, because Federico has told her so, on many warm nights when she meets him while hurrying home from the *World*. He dances alone on the avenue with the precision and lightness of a twenty-year-old. He never looks for applause. He doesn't ask for loose change. He doesn't flirt. He dances for himself. He dances to avoid going home to the apartment where the only resident is himself. He dances to ward off loneliness.

Helen closes the drapes, whispering a *"Buenas noches,* Federico." She moves back through the dark apartment. She thinks about a cigarette, decides no, and returns to bed. A few minutes later, she is asleep.

A few minutes after that, the telephone rings.

### 2:17 a.m. Josh Thompson. Union Square, Manhattan.

He is staring at George Washington's iron ass in this deserted park and the rain starts hammering the poncho. The last leaves are falling. A stray dog hurries from tree to tree, with nobody ready to pick up his crap. He's my brother, that dog, Josh

Thompson thinks. All alone in a cold rain. At least Josh is wearing two sweaters. And the poncho is pulled taut over his stumps, with the gun steadied by his hands. The dog has nothing. And it's colder now. He tells himself to suck in the wet air, suck the rain. Thinking: I did too much time sucking sand.

He closes his eyes and he's in a Humvee and the sky is white and the sand is white, blinding him, and they're all talking nonsense, making jokes, trying to see in the white, trying to see wires coming out of the sand beside the road, and his lips are dry and burnt and the snot is like tiny rocks in his nose and his throat is dry, and someone passes a water bottle and Josh takes a swig, and on they go, into the dry killing whiteness. The dryness soaking up all wetness. And sometimes he even gets a hard-on.

Thinking: I gotta have payback.

Thinking now: Allah took my legs. Took my balls. And not just Allah and the people who love his sorry ass. All kinds of Americans too. Never could get payback. Not from the Iraqis. Not from nobody else.

In Walter Reed that time? The shrink said to him, Make a list. A payback list. Get it out of your head, the shrink said. So he put down the names. Put down the Americans too. Bush. Cheney.

Rumsfeld. Franks. The lieutenant too. Armstrong. He thinks: That was stupid, putting him on the list. He was dead. Killed the same time I got it. Stupid bastard, riding us straight into a white sandy road with wrecked cars all over, and wrecked houses too, like he was Bruce Willis in a fucking movie. He was in Iraq three weeks and thought he was a little Patton. He charged us right into it. The IED blew his fucking head off. So there's no payback for him. I'll never see his squinty-ass little eyes again. His mouth with no lips. Just a line is all. Telling us, Go, go, get in there, and then kuh-fuckin-boom! Killed Whitey too. And Langella. And Alfredo Salinas. And Freddie Goldsmith. Me, I'm the only one that lived. To come to this bench in the fucking New York rain, just behind George Washington. To say, out loud, to an audience of raindrops: *The towelheads took my balls.*

They took his wife too. Took Wendy and the little girl, Flora. He hardly knew that little girl. She was what? A year old when he went to Iraq? So he could get a reward at the other end, get the G.I. Bill, get educated past what he was and where he came from. To make a good life for Wendy and Flora and whatever other kids they'd have. He sees Wendy holding Flora at the airfield in Texas while the band played and everybody saluted, and Flora was bawling, the tears just pouring down her face, her mouth like Jell-O, pointing a chubby little finger at him, and then Josh Thompson followed the others right on the plane. He waved from the door. Wendy waved back. The girl bawled. Then Pfc. Josh Thompson was off to the war. Wendy wrote him letters. Every day, then three days a week, then every Sunday. She sent him pictures of Flora too, in a bright little new dress, standing up and holding the couch, bigger each time, the brown eyes always sad. Josh cried each night after seeing new pictures. Cried quiet, not making a sound. Cried into the pillow.

Most soldiers knew the computer, but not Josh. His shit-ass school had nothing. But one of the guys, Norris, helped him get online and Wendy sent him some video through that, he didn't know how, and Josh saw that Wendy was getting fat, in a big oversized yellow dress, pure Target, or Walmart, a dress like a yellow tent, and her face was all round, and her tits bigger, and Josh Thompson wondered: Who took the video? Norris showed him how to write an e-mail and he asked his wife. Wendy said it was a woman friend from church.

But trying to sleep, he wondered: Was it some guy took the video? Some guy from the base who makes the video, waits till little Flora is asleep, and then Josh sees Wendy in the living room, and she's doing what she did with him one time, but with the guy sitting on the couch, Wendy kneeling on the floor, on the rug.

That night, Josh masturbated in the dark tent, seeing himself on top of Wendy, jamming it home after she blew that guy. Josh playing with his pud, which is what almost everybody did at night because none of them could go anywhere in Iraq to get laid. If you slipped off the base, looking for Iraqi pussy, they buried your body without a head. So every night in Iraq, thousands of guys just beat their meat. The last resort of the lonely. Coming in a Kleenex. Or a washcloth. Or a sock. Some guys scored with the women soldiers, even married them so they could get laid before dying. The way Josh almost died. He closes his eyes. Pay you back. Sees the blinding light, the explosion, shrieking voices of people he can't see. Others quiet. This one's alive! *Morphine!* Stretcher! A chopper then, followed by a blur, and he woke up in Germany. How many days later? Sixteen, they told him. And Wendy was there, out in the hall, that's what the medic told him. The room bright, with blue trim on the windows. You want to see her now, your wife? Talking very carefully. Yeah, Josh Thompson said. Yeah. The medics unfolded a portable screen to give them privacy and Josh saw that there were eight or nine other guys in the long room, all on beds. Each one totally fucking alone.

Wendy came in, wearing the yellow dress from the video and her hair all curly and too much lipstick, all curves and flesh. She was breathing hard, her eyes full of tears, and she leaned over and kissed Josh on the mouth. He couldn't smell her. He couldn't smell anything, and still can't. There was a buzz in his head too, like a dentist drill.

–Hello, baby, she whispered.

–Hello, Wendy, baby.

–I'm so sorry, Josh.

–Me too.

She started telling him that the church raised money to send her there to Germany, that everything was okay with Flora, she was staying at Wendy's mother's house in Norman, that she was praying for him too. Everybody was praying for him. The whole state of Oklahoma was praying for him. She had cookies from the church for him and the other guys. She had flowers. And a book about the Hornets, who played two seasons in Oklahoma City after Katrina. And, oh, it was in the *papers,* she said, what happened to you.

–Can I go home now? he said.

–Not yet, the doctor says.

Josh pushed a hand under the sheet and blanket. There was a thick pad of gauze where his penis used to be. To the side, left and right, more bulging bandages. He wiggled his toes, or thought he did. But there were no toes, because there were no feet and no legs. Jesus Christ.

—Let me see it, Wendy said.

—No.

—I need to see it, she said, her voice colder. I'm your wife.

—Wait till it heals.

She came around to the side and lifted the sheet and blanket. Her eyes grew wide with horror, her eyebrows arched, she made a choked sound in her throat. Then she squeezed his hand, covered him again, seemed to melt a bit, and walked heavily to the door. He never saw her again. She went home to Norman and closed the house and picked up Flora and went away. She divorced him by mail a year later when he was in Walter Reed. On that day in Germany, the cookies were great but he couldn't smell the flowers.

And now he's freezing in this park in New York fucking City. The rain harder. The MAC-10 icy to the touch of his bare hand. The second clip is cold and hard against his gut. Thinking: Payback.

And wondering where that little girl is now, his daughter, little Flora, and whether her eyes are still sad.

George Washington is all green and shiny with rain. Beyond him, a red light blinks on but there is no traffic for it to stop.

He unlocks the wheels and rolls to the edge of the park. Something called Filene's Basement is one way, a Staples store the other. The rain lashes his face.

A black guy in a hoodie comes hurrying across the drowning street. He is hatless, without an umbrella. The hood keeps falling back in the wind and he keeps brushing it forward. He's about the same age as Josh Thompson. He sees the wheelchair and his eyes go wide.

—Hey, man, Josh says.

—I'm busy, muthafucka.

—I'm just wonderin', is there a place I can stay around here?

The black man points down a wide two-way street.

—Try down there. Might be a hotel. A church. At the end, they's an overpass called the High Line. The fuck knows?

Then he looks behind him, and hurries away, heading uptown. And disappears down some stairs.

Josh rolls into what a sign calls 14th Street. He lowers his head and moves into the wind and rain. It ain't sand, he says out loud. It ain't sand. It's wet.

It's rain. What I wanted so bad back there in Iraq. He crosses other avenues and passes many shuttered stores. No sign of a hotel. But across the street, there's a church. Our Lady of . . . something. Goo-add-a-luppy? All the lights are out. The Mexicans back home got a church with the same name. Or like Salinas in Iraq, with a Virgin Mary medal around his neck. It didn't save him.

Then in the distance, on the right-hand side of the street, he sees minarets. He stops, his heart pounding. One big minaret, and a dome, and others around it, high thin towers where they can chant their fucking prayers. Just like in Sadr City. His hips are hurting now but he moves faster.

A neon sign says: ALADDIN.

Then: LAMP.

Aladdin's Lamp.

He hears another word.

Payback.

*2:19 a.m. Beverly Starr. Eighth Street, Gowanus, Brooklyn.*

She eases back from the drawing table, then pushes hard against the black Girsberger chair, the one she thinks of as her second spine. She exhales, takes another breath, holds it, lets the air out more slowly. Then stands. She stares down at the large painting on the table. On thick illustration board. Made of grays and blacks. Bold slashing blacks. A young black woman, infant in arms, small boy holding her skirt. An old junkie with a shirt hanging loose on his bones. A middle-class white man with a lumpy suit, his face sagging in defeat. An old soldier with a steel helmet and combat fatigues. The eyes of each of them full of fear, abandonment, injury, shame.

Beverly Starr steps to the side, a brush in hand, thick with a load of gray casein. She first goes left, then to the right. The eyes follow her. As she wanted them to. Eyes she hoped were full of questions. *How did this happen? How did I end up like this? How did I get to be a wanderer in empty streets? Can't you see we need help? A roof over our heads, a warm bed, a stove, food?* Beverly has lived with them for weeks, has sketched them from window seats in coffee shops, has seen them waiting for food-stamp cards outside welfare offices, has frozen them in memory with her own blinking eyes, using the blinks as if they were shutters in a camera. A trick learned long ago from a sidewalk artist in the Village.

Here they are.

The homeless.

On a street as empty and menacing as any in Batman's Gotham.

She moves in on the painting, and with her brush she blurs the details of the soldier's hands. Too literal. Too comic-book-y. Does the same for the middle-class man, then lifts a smaller brush and makes a subtle crack in one lens of his glasses. Thinking: Don't fuck it up now. Don't overfinish it. She pauses again, and abruptly thinks: It's done.

She slips the two brushes into a large jar of water, shaking the paint loose. Then she lifts a black lithographic pencil from her tabouret and signs her name in the lower right corner. Boldly. Proudly. The first time in too long a time that she has done such work. Doing it for a benefit instead of an editor. To help raise money for the homeless. Tonight.

Another goddamned deadline kept. With hours to spare. Thank God for water-based casein. Quick-drying acrylics. Someone is coming at nine, to carry the painting away for a quick scanning and a framing job, and delivery to the committee in charge of the benefit. The painting will be auctioned off. The scanners will turn it into a poster and all benefactors will receive personally framed copies a few weeks later. She thinks: This is the moment in the old days when I would have had a cigarette.

She stretches, moves her shoulders like rippling gears. Then glances at the Mac. Her true workshop. The homeless painting is the first work she's done away from the Mac in two years. But she can't sleep now. She has more work to do. She rolls the chair and sits down facing the screen. There's a page on the screen, half the panels in black and white, half in color, alternating real world, virtual world. Page 5 of *Like Mama*. For *Vanity Fair*. Splash page, and four strip pages. All about a mild-mannered English teacher named Lois Trueheart, early forties, a spinster, like her creator. She's been driven half mad by the way all the girl students use "like" in almost every uttered sentence. Sometimes twice. Or three times! And how they add question marks after statements of fact. As if all fact were conditional.

On Beverly's splash page there's an aerial shot of New York City, showing the skyscrapers, Central Park, the East River, parts of Brooklyn and Queens. Voice balloons are rising over the city, some large, others tiny, hundreds of them, many millions of others just suggested, all saying likelikelikelikelikelikelikelikelikelike... In class, in the corridors, in stores and churches and bars, on the streets, in the subway, maybe even in their sleep... *He calls, and I'm, like, scared?... I finish*

106

*and I'm, like, happy?...He's handsome, but he's, like, thirty?...I look at it, and it's, like, awesome?* One four-letter word blurring the city's soundtrack, part of the pasty verbal mush, and on the splash page it's crowding the sky among the many towers.

Is that girl scared, or is she *like* scared?

Is this one happy, or is she *like* happy? The guy is thirty, or like thirty, and his schlong is, like, *awesome?*

Where the twin towers once stood, an immense new steel and granite edifice, ominous, primordial, carries the name of the story: *The Charge of the Like Brigade.*

In a small panel at the bottom, Lois Trueheart holds her head in her hands, wracked with despair, alone at her desk in an empty classroom. On a blackboard behind her are the words "Precise, Clear, Exact." Those words that mean, like, nothing to millions of young women. She clicks to the following page. A gigantic gray finger enters through the window, a finger with the cross-hatched texture of stone, and touches her clenched hands. Then Lois is swept up and out the window, into the sky, whizzed to the far reaches of the galaxy, all the way to the Fortress of Exactitude, where she is placed before the ancient deity

Gramaticus. He gives her the sacred task. To cleanse the English-speaking world of "like." By any means necessary. She will become...*Like Mama*.

Beverly Starr laughs. A gust of rain sprays the room's two windows. Hard and tiny pieces of the sky, drowning and silencing the earth, one pellet for each "like." Millions. Billions. Cluster bombs from God or Gramaticus.

She lays down the stylus she uses for details, moves the chair back with her flat butt, hits "Save," and rises. She is barefoot, in jeans and black T-shirt, inhaling the damp warm stale air of the room. She caresses the frame of the tablet/monitor, turns, runs the tips of her fingers over the top of the scanner. She glances at the painting of the homeless. They are, like, hurting. She places it on an easel, revealing a sheet of two-ply Bristol taped to the immaculate white surface of the table. Panels are drawn in blue pencil, lines laid for lettering. In the drawer to the right are the old tools of her trade: two Winsor & Newton sable brushes, two steel-nib pens, a crow quill, various pencils and erasers, markers and technical pens, an X-Acto knife, a single-edge razor blade, an old bottle of Higgins ink, with a jar of white beside it for corrections. The Luxo swing-arm lamp is off now, but it contains a fluorescent bulb and an incandescent one, balancing each other so that color stays true. There's a T square too and a steel ruler, eighteen inches long, and a clear plastic triangle. She thinks: The tools Caniff used, and Will Eisner, and Noel Sickles. Tools I don't use anymore.

She crooks her right arm as far as possible across the top of her head, grips the elbow in her left hand, and bends to the side. Twenty times. Facing a ten-foot-high mirror, she reverses hand and elbow and bends the other way. Her body is still lean and hard, buttless and almost titless, but she wears the same size 8 she wore at nineteen.

In *Like Mama,* Beverly uses herself as the model for Lois, an exclamation point in a Catwoman suit, improved by art into a 34C cup. The character has a secret lab in Red Hook, where she invents her own tools for the crusade: a stylus-sized secret weapon, with a button she can press when it's slyly aimed at one of the Like Brigade. The girl says "like" and her thorax freezes, her eyes widen, she can't finish a sentence? Like Mama presses the button again, and the young woman can speak, which she does nervously, until she says "like" again, and click! Frozen silence! Panic? She resembles a dog who has encountered an electric fence. Maybe the girl even gets what happened, connects "like" to paralysis. But Like Mama doesn't stick around for Pavlovian results, as puny as this one might be. She is returning to the beginning of this, far from Brooklyn, in distant California. Google has taught her that Valley Girls were the Muslim Brotherhood of this linguistic perversion. Now they are Beverly's age (or the same age as Lois Trueheart) and still talking that way, making it seem *normal* in certain households and class-rooms, and Beverly realizes that she will need to invent a Weapon of Mass Obstruction. And *then...*

Now, listening to the rain, Beverly Starr looks down at a narrow blue padded mat spread across the floor. She kneels on the mat, stretches forward, facing the floor, her hands flat beside each shoul-der. Then she rises, arching backward, pushing against the floor, forcing her back to crack. She is facing the Mac, a kind of supplicant, and when she comes up she can see the packed shelves of the Collection. And remembers trying to sell *Bush-whacker* to that guy from the *World:* The editor. Briscoe. The one-shot strip was about a woman who had the mysterious power to remove clothes from anyone. She chooses to strip clothes off George W. Bush. There he is with a bullhorn at the ruins of the World Trade Center, and the res-cue workers are all laughing or smiling, and Bush is naked. His limp pecker hanging there. Yelling

"Bring 'em on!" The crack of his ass is withered. He stands with Condoleezza Rice on the White House steps and she's got a big grin, and Bush is balls-ass naked. He visits troops for Thanksgiving dinner in Iraq, and they are all laughing, and Bush is holding a tray with turkey and stuffing, his schlong resembling a week-old piece of broccoli.

Remembering: When she went to Briscoe's office at the *World* and showed him the printouts, he laughed out loud and then said he couldn't use them without folding the paper an hour after they came off the press. But he was having a dinner party that night at his place in SoHo and she was welcome to come if she had time. Why not? She was single. Free. No deadline. There were eight guests at the table in Briscoe's loft: a political operator and his wife, a professor of French history from NYU and his wife, an unhappy woman novelist and her unhappy female companion, the painter Lew Forrest, and Beverly. The chef was from the French Culinary Institute, a man handsome in a vaguely sinister way. Forrest and Briscoe and the professor exchanged jokes in French. Beverly imagined her own mother at this table. Hawk-faced, her mouth a slash. Sneering, bitter. Muttering: *Speak English, you schmucks.* Full of the endless anger of the South Bronx, anger at the Depression, anger at the rich, the deck stacked

against them all. Heard her: *You wanna be what?*
*An artist? Yeah? Go downstairs, sit on the railing,*
*you meet plenty of artists, baby. Bullshit artists!* Until
one son went off to the army and died in Korea
and the other son found heroin and died in Attica.
And I invented Beverly Starr. Good-bye, Ruthie
Rosenberg. Hello, Beverly.

In a corner, Briscoe introduced Beverly Starr to
Forrest. The older man's eyes were glassy, but he
seemed alert and amused.

–Are you related to Brenda, the great reporter?
Forrest said.

–In a way, yes.

–I always liked her stuff.

–So did I, Beverly said. And yours too. I have a
print of *Chelsea Hotel, Evening* in my studio.

–No kidding?

He smiled in a pleased way and then turned to
the political couple. Parties are always like that.
You start a conversation, but almost never finish it.
Beverly did like the people, or as much as she could
learn about them, which wasn't much. They all
had good faces, character digging into their flesh,
and she slipped away to the john twice to jot
sketches on index cards when the light was too
dim for her use of the blink. She was still smoking
then and slipped onto Briscoe's terrace for a fast
Marlboro Light, looking out at the city and the

dark river and the moving line of cars on the Jersey shore. That night she felt that New York and its buildings and its people and its nervous style would last forever. Before they sat down to dinner, Briscoe showed her around, and Beverly saw the way he had organized his library, New York, Italy, Mexico, and so on, and the next day she started doing the same here in her house on 8th Street in Brooklyn. The house that was not yet paid off. The house purchased with her work.

So tonight, three years later, the house paid off, cracking her back, doing sets, she can see each section rising from floor to ceiling, covering the entire wall. The Collection. Her collection. The first section on the left, near the draped window, has the early classics in hardcover reprints, old comic books, or in retrieved pages from ancient newspapers, all covered in protective plastic. Winsor McCay and *Little Nemo in Slumberland* or *Dream of the Rarebit Fiend;* Herriman and *Krazy Kat;* Milt Gross and *Count Screwloose of Tooloose* along with *Nize Baby; Max and Moritz* from Germany; *Mutt and Jeff; Happy Hooligan; Bringing Up Father,* with the amazing George McManus holding the pen. Briscoe even had a McManus original on his wall. They invented comics, those guys, and, in a way, the movies, since comic strips are really frozen movies. At the party at Briscoe's she

asked Lew Forrest if he ever knew the painter Lyo-
nel Feininger, who once drew a knockoff version
of *The Katzenjammer Kids.*

—I did, he said. He was a wonderful painter.
But as a comics artist, I liked Harold Gray better.
Daddy *Warbucks!* Punjab and the Asp! What
blacks! What a sense of... night. All the communists I knew just loved *Orphan Annie.* How could
the *Daily Worker* have invented a better epitome of
savage capitalism than Daddy Warbucks?

Momma would have agreed. To her, every rich
guy was Daddy Warbucks. She hated the communists too, because she hated anyone who believed
in the future. And every one of her own kids was
an orphan, even when they lived at home. Kids
not like Annie, with a rich protector to watch her
back. But kids like me, who found work at sixteen,
clerking in a Walgreen's, then took a furnished
room for twenty-five bucks a week, and started
drawing comics. Nobody watched my back, not
even the young dummies I fell in love with.

The second book tower holds Sickles, when he
was doing *Scorchy Smith,* and all of Caniff's *Terry
and the Pirates,* almost all of *The Spirit.* She thinks
of them as the books of the Gold Testament. Even
Briscoe, who loved newspaper strips and hated
comic books, knew how good *The Spirit* was.
Then the superheroes, Captain Marvel, Plastic

Man, Sub-Mariner, the Human Torch, Batman, Sheena, the Young Allies, and, above all, Captain America. No Superman, who was a fucking bore, living in Metropolis, where there were no shadows. At least Batman lived in Gotham, which was all shadows, put there by Jerry Robinson even if signed by Bob Kane. Metropolis was Minneapolis. Gotham was New York. But this tower of shelves is really Muscle Beach, and the star is Jack Kirby. He came crashing off the page, the toughest Jew on the Lower East Side, making his heroes do things nobody had ever done before. Baroque, full of violent power. Punching, heaving, in mortal combat with the Red Skull, that filthy Nazi saboteur. The first American heroes on steroids. All before Beverly Starr was born.

*Forget all this childish crap,* Momma said that time. *Learn to type. To take shorthand. Then get a job in an office!*

Until the day Ruthie Rosenberg came home from high school, and her comic book collection was gone, bundled up, hauled away by Momma. The girl went bawling to the street, searching in garbage cans, and the lots, and never did find her treasures. And knew she had to get out of there, go off on her own, because if she didn't she was sure to kill Momma, and make page 1 of the *Daily News.*

She built up her collection in the furnished room, started her life in the comics business, and now thinks: Who was that guy took me home that time? Some kind of banker. He looked around the studio, and said, You read *comics?* She said, I write comics. I draw comics. Lawyers read law books, right? He never came back. Ah, well... Gotta get a Depression story going. Put Momma in it too. Find some way to forgive her...

Beverly is in the second set of the back crunchers when she hears through the rain the sound of the F train moving on the trestle over the Gowanus. Kudda-kuh-kudda-kuh-kudda-kuh, *pock*, kudda-kuh kudda-kuh. *Pock*. The wheels sounding hollow, warm, not steel on steel. Lionel trains. The *pock* like a drummer's rim shot. An accent. High above the steel girders of the Kentile sign and the one from Eagle Outfitters. Brooklyn's Eiffel Towers. Thinking: Roy Crane wrote the best sound. Caniff never tried. And Eisner was best on cities, on shadows, on nights slick with rain. Nights like this. Nights when Denny Colt rose from the mausoleum in Wildwood Cemetery. Which she knows must be the Green-Wood, the most beautiful of all cemeteries. Right here in Brooklyn. Hell, with a little effort, she can walk there from this house. My house.

She knows the Green-Wood is beautiful, because she's walked among its tombstones on summer afternoons. Leonard Bernstein is there, and Fred Ebb, and George Bellows, and William Merritt Chase, and George Catlin, and Lola Montez, and Joey Gallo, and, what's his name? Boss Tweed... and yeah: Denny Colt. Gotta do a comic about the place someday. A girl dies too young. She wakes up in the Green-Wood. Calls it "The New Neighborhood." She meets all of them, even Denny Colt... In real life, Beverly never did find Denny Colt, although she tried, and slept with three guys who looked like him, even asking each of them to wear the fedora and little mask that changed Denny Colt into the Spirit. She even made love to one of them under the stars in the Green-Wood, for Chrissakes. Life never does imitate art.

Gotta go to work, she thinks. Gotta finish the story. Can't sleep now. Gotta be awake until nine, when the guy comes for the pickup. Sleep now, I'll be like granite when he shows up. Gotta work until eight. Breakfast. Watch some *Morning Joe*. Make the handover. Then sleep until four.

The thing tonight is cocktails, with snacks.

Like eating Crayolas.

One thing I learned in this life: If you're going

to a benefit, better eat before you go. Like going to Momma's house for dinner. Before she did the world a favor, and died.

### 2:20 a.m. Ali Watson. Manhattan Bridge.

He pulls onto the bridge with the lights of the skyline visible on the far side. Left hand on the wheel, his right hand is flicking the handheld radio, trying to get the special operations division channel, then the Sixth Precinct, in Greenwich Village. A garble of voices, male, female, abrupt bulletins about small emergencies. Can't find it. Must be 'cause I'm between Brooklyn and Manhattan... Left message. Cell was on Cynthia Harding's answering machine too...Nothing.

The bridge is almost empty in the driving rain. An N train goes by, heading back into Brooklyn, next stop Atlantic-Pacific. Where all the Mexicans change to the R, to get off in Sunset Park. He remembers when they just called it the Sea Beach Express. Three beautiful words, full of summer. Sea Beach Express. Almost empty at this hour. Cleaning ladies and dozing drunks. Down below, the East River's empty too. A lot fewer yachts since the collapse on Wall Street, and none at all past the midnight hour. In the late morning, there's an occasional Circle Line boat jammed with tourists. He took the tour once with Mary Lou. Just for the hell of it. Two New Yorkers playing at being tourists. They sailed around the island. Under the bridges. God, she was beautiful then. With a smile that could crack open a safe. In her second year at Hunter, talking about being a lawyer, maybe running for office. Sure didn't want to get married. Not to me, anyway. Not to a cop that was a Muslim. Fuck no. And then she got pregnant...

The cell rings.

—Watson.

—Reilly, from the Sixth. You called about Patchin Place? There's a fire there. One alarm.

—A fire? Jesus Christ...I'm on the Manhattan Bridge. Be there in ten, twelve minutes.

He clicks off. Tries the operations channel again. A fire. On Patchin Place. Oh, my Mary Lou, he thinks. Please be gone. Oh, please be safe. Please be waiting for me outside, so I can drive you back home, so we can climb into bed, so we can be warm on this cold night. Please, Mary Lou. Please.

Then in the rearview Ali sees lights coming closer, real fast. Hey, pal: I'm in the left lane. You got lots of room. No: he's playing games.

Tailgating. On the Manhattan Bridge! In the fucking rain!

Now his brights are on, blinding Ali, flooding his car with light.

Ali slows down.

Pass me, muthafucka.

And then a yard behind him the tailgater rips to the right on the slick bridge, and Ali glances at him. A BMW. A black-haired white kid. Maybe twenty. Maybe younger. Someone beyond him in the passenger seat. A girl, for sure. The kid's laughing, eyes cocaine-wide, and then he races past. Foot harder on the pedal, and there's a taxi up ahead. The kid wants to pass the cab, racing for Manhattan, for Canal Street. Speeding to SoHo or Tribeca. Or the Meatpacking District. But he clips the cab, spinning it off to the right, and then the BMW swerves, and hits a steel restraining wall, and flips and turns, once, twice, then comes to a tumbling thumping halt on its roof. Filling two lanes. Ali stops three feet from the wrecked car.

Fuck.

He puts the Mazda in park, red lights blinking, turns off the ignition, grabs a heavy-beam flashlight, gets out. Waving the flashlight at oncoming traffic. The taxi is backing up, righting itself, leaving a path.

Ali glances into the crumpled BMW, still waving the flashlight. He sees the driver and a young girl splayed on the inside of the roof, which is now the bottom. Blood moves in a lumpy way from the driver's mouth. The girl's neck looks broken, her shirt near her waist. She's not wearing panties. Neither of them wearing seat belts. The motor is running, as steady as the rain. They look very dead. He touches the driver's wrist. Warm. Then stops himself. No, wait for whoever gets the squeal. For a moment, he wonders how many dead people he has touched in his life.

Then he taps 911 on the cell.

*Wait for me, Mary Lou. Wait, my darling. I'll be a bit late. Wait.*

He reports the accident, clicks off. Then glances at the ruined car. And imagines the parents getting the news from a tired cop. Two hours from now, the phone call at the wrong hour, the hearts thumping in alarm, hands lifting receivers. Seeing the boy at four, the girl at three, running barefoot in a backyard on a summer afternoon, splashing in surf. Seeing New York from the Circle Line. Full of amazement. Staring at the phone. Then sobbing, collapsing, falling, screaming.

At least it's not Malik.

The rain falls hard.

### 2:22 a.m. Consuelo Mendoza. The N train to Brooklyn.

She is wearing a thick brown polyester jacket, cloth gloves, a watch cap. She speaks good English, but usually thinks in Spanish, and knows that at this hour of the night, on this night of all nights, she must be extra careful. *Por seguro.* She carries no purse, nothing to tempt some *pendejo.* In her hidden belt, she has 207 dollars in cash. In her jacket pocket, some change and a MetroCard. The last payday. The last night of a job she has held for seven years. The thick down jacket hides an immense gouge in her stomach, an emptiness put there by her boss. There were many consoling words from the woman who was her boss. But the hole is still there. Getting larger.

The windows of the train are streaked with rain, racing left to right instead of top to bottom, as they cross the Manhattan Bridge, high over the river. The train turns and an empty plastic Diet Pepsi bottle rolls from one side of the car to the other. Just another passenger, lost and empty. Two men move to a window, looking down at something. Bright whirling lights. An accident. The train keeps moving. The men can see nothing now and one returns to a seat. A sleeping Chinese man lurches and almost falls from his seat. His eyes widen, and then he gazes around the car, relaxes, and returns to sleep. An unshaven white man in a Giants jacket stares at something in the back of his eyes. There are three other women on the train as it comes down off the bridge into the tunnel. The rain now makes paths from top to bottom. Usually, her friend Norma is with her, and they can talk and make jokes in Spanish. But Norma was laid off two weeks ago and still doesn't have a new job. She helps out at a taco van in Red Hook on weekends, but that's not a real job. The last year, lots of people lost jobs. Maybe tonight was just her turn. Just like that. Paid in cash by Sara, the Colombiana, as always, so they'd have no records at the cleaning company. I'm carrying the money alone. And alone, Consuelo tries to look small, insignificant, worthless, homely, avoiding all eye contact, especially with the men.

The train pulls into Atlantic Avenue–Pacific Street, and several people get up. Down the car, near the middle door, she sees a sign:

IF YOU SEE SOMETHING,
SAY SOMETHING

Consuelo Mendoza never sees anything that they're talking about. No crazy Arabs. No guys with guns or bombs. She sees a lot of other things. But no *musulmanes locos*. The train waits, with doors open. Down the aisle are two other women, one of them Mexican. Or maybe Guatemalan. She has an Indian face, like Consuelo's. Sad too. The R pulls in, the doors open, and more people hurry into the N. On the platform, dozens of others start pushing into the R, which is always late. On one of the benches, Consuelo glimpses a white *vagabundo* in clothes made shiny by filth. No socks. Stretched out, one sneakered foot on the cement floor, one arm hanging. There are many of them now. Homeless. Jobless. *Borrachos, adictos,* most of them, but not all.

In her work building back in SoHo, she and Norma weren't the only persons fired. So were the men who worked there days, and sometimes nights. All the women too. Many worked late, sweating, ruled by the computer, sometimes joking. But when she arrived at seven sharp on this night, they all were gone. She cleaned anyway, sensing it was over, but not knowing for sure, didn't call home to Raymundo, didn't want him to worry, to lose sleep, to fret. He is such a sweet man. All evening, she didn't do anything except her job. While the emptiness began to widen in her belly. She ate nothing, took nothing but water. Her head was buzzing with unspoken words. We all knew what was coming. We knew for weeks that if the men left, if the office closed, if the computers were all blank, there'd be no garbage to empty, no cardboard coffee cups, no half-eaten sandwiches, no banana peels, no apple cores, no empty soda bottles, no pizza crusts. No floors to sweep and mop. No work. What will we do?

Raymundo is home, right this minute, sleeping in their bedroom, the three children in theirs. She and Raymundo will sleep together for three hours tonight and then he will rise up in the morning dark, *mi Dios,* whispering, walking in socks to make no noise, and wash and get dressed and take the train to his job in the coffee shop. Does she tell him when he wakes up that she has lost her job? No. Then all day at the coffee shop he will be sick in his heart, in his hands, in his belly, like me. The coffee shop won't be the same. Usually, he would be there all day, starting at six, finishing at five, hurrying home, where they would kiss and she would show him the food in the pot, and then hurry off to her job. In the coffee shop, he cooks sandwiches, ham and bacon and cheese and eggs. All the stuff the *gringos* love. Sometimes a club sandwich with turkey and lettuce and tomato and bacon. He slices and toasts bagels. He fills many cardboard cups of coffee.

*Carajo,* how can I tell poor Raymundo? How

125

do I say I lost my job? Wake him up? Take him out to the hall when he wakes up in the dark? So the kids don't hear?

No, he'll be sick.

I'm sick.

Right now.

My stomach is turning over.

My heart beating.

The N train pulls out. One more stop, and then a final stop on the local. The familiar stations of the R pass in a blur of black poles and flashing lights. Union Street. Fourth Avenue, Prospect Avenue, 25th Street. She sees the signs before she sees the stations, some trick in her head. The stations changing the way their luck is changing. But she knows from Mexico that you can't trust in luck. You will not kneel before Nuestra Señora de Guadalupe and the next day win the *lotería nacional*. You will not be told you have cancer and then pray and pray and pray and find that you are clean again. You make your luck. You work for your luck. You work and work and work and work.

Then at 36th Street, she rises to change to the R. The Chinese man gets up and yawns. The woman who looks Mexican grabs a pole and angles to the door. The angry-looking *gringo* stays there, his fingers laced, his knuckles white, staring at nothing. Consuelo thinks: Who can I go to? Who will help me find a job? Who can save us? The Diet Pepsi bottle rolls across the floor. Consuelo follows it with her eyes. Looks up. Sees a sign:

SI VES ALGO,
DI ALGO!

If you see something, say something. The bilingual train stops. The doors open. Here is the R. She boards it, notices the usual people. Latinas and Chinese, a few *gringos*. Like most of them, she remains standing, until the train reaches 45th Street. She leaves the train and moves quickly along the platform to the revolving door that leads to the stairs and the street. The dented metal bars on the door need painting. She moves quickly with the other women, Chinese women, Mexican women, some Dominicans too, *por seguro,* some from Ecuador. Up the stairs. Into the rain.

She sees the familiar signs. El Reencuentro restaurant. Mega Car Service. The Sprint Payment Service. The Tlaxcala Estila barbershop. They all start up the hill, the Chinese heading for distant Eighth Avenue, Consuelo and most of the other Latinas one long hilly block to La Quinta. This street is safe, with people here most of the time, even in the rain. You can see a police car every twenty minutes, maybe, just cruising along. Some other streets are not so safe. She reaches Fifth Avenue, and knows where everything is, even when the stores are closed and the metal shutters rolled down tight. Zapatería México. Tacos Matamoros. Cancún Fashion. The travel agency with a sign that says ENVÍA DINERO A MEXICO AQUÍ. They haven't sent money back home since little Timoteo was born. Now four years old. And the middle one, Marcela, is ten. The boy loves her. Always giggling when she tickles him. Following her everywhere in the house. What will happen to them?

She turns right, heading south, hugging the wall to avoid the rain. Her bare hand clutches the key chain in her pocket. She sees the sign on the corner of her street: School Daze. Where everybody buys clothes for kids, the boys downstairs, the girls right inside the door. Beside it and on top of it, the apartment house called Roma rises five stories, the shades drawn in every apartment, no lights burning.

Abruptly, from a shadowy doorway, a black man appears, his back against the door. She gasps, says *Oh*. He wears a thick black beard. His eyes are as surprised as hers must be. His skin is wet.

–Don't worry, he says. Just keep going.

She moves out toward the avenue and hurries along, not too fast, so she won't show fear. But

she's afraid. Where is the police car? Where is anybody? At the corner, in front of the Toda Moda
shoe shop, she sees the lights of the Korean store a
block away, burning as always through the night,
and thinks she can run to its safety. They know
her there. In the daytime, after school, her oldest
son, Eduardo, works there, delivering orders,
sweeping. The customers call him Eddie. The first
American child. Fourteen now. Almost as tall as
his father. And we were here only a year when he
was born. Eddie is one reason Consuelo likes the
Korean store. When she doesn't have time to go to
the cheaper store on 42nd Street down by Second
Avenue, she buys serrano chilies there and nopales
and tortillas.

She turns and looks back.

The black man is gone.

She moves quickly into her street, stops before
the shuttered unisex barber, looks for slow-moving
car headlights, sees none, looks for the bearded
black man, sees no one, and dashes across the wet
street to her house. She jams the key into the
downstairs gate. Turns it. Goes in, flicks the small
lever that locks the door, and slams shut the iron
bolt that Raymundo always leaves open for her.
Goes through the second door, locks that behind
her, stands there for a long moment, breathing
hard. Home. Safe.

She hangs her hat on a wallpeg, shakes her hair, unbuttons her jacket and pulls off her scarf and hangs them on a separate peg. Raymundo's padded tan jacket is on the third peg. She slides off her wet shoes, and places them on the floor beneath the pegs. She walks in socks past the stairs into the kitchen. A coffee cup and saucer are in the sink, on top of dinner plates. That is part of their deal. She will do the dishes. Over the years, Raymundo had washed so many dishes, before becoming a cook, that he told her once his only wish was that he never wash another dish. She smiled and hugged him, and said, Okay. He said, No, no, it's only a joke, *un chiste, mi vida,* but she said, No, I do the dishes from now on.

She turns on the hot water, letting it run, squirting some liquid cleanser over the dishes. Four dishes, one each for Raymundo and Eddie, Marcela, and Timmie. The water warms her cold hands. She glances at the refrigerator, where photos of the kids are attached to the door with magnets. On the table is a copy of *Diario de México,* the new paper with all the terrible news from the old country.

EJECUTAN
A TRECE

Thirteen more killed in the drug war. Usually along *la frontera*. This time in Mazatlán, to the south. It's as if Raymundo is sending a message: We can't ever go back to that country. Our lost country.

She thinks: Oh, how will I tell him?

She thinks: And what will we do?

She tries to remember Mexico. To forget their two floors in this house, the kitchen and the room with the TV and the garden on the first floor, the bedrooms up one flight. To forget Sunset Park. Writing the rent checks. Addition and subtraction. Clothes for the boys. New shoes for Marcela. Instead, she pictures birds in the morning in the house in Cuernavaca. She is seventeen again, working up north in Cuernavaca, and sending money home every two weeks to Mama in Oaxaca. She sees the stone house in Cuernavaca, with light streaming into the rooms while she mops, and the pool blue and glassy and the birds singing. Señor Lewis said one time that birds were the first musicians. He was right. And on the second floor, Señor Lewis is in his studio, sipping coffee, painting in shorts and T-shirt. She sees the narrow bed against the studio wall. The bed where—

Señor Lewis.

Perhaps he can help.

She has his address in New York, from fifteen years ago. She has never gone to see him. Not once. Not after —

Señor Lewis.

His kindness. His heart.

She thinks: I don't even know if he's alive.

I must try to find out.

### 2:28 a.m. Malik Shahid, aka Malik Watson. Sunset Park, Brooklyn.

Rain and rain and rain. Malik moves with caution, his kufi behind him in a sewer, his shoes soaked. Here nothing grows. Paradise is a garden, says al-Quran, but this is not Paradise. Here is only concrete and slate and asphalt, skeletons of trees, dead cars whose floppy airless tires caress stone curbs. He thinks: I am alone in rain and night. I hear the tearing sound of cars above me on the expressway but can't see their lights. A few taxis, roof lights saying "Off Duty," move south to their garages.

Under his watery canvas jacket, Malik hugs the plastic bag from the Korean store, lowers his head, moves through black shadows. He needs to vanish. After tonight, after the holy mission of redemption, he must disappear. To make the final cleansing on Friday night. Holy night. With Glorious, or without her. With the child, when all is over. Yes. Above all, with the child. A boy, they told Glorious at the clinic. A son of Islam. *Inshallah*. Me and the boy. To the sacred places. Now he sees sleeping bodies under spread blankets, scrunched up against ugly girders that support the expressway. Shoe-covered feet jut from packing crates. Some mixture of rain and piss finds channels between fractured cobblestones. He sees garbage in black plastic bags, and a banana peel turned brown. A patrol car hurries by, dome light turning, and Malik flattens himself on the dark side of a girder. When the police car is gone, he gazes at the vacant side of the avenue, the one that carries traffic to Manhattan.

And runs.

In the rubbled street leading up the hill, there are three parked cars, each one alone, separate, two on one side, a solitary on Malik's side. Just a few, as always. In summer, hornboys from New Jersey come here for twenty-dollar blow jobs from the filthy infidel women. Jizm in the throat, junk in the veins. On this night, the parked cars seem empty but Malik cannot be certain. He slides into the front yard of a condemned corner house, windows boarded up, and hunches behind the remains of a battered stoop. He peers at the dark parked cars, looking for steam on the windows, or a match lighting a cigarette. Nothing. The Lots are part of a vast project organized by some developer: housing for yuppies, or for NYU students to share, or for Jersey types who wanted a place to get laid before driving home; an office building too, and an Italian hotel where tourists could pay in euros. The sell: Wall Street just fifteen minutes away through the Battery Tunnel. It was all set to go, until Allah punished America, punished the crusaders, punished the Jews, punished the filthy infidel women with their polluted cunts and sucked-out tits. Allah gazed down upon them and broke their fucking economy, exposed their filth and usury and greed. The project stopped dead.

Now all is gone except a few lonesome old-time tenements, somehow missed by the bulldozers, including the tenement used by Malik and Glorious. The whole area weeps now. It looks like a wet Baghdad. The one he sees in newspapers. On TV. That ruined city. Baghdad without the Muslim dead.

He says out loud: Be there soon, Glorious. We got things to do. Hey: the rain is lighter now. All of a sudden. A message, for shit sure. Gotta go home. Gotta get dry. Gotta bundle these clothes. Gotta chop this beard. Gotta sleep. Can't sleep, then hold the tits of Glorious, bursting with God's milk. Oh. And enter her. As you have willed it, my beloved Allah. No papers from any authority. Just your will. You created women for us, didn't you? Glorious doesn't believe it, doesn't believe anything, not Yahweh, not Jesus, not Buddha, not Allah. She's not into it, she says. Won't even wear a *hijab* out in the street, to cover her hair, to hide it from the lusting eyes of strangers. Why not? He didn't ask her to wear a *chador,* covering her face, even her eyes. Just the hair. She says no. He keeps telling her that belief will come, that she will accept, will submit. Thinking: She's a puppy, that's all. One morning she'll wake up and understand everything and accept Allah. But now she says something like What's all this shit about submitting? Submitting to what? To who? And Malik always says: Submitting to Allah's order, Allah's rules. Told in al-Quran and the Hadith. And she says, You mean, submitting to *you,* right? And laughs.

That's the way she is. An example of *jahiliyah.* Ignorance of God. She knows as much as any puppy. She should be nasty but she isn't. She's got a good heart, Glorious, but she's her mother's daughter. The mother that named her. A filthy woman for sure, who lived with a Muslim, some asshole who pledged allegiance to Elijah Muhammad and his Lost-Found bullshit Nation street hustle. She left him because she loved junk more than the creed passed to us by the Prophet. Malik remembered talking about such traitors as heroin-fidels. The mother went on the stroll, Glorious told Malik. Probably fucked a thousand guys, at least. Poor Glorious doesn't even know who her father is. Some dude threw a load into her mother's belly and moved on. Maybe even a white dude, 'cause Glorious is tan, not black.

Later, after Glorious was born, some other dude threw the mother the virus. The usual shit started after that: moving around, shelters, different dudes moving in with the mother and trying to fuck Glorious, foster care, one school after another, until finally Allah put the mother out of her misery. Just last year. Around the time Malik met Glorious in Newark. Even now, Glorious wakes up calling for her mother. Imagine. Not Allah. Her filthy mother. Malik thinks: I never cry for mine.

Then Malik starts to run through the Lots, staying low in the black emptiness, avoiding the open spaces, the deep gouges in the dirt, the sudden drops into basements where the houses are gone, one mound of rubble following another, one three-story house with only one roofless story left, an abandoned car without wheels or windows, a fuel drum on its side with charred wood from a dead fire spilling out. Up ahead: the tenement. No lights burning, even on the fourth floor, where Glorious is waiting. Nobody else lives in the tenement. The buried power line comes from the far side of the site, where an abandoned construction trailer awaits workers who went away when the money ran out and may never come back. Malik laid the power line himself. Stole it off a pole. Learned how to do all that when he worked a summer job upstate, near Canada. Malik and Jamal. He was into computers, Malik was a student, just starting at CUNY. But he was Jamal's student too. A student of Islam. The true Islam. More and more they moved from the banalities of the mosque to the thinking of Sayyid Qutb. To Hassan al-Banna. To the true children of the Prophet. To the brotherhood. To jihad.

Now he reaches the back side of the tenement. He faces the side wall, pale, jagged, broken into rectangles of old paint, the colors of rooms that are now gone, slowly washing away in the wind and weather. In the daytime, the walls are weird and beautiful: baby blue, bright red, one wall all black. The people who painted them are all gone now. Now Malik reminds himself: Be careful. He goes to the back door, facing the rubble where the yard used to be. He grips the big key for that door, a small one for the apartment on the top floor. He is jittery. You can never know if some crackheads made it into the building.

Malik inserts the large key, pauses, leans gently on the door, listening, while wondering where Jamal is now. He is sure his old friend, his instructor, is still in the house he bought in the lower part of Park Slope. Bought with money he started making as a designer, after the friendship broke, after Jamal made the *haj*, with some help from his father, the X-ray guy. And came home a different man. Calling himself a lover of Islam, a hater of jihad. It must have been Jamal's wife that changed him. Another American bitch. And her having a kid. Or maybe it's a cover story, a way to exist here as if he were another dumb American nigger, working away, but keeping jihad in the most secret place in his mind. Malik wants to believe that. But he simply doesn't know. He will have to find out. When this night of red rain ends.

Now Malik inhales, turns the key, leans close, listens. Then exhales. No sound. He looks behind him across the Lots through the rain. Nobody. He slips inside.

He hears faint groans and creaks from the black empty building above him. He has learned that such sounds are normal on nights of hard rain or stiff wind. Still, this night is different. He waits with the door shut behind him, letting his eyes adjust to the darkness. In a corner, a pile of discarded shovels resembles a small monument of iron tombstones. He closes his eyes and remembers the chant recited each night by him and Jamal and Atub. They took turns with the first name, then all three repeated it, heads bowed in submission, barefoot, kneeling on the floor of whatever place they were in.

Khalid al-Mihdhar.
*Khalid al-Mihdhar.*
Majed Moqed.
*Majed Moqed.*
Nawaf al-Hazmi.
*Nawaf al-Hazmi.*
Salem al-Hazmi.
*Salem al-Hazmi.*
Hani Hanjour.
*Hani Hanjour.*
Satam al-Suqami.
*Satam al-Suqami.*
Waleed al-Shehri.
*Waleed al-Shehri.*
Wail al-Shehri.
*Wail al-Shehri.*
Abdulaziz al-Omari.
*Abdulaziz al-Omari.*
Marwan al-Shehhi.

*Marwan al-Shehhi.*
Fayez Banihammad.
*Fayez Banihammad.*
Ahmed al-Ghamdi.
*Ahmed al-Ghamdi.*
Hamza al-Ghamdi.
*Hamza al-Ghamdi.*
Mohand al-Shehri.
*Mohand al-Shehri.*
Mohamed Atta.
*Mohamed Atta...*

A prayer.
Our prayer.
A prayer for our martyrs.
All waiting for us in Paradise.
*Allahu akbar!*
Now Malik can see, if only the large shapes of
ceilings and walls, as he peers up the stairs to the
first landing. He starts up. Somewhere up there, a
door creaks open on rusting hinges. There is
nobody visible, no sounds of breathing, no crackheads grunting, no pigs with badges from Home-
land Security or the FBfuckingI. No New York
cops. Like my father. Just the wind and the rain.
On the landings, puddles are spreading from
apartments without windows. The writhing
unreadable graffiti on the walls hasn't changed.

On the second flight of stairs, the entire banister is gone, used for firewood in the iron barrels of the empty lots, and Malik hugs the walls. A damp rotting smell is everywhere in the vertical cave of the stairwell. Water leaks from another doorway without a door. He listens as if he were a cat. He hears the distant hum of the expressway. The beep of a horn. Silence, except for the rain. Thinking: I'm coming, baby. I got money, gorgeous. Like I promised. Tomorrow you see a doctor. Tomorrow you go to a warm place.

On the top landing he goes to what was the front door and inserts the key in the lock he installed himself, bought from a locksmith up on Fifth Avenue. The same key can open the bedroom door, with its separate cylinder. Nine hours earlier, Malik locked Glorious in the bedroom, with its tiny closet of a room holding a toilet and nothing else. Afraid that she would go wandering and trip or fall and hurt herself. He lets himself in through the front door, and quickly locks the door again, using his free hand to smother the sound of clacking steel.

Sleep, my Glorious.

Be there soon.

Sleep.

Some clothes hang from a steel rack outside the hall bathroom, a flannel shirt, fresh jeans, socks looped over the bar. Sleep, Glorious, Malik thinks. We have things to do tomorrow. To get you to a hospital at last. To a doctor. He slips into the narrow bathroom, and begins to undress in the dark. He urinates, hoping the sound of water puncturing water does not escape the room. He is very cold. From a plastic milk crate on the tiled floor, he removes a flashlight and a pair of scissors. He tests the flashlight, then shuts it off. On the chipped sink, he lays out some things from the Korean store: a razor, a small can of shaving cream. He hopes he can remember how to do this, after so many years. And there's no hot water. The rusted boiler in the ruined basement holds no water. Somehow the pressure still moves cold water to the top floor. Malik holds the bag from the store under his chin and begins to chop away his thick beard. The hair is wet and wiry and tough. His body shakes from the cold. After a while, he runs a hand over his chin, feels a kind of bumpy fuzz, then switches on the flashlight. He doesn't know the face in the cracked mirror. He covers his jaws and chin with cream and begins to shave. He nicks himself in three places, wipes the blood with the back of a hand. My father's blood. Her blood. Soon it will be the boy's blood. The blood of Glorious too. Our blood. Allah's blood. Then he feels the smooth cheeks, makes a square cut for side-burns, and shuts off the light.

He shudders again from the cold, lays down the razor and the bag of hair, and steps into the shower. He doesn't want to do this. He'd rather fight some-one in the lot with bare hands. Not this. But he must. He must wash away the filth of infidels. This water will not hurt him. Inshallah. He reaches around for the shrinking bar of Dove, lying on its metal tray fas-tened to the water pipe. He turns the tap. His body feels a small death. He tells himself: Paradise is a gar-den with a stream running through it. Hell is another place, which Allah suggests to us through our living. And must be full of ice. Malik starts to pray as the water courses slowly down his body.

Khalid al-Mihdhar.
Majed Moqed.
Nawaf al-Hazmi...

He lectures himself: When we conquered Spain, we taught the infidels how to wash. And there was no steam heat in Andalusia or boilers in the basement. I would remind Mama when I was twelve or thirteen or fourteen that Islam civi-lized the world. Taught the filthy Christians to wash, Mama, taught them to read, taught them numbers, Mama, and architecture and music. Taught them for eight hundred years. And Mama would laugh, and say, If the Muslims were so damned civilized, why did they circumcise little girls? And why did they round up your ancestors in Africa and sell them to white folks? How is that civilized? And young Malik would say, Allah knows. Allah was testing all of us. And she would laugh. And say: Allah should get a life.

Bitch.

Now he soaps his hands over and over again, digging his nails into the Dove, soaps his hair, soaps his armpits, his ass, and his balls, grunting silently, using motion to warm him. The trickling water falls upon his shoulders and he splashes it roughly, feeling cleansed, purged, ready again for the mission, ready again to go forth as a member of the brotherhood. Ready for one final purge. Ready to die.

He turns off the shower, steps onto the cold tiled floor, and grabs a towel, the only towel, one that smells of Glorious. He feels his cock getting thicker, harder, and now wants the warmth of Glorious, Allah's gift; wants to lie behind her, to kiss her neck, to hold her swollen tits, to feel her ass grinding against his groin, to plunge his cock into her wet cave. He takes the key from his trousers, pulls on dry socks for warmth, wraps the

damp towel around his shoulders, lifts the flashlight, and pads down the hall to the bedroom.
Thinking: She'll be shocked. She has never seen
me without my beard. I must be silent. I must be
gentle. Above all, I must not scare her. She's my
woman. She's carrying my son.

He unlocks the door and steps into the darkness. The room is full of a black wind. The cold is
bitter. The cold is unforgiving. He switches on the
flashlight. There is nobody in the bed. The covers
are wild and rumpled and stained with something
dark that he knows must be blood. A pillow lies
on the floor. He moves the light and sees that the
window is open.

No.

—Baby? You here someplace?

No answer.

He walks to the open window, the towel falling. *No.* He stops a foot from the window. His feet
are suddenly sticky. No, please. No...The rain
has ended but the wind blows harder. But now he
does not shudder. He feels that his body is made of
ice. *No.*

He steps forward, his feet making a squishy
sound, and lays a free hand on the icy windowsill.
His breath expels a small cloud of steam. Finally
he leans forward and looks down. Four stories.

He sees the naked body of Glorious on a carpet

of rubble. Her luminous brown skin glistens from the rain. She does not move. In the crook of her left arm is a tiny child. Like a doll. The child does not move either.

Malik jerks backward, then falls hard to his knees. He faces the empty sky, and begins to howl.

### 2:29 a.m. Sandra Gordon. Her apartment.

She's awake again, out on the balcony, high above the glistening street. The plants are all dead, or dozing through winter. She's wearing the heavy down coat that Myles Compton bought her that cold spring day a few years back, explaining that it was to keep her Jamaican blood at room temperature. She laughed then. Jamaican blood. Why not New York blood? she said. I've been here longer than I ever lived in Jamaica. Longer than you, Myles, ever lived here either.

Now he's gone, lugging his credit default swaps and his derivatives or whatever the hell he was into. Gone. A fugitive now like ten thousand other rich grifters. He won't call me, she thinks. He won't e-mail. He won't do anything that will help them track him down. For sure, she thinks, the people on his trail will be listening to me too. Gotta change this number. The e-mail address too. They'll catch him anyway. The Feds. Interpol. The Bulgarians. Whoever. Ah, Myles.

Where are you, Myles? She turns and slips back into the dark living room, sliding the balcony door shut. She unzips the coat and drops it on the carpet.

Thinking: I can't ever do this again.

## 2:31 a.m. Ali Watson. Patchin Place, Greenwich Village.

He turns left off Sixth Avenue onto Greenwich and sees an open spot along the curb on the right. When he was young and tending bar in a joint called Asher's, the summer after he took the cops' test, he often walked past this spot when the little park was one of the saddest buildings in the city: the Women's House of Detention. Day and night, women in the House of D. would yell down from their cells to young men or older women who were holding babies for them to see. Most of the women in the cells were caught hooking or dealing drugs. Their mothers were scolding them from Sixth Avenue. Many men on the sidewalks were really only older kids. *You take care a' him, Buddy. Feed him good, Momma. No crap now, JoJo . . .*

The building is now gone: replaced by a park,

and on an angle through the wet leafless trees Ali Watson can see two fire engines, three police cars, a gathering of people in black silhouette. He can see the helmets of firemen bobbing in and out of the handheld lights. He pulls down the sun-blind mirror, with its NYPD placard facing the street side, clamps his badge on the top of his coat collar, gets out, pats his cell phone, locks the doors. Thinking: *Jesus fucking Christ.*

The rain has stopped now but the street is wet and glassy, reflecting a garish mixture of red lights and brights. And there in front of him is Patchin Place, a gated dead-end street between Greenwich and 10th Street, where he has so often dropped Mary Lou or picked her up to go home. The iron gates are open, hoses on the ground. Other residents of the small dead-end street are outside the gates, flanking the entrance, coats pulled tightly over nightgowns and pajamas, drinking coffee, smoking. All alone, a fat bare-legged white guy with a coat on top of a bathrobe seems to be eating a bowl of cereal. Watching. In a separate cluster, men and women aim cameras or cell phones, scribble notes: the reporters. Ali's breath is coming in tiny gasps. The front door of the house is open. Hoses snake from fire hydrants up the few steps into the Harding house. Three windows are open on the top floor. Lamps move in jerky patterns inside all floors. The air is gritty with smoke and ash.

*Oh, Mary Lou. Let them tell me you're at St. Vincent's. Let me know that you're okay.*

He walks to the front gate. He sees that each corner of the short street is blocked by a squad car with its red dome light turning. A lieutenant from the Sixth Precinct, a guy named Brennan, spots him. And comes up to him, taking his arm.

—Hey, Ali, he says softly.

—How bad is it, Joe?

—Pretty bad.

*Mary Lou. Mary Lou. Let me drive you home now.*

—Exactly how bad?

—Two dead. Then the fire after.

—Is—

—Yeah.

Brennan hugs Ali, tries to move him away from the house. Ali sags, then stiffens. The reporters, some street cops, an old lady in a man's overcoat: all are now watching. Tiny orange digital lights flicker like eyes. Ali gives Brennan a soft push and starts for the steps.

Just as a man in a civilian overcoat, a fedora, collar up, steps out of the building onto the top of the small stoop. Ray Kelly. The commissioner. He sees Ali, removes gloved hands from his pockets. There are two other cops behind him, blocking the narrow doorway. The odor of burned wood and fabric is stronger here. But clearly the fire is out. Kelly comes down the steps and goes directly to Ali Watson.

–Don't go in there, Ali, Kelly says softly.

–For Chrissakes, Ray. It's my *wife!*

–I know. That's why you're not going in.

–I gotta—

–It's an order, Ali. Come on. We'll take a walk.


**2:32 a.m. Sam Briscoe. His loft on Greene Street, SoHo.**


The phone rings in the darkness. From his bed, Briscoe glances at the night table. The bright green phone with caller I.D. From the paper.

–Sam here.

–Mr. Briscoe, it's the desk and—

–Put him on.

Briscoe sits up, swings around with his feet on the floor. Then he hears Matt Logan's voice.

–Sorry to bother you, Sam. But we got a big one.

–Tell me.

–A double homicide in the Village. One of them we think you know. Named Cynthia Harding and—

–What?

–And her secretary, a black woman named Watson. Mary Lou Watson. Her husband's a cop. Fonseca's at the scene. No details yet. How they died. Suspects. *Nada,* Sam.

–Call Helen.

–She got here ten minutes ago.

Briscoe switches on the lamp.

–The paper's locked up, Logan says. Maybe we can do a wrap, front and back.

–Yeah. Call Billygoat at the plant. See if we can do the wrap. Have Helen write the lede. Fonseca can write the scene. The clips should have a lot of stuff on Cynthia Harding, charities, the public library. Two husbands.

–Right.

–One more thing, Matt. Tonight she had a small fund-raiser at Patchin Place. For the library. I know because I was invited, but couldn't go. See if Fonseca can get a guest list, then you know what to do.

–Right.

–I'll get dressed and head to Patchin Place for a bit. Maybe call in a few things. Then I'll come to the paper. And Matt? One more thing.

–Yeah?

–Tell Helen she can smoke.

Briscoe hangs up. Mumbling in the emptiness of the loft. Jesus Christ. Jesus Christ. Cynthia?

151

Dead? Christ Allfuckingmighty. *No.* It's bullshit. *No.* Wrong address. But Matt has Mary Lou's name too. Oh, Cynthia...If I'd gone to the party, maybe I'd have picked up something, something wrong in the rooms, something about the guests or the mood. But hell: Cynthia's a grown-up. She knows what to look for too. So does Mary Lou. She sees like a cop. Like her husband, Ali.

Briscoe moves quickly to the bathroom, splashing water to wake himself up. Dries himself while looking out the back window. The rain is over. *Cynthia? Cynthia dead?* His heart is beating furiously. His stomach contracts, expands. Cynthia. My Cynthia. He sees fragments of her face. Many angles, always shifting, depending on age, emotions, the light. He sees the intelligence in Mary Lou's eyes. And her permanent skepticism. But Cynthia...Oh Jesus fucking Christ.

He pulls on socks, the gray trousers, thinking coldly now, becoming the newspaperman again, the craft that always protects him. Murder at a good address always leads the paper. Then remembers his breakfast meeting with the F.P. Eight-thirty in the morning. Very important. I'll bet. Yeah. Briscoe knots his tie. He is filled with a sudden rush of things ending. *Cynthia Harding is dead.* Along with Mary Lou Watson.

*Oh.*

Going cold again. Displacing the human. Displacing the enduring privacy of his life, and hers.

Cynthia Harding has been murdered.

He shoves some files in his leather bag, grabs a fedora and trench coat, and goes down to the street. He finds a cab on Sixth Avenue. He and the driver travel uptown in silence. The man doesn't play the radio as he moves north through the emptiness. Briscoe loops the chain of his press card around the collar of the coat. He gets off at Barnes & Noble on the corner of 8th Street, overtips, hurries toward the aura of bright white police lights and red domes. He sees the group of curious citizens, the cops, the firemen, the huddle of reporters. A few nod. He nods back. Fonseca is there too, and Briscoe motions him aside.

–How bad is it?

–Pretty bad, Fonseca says, looking at a notebook. Both women stabbed to death, Mr. Briscoe. Kitchen knife, maybe. There's one missing from one of those racks. The cops are searching sewers. It looks like the Watson woman got it first, in the hall outside the bedroom door. Then the Harding woman opened the door, they figure. And she got it. She was naked under a bathrobe. The Watson woman was fully clothed. There's blood all over.

–God…

Briscoe inhales the wet ashy air, lets it out slowly.

—Watson's husband is a cop, Fonseca says. Ali Watson. Ray Kelly was here and took him away somewhere, I guess to comfort him. Wouldn't let him in the house, for obvious reasons. I got a picture of Kelly and Watson on my cell phone, sent it already.

—Ali Watson's a member of the Joint Terrorism Task Force, Briscoe says. Tell Helen, but tell her I said she shouldn't put that in the paper. I'll tell Matt to keep Ali's face out of the paper too. Who knows what he's working on. Do they have any suspects?

He hears his own voice. Cold and flat, with a slight tremble.

—I don't know, Fonseca says. They're not saying much at all. The women were killed, then whoever did it used some kind of an accelerant to cover himself. Maybe from some kind of old-fashioned oil lamp. If it's a him. The firemen kept the damage to one room, top floor. Mostly scorching.

The bedroom, Briscoe thinks. Up past the paintings by Kuniyoshi and Lew Forrest.

—Who's running this? he says.

—A lieutenant named Brennan.

—He's a good cop. Tell him you know there was a party here last night, a fund-raiser for the library. Ask him if he has a guest list. If he lets you, then write down the names and we'll call each one of them. Don't do any of this in front of the other reporters.

–Right.

–Also ask if he's got the name of the caterer. And the waiters. Cynthia Harding always used a caterer for these things. They'd be the last to leave. Or one of them maybe stayed. If Brennan won't tell you shit, then do a sidebar right here, while you're waiting. Neighbors, everything. On the scene itself.

–Someone said that E. E. Cummings lived here. And John Reed.

–And a bunch of other people, including Anaïs Nin. I'll edit your piece and fill in any blanks.

–Great.

–See ya, Briscoe says, and slips away, walks to Greenwich and hails a cab.

**2:33 a.m. Bobby Fonseca. Patchin Place.**

He watches Briscoe go, then searches the corner crowd for Victoria Collins. No sign of her. His heart sank when the cell phone found him in the taxi. Matt Logan. Double murder in the Village. Go. He thought Victoria would be furious. Instead, she was excited.

—I want to go with you, she said.

—You got a press card? Fonseca said.

—An old one, a student I.D. from Columbia. Laminated. And—

—You probably can't get very close, he said. The cops—

—Come on, Fonseca. Let me try. I can work the neighborhood. Talk to people who might have known the victims. Whatever. I'm a good reporter. And I got this little recorder too. I can feed you my notes. Please.

The "please" got him. He leaned forward and told the taxi driver to take them to Sixth Avenue and 8th Street instead, and she squeezed his hand. At the scene, he got past the police line and she didn't, but he saw her talking to people beyond the line, knowing she held the tiny recorder in her hand shielded by a small notebook. Hands bare. Scribbling notes. As he was soon doing. Fonseca thought: She *is* a reporter, for Chrissakes. Why didn't someone hire her? Why'd they hire me?

The details came fast. From a uniformed cop. From a lieutenant. The air grainy from the fire, which was out. He called in notes as he got them, unloading to Helen Loomis. He went over to the edge of the gathering crowd, found Victoria Collins, took her notes, thanked her, pecked her cheek like a colleague. A *Times* guy showed up. Somebody from AP. Then Fonseca was back at the gates. Not feeling the cold. Full of the rush. A big one.

Then he saw Mr. Briscoe. Wondered why he was here. The boss. Fonseca saw pain in his face. Gave him a fill. Heard his directions. Saw him walk off. Thinking: Who the fuck am I to feel sorry for Briscoe? But I do. And I don't know why.

Victoria. Hey, there she is.


*2:36 a.m. Sam Briscoe. A taxi.*


His head throbs. Two dead. Stabbed and sliced. Fresh blood on the floor. Eyes wide in shock, for sure. Oh: my Cynthia.

And turns the switch in his head. Thinking. What's the wood? Think about wood. VILLAGE HORROR. No. Maybe. VILLAGE SLAUGHTER. Too many letters in "slaughter." Think about wood. Page 1, page 1 . . . BLOODBATH, with a subhead, *Socialite, Cop's Wife Killed in Village.* And the press run. Gotta tell Billygoat at the plant. A hundred thou more. Maybe two, if we replate completely for another edition. A head shot of Cynthia Harding. And Mary Lou Watson. Side by side. Back page, the kid's photo of Ray Kelly and Ali Watson.

Maybe the kid shot them from the rear. Ray with his arm across Ali's back. The wet street. Cynthia smiling.

Then thinks: Stop, you asshole.

Stop.

You loved this woman for three decades...

The cab pulls up at the newspaper. West Street now busy with groaning early-morning trucks. He pays, rushes through the one unlocked door, is waved to the elevator by the black security guard. Into the city room. Almost running. Right to Logan.

–How much time we got?

Logan glances at the old clock.

–Maybe forty-five minutes.

Briscoe pulls off his hat, coat, and jacket, throws them on a desk. He waves at Helen Loomis. She is smoking. Flourishing the cigarette, nodding thanks.

–The kid got the guest list, Logan says.

–Great.

–Guess who's on it?

–Tell me.

–Our brave publisher.

Briscoe makes a percussive sound with his mouth. *Pah!*

–You're kidding me.

–I'm afraid not.

—Give me some time. I'll call him and get details. What's the wood?

—Maybe THE LAST DINNER PARTY. No gore, except in the subhead.

—You're a fucking genius, Matt.

Briscoe walks away and stops at the desk of Helen Loomis. She looks up, a smile on her face. She's using a coffee container for an ashtray.

—Matt tell you about the party list? he says.

—Yeah, I'm calling them now.

—I'll call the publisher, Briscoe says.

—That's what I figured.

—I'll read the obit at my desk.

—Sure. By the way, Sam. You're in it. Among the various boyfriends.

—Not in this edition, Helen.

—Sam, it'll be in the *News,* the *Post,* and the *Times.* You can't leave it out.

Briscoe sighs.

—But I buried it with the names of other boy-friends, Helen says. The ones that made the gossip columns. And by the way, the Fonseca kid just dictated a scene sidebar. Very good — tight, great details. It ends with the cops carrying off two computers. I figure one for each vic.

He thinks: One of them contains the last e-mail I ever sent her.

–Thanks, Helen. For everything, but especially for showing up.

He hurries to his office, dumps his clothes in a chair, turns on the lights, opens the computer. Still standing, he checks the *Times* website. Nothing yet. Same with the *Post*. He doesn't bother with the *News* website because he can never figure it out. Then he sits down, looks for the phone number. Richard Elwood. He dials. Busy signal. Christ, the news is spreading.

He looks at the paper. The wrap will take a while. Fonseca's story about the murdered kid from Stuyvesant. The Doom Page. All old news now. He dials Elwood again. This time the young man answers.

–Yes? he says, his voice distracted.

–Briscoe here. I'm at the paper, Richard. You might have heard about what happened on Patchin Place.

–Yes, he says, his voice lowering. I was just on with some cop. It's a horror, Sam. She seemed like a nice woman.

Briscoe thinks: You mean Cynthia, of course, not Mary Lou.

–Do you want to give some sense of the dinner party to a reporter? Just atmosphere. What they talked about. No direct quotes, or I.D.

—I don't know. Let me think about it.

—We're on deadline, Richard.

—Deadline? I thought the deadline had passed.

—We're doing a wraparound. Four pages.

—A wraparound? How much will *that* cost?

—You can sell a hundred thousand more. We have stuff nobody else has. They'll blow it out on the morning news shows. If we can get it to them around nine.

—A hundred thousand more copies? That's a lot of paper.

—It's a lot of news.

Elwood exhales, pauses.

—All right, give me a few minutes to gather my thoughts. And Sam? We're still on for eight-thirty. It's very important.

Elwood hangs up. Briscoe writes his name and number on an index card, walks out to the city room, and hands it to Helen Loomis. She is lighting a fresh Marlboro Light.

—Call him in about five minutes, Briscoe says. As much detail as possible. Who was there, what was said, what was served for dinner, what they talked about. Everything.

She nods, focused by nicotine and urgency. Briscoe walks over to Logan.

—Tell Billygoat to print a hundred thousand

more, with the wrap, he says. And be ready for a replate, if they make an arrest.

—*Yes,* Logan says, smiling and making a fist.

Neither mentions the tabloid joy of murder at a good address. But Briscoe feels the rush, the adrenaline pumping. And then walks to his office consumed by shame.

**2:37 a.m. Malik Shahid. The Lots, Sunset Park, Brooklyn.**

There was no time to wash the body. No washing table there in the mud. No time to braid her hair either. No need to squash out the shit or piss or other filth; there was nothing inside her at the end, not even the baby. Malik knows he should have washed her three times, or five, or seven, always an odd number. But he is sure that the rain has washed her pure. He is sure of that. She was pure enough for Allah. Cleansed by rain sent by Allah.

Standing above the grave, he spoke scraps from the *takbars* too. *O Allah*: *let the one thou causeth to die from among us die as a believer* . . .

Malik wants to believe that Glorious died as a believer. When he covered her with the wet dirt, he whispered, *Minha khalaqnakum*. And added, *And into it we deposit you...* He wants Allah, in all of his mercy, to forgive Glorious Burress. For her puppy's doubt, for her scorn. She was a child herself.

But nothing has been easy, on this night of death. He dug the trench with a shovel from the hallway, grunting, moaning. Losing feeling in his hands. He brought down the bloody sheets and wrapped her in them, making a shroud. The boy's flesh was already cold, still tied to her by the cord. He placed the boy facedown on her rain-washed body, both of them like ice, moved her arms so that she was holding the baby, hugging the boy into eternity. Then he moved the sheet over her head, covering her face, and tied the ends beneath her neck. Praying all the while. Ending with *Allah is most great,* four times.

Then he climbed the stairs one final time, gathered what he needed into a backpack, scattered what was there as if it had been a crack house. He thought about spreading alcohol and setting it all on fire. And decided, No, that would attract police and firemen. Then he came down through the dark hallways, paused for a final prayer. Now he sets off into the night without end. Night of godly avenging horror. Night of red rain.

### 2:42 a.m. Myles Compton. New York State Thruway.

There is almost no traffic on the thruway. The driver is following orders: driving just above the speed limit, because his passenger doesn't want a delay caused by a state trooper. No ticket either. No record. Myles doesn't explain any of this to the driver and the two men don't chat. The digital clock on the dashboard changes by the second. Myles keeps repeating his new name, silently, like beads in a rosary. *Martin Canfield, Martin Canfield, Martin Canfield*...And in a silent echo of long ago, adds an ironical coda: Pray for us sinners, now and at the hour of thy death...

For a while in the past two months, he even thought of going back to his real name, his birth name, his baptismal name. Michael Cooney. The one he changed when he arrived on Wall Street. The name that was too Irish. Who the hell would invest money with a mick? At least in those years before the Celtic Tiger roared in Ireland. Now that's gone too. And if he became Mike Cooney again, then some smart little prick from the FBI could trace it, and trace me. *Martin Canfield, Martin Canfield*...

—How much longer, driver? he says.

The driver pauses, taps a finger on the GPS, says: Maybe ten minutes, sir.

—Okay, Myles says. They'll wait. Just don't speed.

—Yes, sir.

Myles slouches lower as the interior of the limo suddenly brightens. He feels a moment of fear. The Bulgarian's eyes. But a pickup truck passes on the left. No passenger. The driver in his thick plaid shirt doesn't look. Within seconds, the truck becomes two red eyes far ahead of them.

*Martin Canfield.*

He looks at tree branches whizzing above him, a stretch of emptiness, more trees, conical, dark and full, pine without Christmas ornaments. He thinks: My guys will be pissed at me today. All charged as co-conspirators. They'll probably think I was turned. All except the fucking Bulgarian. Sorry, guys. Blame me, okay? Just don't come looking for me. Don't find me.

He knows that Sandra won't even try. Too proud. She would no more pursue a man than she'd stick up a blind news dealer. Maybe that's why... Does he love her? Maybe. Probably. Whatever the hell love means. For sure, she didn't want a dime from him. Never asked for stock tips. Never asked about his business. A lot of women he knew were creatures of appetite and opportunity.

Sandra, no. Maybe later, a year from now, the man formerly known as Myles Compton can call from somewhere. He could ask her to meet him in another place, and they could drive to Martin Canfield's house, and...Nah. She'd hang up.

Christ, he thinks, it's harder to run from a woman than to run from an indictment.

The driver passes an exit sign and begins to slow. He pulls right, onto a ramp. Myles glances behind him through the tinted rear window. No other cars have turned off the thruway. He leans back, closes his eyes. In his mind, he sees the Lear-jet waiting on the landing strip. The pilot is standing by the door, glancing at his watch. The limo pulls over, and Myles gets out. No bags. A brief-case is all. Business trip to Toledo. The pilot says: Mr. Canfield? Then he sees himself tightening the seat belt and hears the engine revving up.

The limo driver makes several turns, and then is on a dark country road. Two lanes. Myles watches now. They pass houses whose windows are all dark. They pass some shuttered country stores. Another turn.

Then the driver leaves the two-lane road, into a lane with a painted sign for a place that ends in "Farms." He drives slowly now, then passes a dark house, moves into a parking area just beyond, and stops. The area is fenced by trees.

—One moment, sir, the driver says.

He steps out, leaves the door open, walks back toward the house.

Myles thinks, sucking saliva: This is not an airfield.

He pushes a button to lock the door beside him, his heart pounding now. He reaches across the front seat for the open front door.

Then a hand is in the car, and it's holding a pistol.

—Out of car, a voice says.

—Who are you? Myles says.

—Out.

The pistol is aimed at his head. Myles lifts the door button, pushes down on the handle, steps out into the rain.

There's a second man on the far side of the car. He walks around to face Myles.

—We take walk, he says.

And gestures to the woods.


**3:10 a.m. Ali Watson. Fort Greene.**


He can smell her everywhere in the house. Aromas more powerful than when he left, an hour or so ago. In the kitchen. On the stairs. In the sweetness of hand soap in the parlor-floor bathroom. There are traces of her cooking in the air, her breath, her skin. The perfumes of Mary Lou Watson. His body is clenched as tight as a fist. He knows he will have to leave.

His gun lies on the kitchen table, jammed into the holster that fits under his arm. He stares at the pistol. He knows he must carry it back into the night. And use it to find the person who stabbed his wife to death.

And remembers many of the people he has met after slaughter in this city, wives, lovers, husbands, boyfriends, children: the whole broken lot. All wrecked by the death of love. Life blown out of the ones they loved, or sliced out of them, or battered, or gouged. In their presence, working his imperfect craft, Ali was always low-key, knowing that force or threats or accusations never worked when the goal was to find out what happened. He wonders now how long it took the survivors to find sleep. He imagines them reaching for pills or whiskey, reefer or smack, anything that would obliterate memory or consciousness. In memory, every one of them talks about revenge. Some loudly. Some bitterly. Most often in whispers. The baffled children simply weep. But every one of them must have known that there were some problems you could not shoot.

He opens the refrigerator, looking for the bottle of Diet Coke that would scour the ash in his mouth. And sees Mary Lou there, too, in the neat Ziploc bags of cold cuts, the jars of sugarless jam on the door, the plastic cup of fake butter: the armory of her campaign against his cholesterol problem and her diabetes. He takes a bottle of water and closes the door. He cannot yet climb to the bedroom. He cannot stare at her shoes and clothing in the closet, or her dresser with its vials and combs and brushes and powders, or the sink with her mouthwash and toothbrush and tube of Crest.

He should not have come here alone. Ray Kelly offered to drive him home in his own car. "We can talk on the way," said Ray, who had talked to many survivors too, starting in Vietnam. But Ali Watson insisted that the commissioner had too much to do. Implying that this horror would be in all the papers. Kelly would have to speak in front of cameras and lights, maybe at the side of the mayor. So Kelly hugged him and whispered that he was very, very sorry. Malachy Devlin, his young partner from the task force, arrived in a raw angry mood, and used Ali's car to drive him back to Brooklyn. He wasn't angry at Ali. He was angry at whoever had caused Ali such pain. Everything was arranged, the kid said. A local squad car would return Malachy to Manhattan. All the way to Brooklyn, they talked very little. Ali Watson didn't want to sound like another mourning example of collateral damage. The kid offered to stay the night. No, Ali Watson said, I'll be all right.

Both of them knowing that he was lying.

Thinking now: I'll have to leave. But for where?

For a moment now in the kitchen, he imagines Mary Lou at the morgue. On her slab. Permanently silenced.

He forces himself to see her when she was twenty-three. Her skin glowing gold in the dim light of that little one-bedroom place in Bed-Stuy, framed by white cotton sheets. He forces himself to feel her warmth again as he held her tightly, full of need, and she again helped melt the ice jam in his heart, the one he had formed to protect himself from the horrors of the world that he was paid to police. She helped him on many nights to build a fence around all of that, to keep it in a separate place, far from home, far from here, far from all these rooms that bear even now the aromas of Mary Lou Watson. Now he has to build his own fences.

Just like that. Gone forever. They will not grow old together. They will never live on a beach by the sea, their hair turned white, dancing in a living room to Billie Holiday or Nat Cole. They will not enter a New York club at midnight and show the poor hip-hop fools how to dance. They will not chuckle together over the endless folly of the world, its vanities and stupid ambitions. They will not hug each other in any chilly New York dawn.

Oh, Mary Lou.

My baby.

My love.

He leans forward now on the table, his forehead pressed upon his folded arms, and his body unclenches, and he begins to weep.

When he is finished, when there are no more tears left in him, Ali Watson sits up. He reaches forward and taps the cold steel of the revolver.

### 3:45 a.m. Lew Forrest. Chelsea Hotel lobby.

He knows it's late because the lobby is empty. He can see it with his ears. Even Harry, the night man behind the desk, is dozing. He can hear the man's faint snoring, a papery flutter. Or the sound of someone blowing into an old Chiclets box. At this hour, it's just Forrest and Camus. At this hour, whatever time it is, the dog is usually a no-no. He's the gentlest and most noble of creatures, but there's always a chance that some knucklehead will barge through the door and Camus will read him wrong and go for his balls. But on nights when Lew Forrest can't sleep, the owners let them both sit here. A comforting solitude, in the best of company. No odors of paint or turpentine. No demands to keep working.

After Camus walked him to 24th Street and back, Forrest did sleep for a while. Then he was suddenly awake, his heart racing, and he knew he'd been dreaming about the war. There were no images alive in his head, no scenes, no faces, but he knew what they must have been, for they had been coming to him across more than sixty years. He was lost in the fog of the Hürtgen Forest. The artillery was roaring. And he was running, running, running. With no way out.

Now he is in the lobby of the Chelsea. No running. No panting. No artillery. From the street, he can hear a few cars, and one bus, all moving east and west on wet asphalt. He can hear Harry's snoring. There is no sound of fresh rain, but he can smell the wetness sliding under the front door. In the old days, the empty lobby was alive with tobacco smells, from cigarettes, cigars, pipes. All banished now by the triumphant armies of reform. There is a trace of disinfectant in the air, so he knows the lobby has been mopped.

Then he hears the elevator kicking in, humming as it rises in its shaft. A pause, as someone

172

boards. Maybe it's that Irish guy who has a hit novel out that I can't even read now. Seems like a nice fella. Another guy who wakes up in the night and needs the air to unlock a paragraph. There's been a lot of those guys here over the years. Now the elevator is coming down. He hopes the passenger is not leading a strange dog. Camus knows all the regulars. But he brooks no arrogant hounds. Particularly phony tough guys. Those runty little dogs with teeth like critics. Camus, after all, was once a member of the Resistance. Or his namesake was.

Lew Forrest hears the elevator stop, with a jerk and a thump. The doors open. Harry whispers his good morning. Then he hears the klok-klok klok-klok of knobby heels. He knows who it is.

–Oh, Mr. Forrest.

Lucy from *ARTnews*. Down from the third floor.

–Good morning, dear, Forrest says.

She comes around and sits next to him. Camus exhales, returning to his position with paws stretched out, head between them on the tiled floor.

–I couldn't sleep, she says.

–Good. That's the best time to work. Wear yourself out and sleep till noon.

–It's not that easy.

—The key is, Forrest says, leave the television set off. It scrambles the brain, whether you're painting or writing.

—Funny, that's exactly what happened.

—See what I mean?

—There was an awful story on New York One. I had it on to check the weather, to see if the rain would end. And there was this story. Very upsetting. Two women were murdered in the Village. One of them was a cop's wife. The other was a woman named Cynthia Harding.

—Cynthia *Har*ding? Forrest whispers, shock in his voice.

—Did you know her, Mr. Forrest? New York One said she was a patron of . . .

He inhales, then exhales.

—I knew her, yes.

—The TV said she raised money for the arts and—

—She did a lot more than that.

—Oh, I'm sorry, Mr. Forrest.

—She owned some of my paintings and hung them down at her home in Patchin Place. She bought them in, oh, nineteen eighty-five? Before anybody was buying them. Before the dough started rolling in from buyers, before I was suddenly hip after fifty years of painting . . . But I first knew her back in the sixties, after I came home from Paris...Or was it Mexico? Anyway, I knew her. She was the same age you are now, maybe. Beautiful, and very smart...Oh, God. Oh, god-damn it all to hell.

She touches his face with both hands.

—I didn't mean to hurt you, she says. I should've kept my mouth shut.

—Yes, the hurt...But it's not about me, Lucy dear. Not even close. It's about her. Lovely Cynthia...

He stands up. So does the dog, who stretches, then shakes.

—Can we go for a little walk? Forrest says. The rain's over, isn't it?

—Yes, Lucy says. But it's pretty wet out there.

—Eh, let's try.

Lucy opens the door, and Camus moves through it, pulling Lew Forrest after him. Harry is with them. Awake now. Protective.

—Don't go too far, Harry says.

—We'll be all right, Harry, Forrest says.

Then he, the dog, and Lucy are outside under the awning. Each inhales the freshness of the rain.

—Just beautiful, he says.

—Yes, it is.

They walk in silence toward Eighth Avenue, following the lead of the dog.

—Can I ask your permission for something? Forrest says.

—Of course.

—Can I touch your face?

She giggles.

—Of course, she says.

He uses his right hand, and runs his fingertips lightly, gently over her brow, her cheekbones, her chin, her nose, and her lips.

—You're beautiful, he says. I thought so.

—Come on, Mr. Forrest.

—You are, he says. I wish I could draw you.

They are still walking toward Eighth Avenue, and stop under the marquee of the movie house.

—But you live alone, he says. How come?

—Oh, I don't know. Maybe I'm not as beautiful as you think. Guys are . . . you know.

—Yeah, I know. Are you lonely?

—Sometimes, she says.

Forrest thinks: That means all the time.

—Don't let it get to you, he says. It's part of the deal, especially in this goddamned city.

He turns to go back to the Chelsea. She holds the crook of his arm. Then he stops again.

—How bad was it? he says. The killings, I mean.

—Pretty bad, she says. If New York One has it right.

—Both of them shot?

—No. Stabbed.

—Oh, God.

He pauses, feels tears welling in his ruined eyes. He flashes on Cynthia Harding's smooth skin, her delicate neck.

—I'm so sorry, Mr. Forrest, Lucy says, squeezing his arm. I should've kept my mouth shut.

—No, no. Don't apologize. Please.

—But I—

—It's not you, Lucy. It's her. And the son of a bitch who did it to her.

Camus senses that something is wrong. He nuzzles Forrest's leg, pulls gently on the leash. And leads him home.

### 3:50 a.m. Freddie Wheeler. His apartment, Williamsburg, Brooklyn.

He sits barefoot in a bathrobe, leaning back in the chair, staring at the blank screen. He has checked the news bulletins online, and they are alive with the killing of Cynthia Harding and Mary Lou Watson. He wants to write, and can't. He knows nothing about Mary Lou Watson. She doesn't even have a Facebook page, f' fuck's sake. But neither does Cynthia Harding. He has never spoken with her, but he does know her. Rich bitch with a press agent. Her name in the papers, the columns, fund-raising for the library, a Brooke Astor knockoff. Never gives interviews. Didn't even know that books are over, that words on paper are over, that nobody goes to the fucking library in the age of Google. Still, why kill her? Why slice her up? Nobody deserves that...

–Stop, he says out loud.

Céline would laugh at you, you mushy air-headed sentimentalist! What makes you think Cynthia Harding was *not* just another New York hustler, chiseling her piece from the charities, lying on her taxes, and always nasty with the help? What makes you think she *didn't* deserve it? For Chrissakes, she was the girlfriend of that son of a bitch Briscoe. That should have been enough motive, right?

And laughs, thinking: Oh, my Céline: I've been doing this too long.

He stands up and stretches. He places a hand on the window frame and stares across the street at the converted four-story tenements, with their black metal chimneys rising from the rooftops like hooded night watchmen. Water drips from cornices. Fire escapes cover the facades...a kind of iron calligraphy...cluttered with dead flowerpots...and one soaked denim shirt that has been there for months. A few lights burn in yellow rectangles behind drawn shades...still awake, or living in fear. He senses the city beyond the corniced rooftops...the sleepless...block after block of loveless imperfect fortresses that have lasted now for a century. So many people are awake...like the rats within the walls. The lucky ones are fucking...risking everything...even their lives. The rest are plotting...scheming...seething.

The way I do.

The way Céline did.

Even Céline needed sleep, he thinks. I must sleep now...be ready to celebrate. In a few hours...must raise a fist in the air...and curse Briscoe...and proclaim the end of the *World*.

### 3:50 a.m. Malik Shahid. Sixth Street, Gowanus, Brooklyn.

He is stretched across the backseat of the car, thinking that all we have is the past. The long-ago past. Medina in the seventh century. The immediate past. Two days ago. An hour ago. The blue Toyota is about eight years old, with a rusting scar on the hood. Definitely not a car worth stealing, either for resale or joyriding. It smells too of cigarette smoke and stale Chinese food. The filthy perfume of corruption. All the way from Sunset Park, Malik had been careful, never speeding, never trying to beat a red light. On Fourth

Avenue, he drove all the way in the center lane. Looking casual. Middle-class. Yeah. Some graduate student from CUNY. Yeah. That's me. Even when a police car eased past him and made a right on 9th Street. He didn't play the radio, didn't want to hear news bulletins on 1010 WINS. No weather report. The rain stopped. The sky gray.

He drove past Jamal's street, went three more blocks, and turned on 3rd Street toward the Gowanus Canal. Pulled over beside a shuttered clothing factory, just past a loading bay. Turned off lights and engine. He pocketed the key, left by some drunken asshole. He wasn't worried about the license plate. Nobody would report this heap of shit stolen. Waited, battling sleep, exhaustion eating his flesh. Alert for cruising patrol cars. Or anyone else who might spot him. Then he climbed into the backseat. The floor littered with beer cans mixed with a child's plastic earthmover toy and a scuffed pair of women's shoes. He opened a window on the right side, about a quarter inch, to allow air to enter. And stretched out to rest. He did not truly sleep.

Sleep would have to wait until he entered Jamal's house on 6th Street, three blocks to the south. Jamal, his closest friend in the years after his conversion, Jamal, who traveled with him to Philadelphia, to Buffalo, to Canada, to all the stops in what they both called the Network. He was my brother then, the older brother I never had. His father was a doctor in Philadelphia, maybe still alive, practicing. Making money off sick black folks. Whites too. After September 11, Jamal was convinced that jihad was the only way. He and Malik started collecting the things they needed. A few guns. Powder. Accelerants. Bomb stuff. Getting ready for a rising.

Even after Jamal married an unbeliever, even after his father helped him buy the Brooklyn house, he still believed that day was coming, the moment when Allah's punishing wind would blow again through America. Malik believed too.

Then Jamal went on the *haj*. And when Jamal came back, he called Malik and said: Malcolm was right, brother. Malik was sure he knew what Jamal meant. Malcolm came back from making his own first *haj* believing that Elijah Muhammad and his Black Muslim cult was a bunch of shit. Pure Islam, Jamal said, was all that mattered. Malik agreed. But Jamal said that pure Islam didn't necessarily include jihad. Their friendship started drying up. Jamal's marriage helped it happen. They stayed in touch for a while. But it wasn't the same.

After services at the mosque in Cobble Hill, even the imam, that timid man, asked them to stay away, insisting that suicide was against the Quran, that if you kill yourself in some action it is *haraam* and you cannot enter Paradise. Later that afternoon, walking in Brooklyn, Malik ranted to Jamal, shouting that the imam was a *mushrig,* a Muslim who betrays other Muslims. He should be killed. Jamal disagreed, softly, politely, a consoling arm upon Malik's shoulders, but Malik raised his voice even higher and they went their separate ways. Malik traveled different roads. Longing for Iraq. Longing for Pakistan. Longing for Tora Bora. For training. For sacrifice. And never going. Finding Glorious Burress instead.

Now Jamal is a designer, a graphic artist, who uses his talent to sell the worthless shit that corrupts the world, even the Muslim world. His infidel whore wife won't allow Malik into their house. They have a child, now about four years old, and the wife is too busy for visitors. Or so Jamal said once when Malik called from Denver. "You're my brother, Jamal," Malik said. "I miss you, man." Jamal chuckled and said, "Yes, but I'm my little girl's father and my wife's husband."

Malik couldn't tell anyone all that he felt about the old friendship. The endless nights of talk. The dissecting of the Quran. The discovery of the work of Sayyid Qutb. The sense of mission, and purpose, and fierce shared anger at all the corruption in America. He never had another talk as intense as the talks with Jamal. Not with anyone. Certainly not with Glorious Burress, that beautiful heathen puppy. Jamal was the one, the channel into truth. He did try to keep Jamal alive in his life. When he called Jamal, the infidel whore wife almost always answered and Malik always hung up. One Friday evening in the previous July, Malik even went to Jamal's street, taking the R train, walking to their block. Looking casual as he passed their house. Hoping he would bump into Jamal as he took a morning walk. Watched for a long time from the doors of the abandoned garage up the street. Rehearsing words. After twenty minutes, he saw them placing bundles and suitcases and a folded stroller into the trunk of a BMW. The wife held the little girl by the hand, the two of them whorish in bare legs and flip-flops. Heard the wife calling to Jamal: "Jerry! *Jer*-ry! We're *late!*" Jamal now called Jerry. Malik turned and walked around the corner, out of sight into Third Avenue, thinking: Maybe they are picking up the imam to drive to the Hamptons.

Fatigue gnaws at him now. Eating the sore muscles in his arms and legs and hands. Reducing him to this boneless body flattened against the

183

backseat. He thinks: I have nobody at all left to talk to. Nobody in the whole wide godless world. Unless Jamal talks. One last time. I will lie here, empty, until the sun comes over the ridge behind me and warms the morning and dries the rain. Then I will rise too, he thinks. To walk the short blocks to 6th Street. To look, to see, to go to Jamal and retrieve what I know is in his house. The stuff of cleansing.

He begins to pray.

Khalid al-Mihdhar.
*Khalid al-Mihdhar.*
Majed Moqed...

And sleeps.


**5:25 a.m. Bobby Fonseca. Avenue B and 12th Street, Manhattan.**

They lie together in the dark, spent, breathing deeply, Victoria's breasts against Fonseca's back, a down blanket pulled tightly to their necks. Gray street light seeps from the bottom of the window shades. The sound of rain has stopped. Both are awake.

–Thank you, she whispers.

—I promise I'll get better.

—Not that, dummy. Thanks for taking me with you. For making me feel like a reporter, instead of a goddamned waitress. For three hours, at least.

He turns to face her, breaking into a smile. His black hair is spiky.

—I'm glad I did, he says. You kicked ass. Made me look good. I told them to give you a credit line.

—Now you tell me?

She sits up.

—I gotta tell my father!

—Not now, he says, leaning on his bent elbow, head in hand, as if addressing her right breast. We don't know if they'll *give* you the credit. I can't order it, y'know.

—He'll increase today's circulation by at least *ten* papers, Fonseca.

Then she laughs and slides back beneath the covers. And is silent.

—I'll be right back, Fonseca says. Where's the, uh—?

She switches on a muted bedside lamp. In the yellow darkness, framed photographs cover a wall, with some front pages too. *Times. Daily News. Post.* HEADLESS BODY IN TOPLESS BAR. A stove. A sink. One wall of books, CDs, DVDs. She points.

—Right there. The blue door.

Fonseca walks naked to the blue door,

shivering in the cold. The wood floor is cold too when he steps past the rug. A small narrow john. Just a toilet, a roll of paper attached to the wall, the seat down. Like an airline toilet, without the sink. He lifts the seat. Staring at a framed browning photograph of a blonde woman. Eyes that miss nothing. From the thirties, maybe? Her grandmother, maybe? Finishes. The woman in the photograph seems to demand he wash his macho hands. No sink.

He steps out, closes the door behind him.

—The sink is beside the stove, she says, her head showing above the blankets. Shoulda warned you.

He washes his hands, uses a towel on a rod above the sink.

Then hurries back to the warmth, the aroma of Victoria Collins. Reaches past her back and holds one of her hands. Silence for a beat. Then:

—A question, he says.

—Yeah?

—The woman in the bathroom: who is she?

—My hero. Martha Gellhorn. She's in the bathroom so I'll see her every morning. And night.

A vague memory stirs in him. Professor Norman's class at NYU...

—She was married to Hemingway, right? Fonseca says.

—Wrong. He was married to Martha Gellhorn.

As a journalist, Hemingway wouldn't make a pimple on her ass.

And laughs. So does Fonseca. She squeezes his hand. His flesh is warm now. They are quiet. Finally, she clears her throat.

—Did you read CelineWire tonight?

—Life is too short for that asshole. He's a nasty little prick that Briscoe fired a couple of years ago. Why should I read his crap?

—He says the *World* is folding this weekend.

—He's *always* saying that. He wants it to be true, even if it isn't.

—Just thought you should know, she whispers.

They are silent again.

—Would Martha Gellhorn read CelineWire? he whispers.

She giggles.

—If it was about Hemingway, she would.

And pushes her butt against him.

# DAY

***8:10 a.m. Sam Briscoe. Third Avenue and East
53rd Street, Manhattan.***

H E STANDS WITH HIS BACK to the Citibank
Building, a steel and glass structure too big
to fail. After three hours napping on the couch in
his darkened office, a quick shave in the john, a
fresh shirt, a glance at the papers, Briscoe is twenty
minutes early for his appointment with the F.P.
The Dominican driver from the car service
explained that traffic is thinner now, with fewer
limousines, not as many cars coming in from
Brooklyn and Queens and New Jersey. Briscoe
doesn't mind being early on this bright cold morning after too much rain and too little sleep. He
would not want to give the publisher an edge by

being late. And he needs to get out of his solitude, to look at other people, to stop thinking for a little while about Cynthia Harding and Mary Lou Watson and the dark horror of the night.

Across the avenue, the publisher's office is half-way up the more than thirty stories of the Lipstick Building, the gleaming tower where Bernie Madoff pulled off his immense robberies. Thus achieving tabloid immortality. Hell, even immortality in the *Times* and the *Washington Post*. Briscoe imagines the gullible rich arriving in a steady, discreet stream to be conned with a smile and a shoe shine. Except Madoff didn't have the soul of Willy Loman. Madoff knew that his victims were rich by most standards, certainly by the standards of his own Far Rockaway childhood. And so they came to him during the boom, believing that Madoff would make them even richer. Acolytes of the religion of more. Obese capitalism. They knew from whispery chats that he had done it for some select friends. He had done it for universities. He had done it for Holocaust survivors and their children and even for Elie Wiesel. Why not ask him to turn their spare ten million bucks into sixteen? His reputation made them believers. And once again, Briscoe remembers Paul Sann's ancient city room creed: "If you want it to be true, it usually isn't."

He turns his eyes away from the rising ovals of the Lipstick Building, with its arrogant red-brown and pink bands, gazes downtown, sees a thirty-ish hatless man in a dark blue overcoat, staring at the page 1 wrap of the *World*. His jaw is slack. And Briscoe wonders if Cynthia Harding had ever arrived on this corner. To cross into the Lipstick Building and ride up the silent elevator to meet Madoff. To create wealth for the library. To create wealth for herself. And Briscoe thinks: Never.

Cynthia was a reader, one who could read human faces too, including mine, read the practiced smiles of others, the rehearsed patter, the movements of eyes, the posture of hands. She knew that books in neat or disordered shelves revealed the character of their owners too, and as a guest in any luxurious apartment always found her way to the library, and was filled with a kind of joy to discover those leathery older volumes whose pages had never been cut. Briscoe was beside her on two such investigations, moving around the edges of crowded parties. She didn't say much, showing him a volume that was only a piece of interior decoration. She never needed to italicize a word. She just moved her brows in an amused way. "Henry James would love these people," she whispered on one such patrol. "His own books have never been opened."

An imaginary flash of her astonished face slices into his mind.

*Oh.*

Her beautiful mind drained of life. And irony. And art. And love. With a knife, on a rain-soaked night.

*You fucker.*

And realizes that he is thinking now about Cynthia in the past tense.

For the first time. And for the rest of his life.

He inhales hard, turns to watch the thickening morning crowds rising from the subway stairs or stepping out of the few limousines, or finishing the last lap from Grand Central. Hundreds of them. And sees past them, or through them, or under them, into a world they don't know ever existed, right here. Where the Lipstick Building rises like a triumphant sneering monument. Briscoe sees the corner when he lived in this neighborhood as a boy, in another century, another world. He sees the great black steel girders of the Third Avenue El rising above the summer street during the war. He climbs the worn stairs at 53rd Street with his mother and goes through the turnstile. He rides all the way to the last stop in the Bronx,

East 149th Street, peering from the front car at the tracks ahead of him, the steel rails stretching to a vanishing point, or making abrupt turns, while Briscoe looks into the windows where other people lived, sipping tea, drinking beer from tin pails, eating or laughing or locked in morose solitude, smoking cigarettes. He sees their heads and shoulders beyond the rooftop canopies, tending flocks of pigeons, or hanging wash.

On another day, he takes the El downtown to Chatham Square and he and his mother have chop suey in Chinatown and walk over to the entrance of the Brooklyn Bridge, his mother gripping his hand, and they are walking across to Brooklyn, just the two of them, high above the crowded river, then walking back that summer afternoon and seeing the skyline for the first time outside of a movie. On the way home, they get off early and stop in St. Agnes to pray for Briscoe's father, who is off at the war.

And then Briscoe sees V-E Day, when he was seven, and the war is over at last in Europe and everyone who lived on these side streets came surging out to Third Avenue, and out of the saloons, out of P. J. Clarke's and the World's Fair and others whose names he can't remember. Retired cops and old bootleggers, butchers and bakers, shipyard guys. longshoremen, shoemakers, plumbers, ice men, thieves, black marketeers, cabdrivers, all of them roaring, singing, drinking. There were even more women than men, most of them crying for sons and boyfriends and husbands who would now be on the troopships steaming back into the harbor. And his mother said, "Now, Sam, *now* your father will come home, Sam. He and his friends, they beat that old Hitler." Nobody said anything about the war in the Pacific that was not over. They took what they could get here, Briscoe thinks. Right where my feet are planted.

And though his father was a New York cop, and could have stayed home, he had to go to the war, his mother explained, because he was a Jew, and Hitler was killing Jews, and so his father had to kill some Nazis back. That's what his mother told him. On the crowded street now, in the rushing Friday crowds, he can still hear her voice, the Irish curl, the Belfast rhythm.

He sees his father too, months later, coming up the tenement stairs where they lived on East 49th Street, wearing his army uniform, a big lumpy duffel bag on his shoulder. Sam was sitting on the third-floor-hallway steps with his friends, all of them eight years old, waiting and waiting. Until Jimmy Hartigan from the first floor started yelling up at them, *He's here, Sam! He's here!* And Briscoe remembers clomping down the flights of stairs, two steps at a time, leaping to each landing, and on the first flight he saw his father, who saw him, and dropped his duffel bag, and the boy leaped to his father's arms, and the two of them froze there, bawling and bawling, man and boy. No words said. The father's body heaving. The boy trembling. The fucking war was over.

Nobody on this Third Avenue morning knows that such a world ever existed. Cynthia Harding knew. She knew because I walked these streets with her and told her all about it. More than once. Blathering away. Hoping I was not coating her with the treacherous paste of sentimentality. We went together often to the only surviving remnant: P. J. Clarke's, another block uptown. Introduced her one night to Sinatra. And Danny Lavezzo, the owner. When we got back to her house, she said to me, with a hint of envy, *You're such a lucky man, Sam. You didn't get that world secondhand. You didn't take a course in it. You lived it.* He thinks: I didn't take a course in Cynthia Harding either. I lived it. We lived it.

Standing now, facing the Lipstick Building, Briscoe checks his watch. Ten minutes more before the meeting. And he remembers walking here with Cynthia one summer afternoon, telling her about walking the same street with his father, who was a cop again. After the war. They passed pawnshops and saloons, full of workers from the slaughterhouses down where the UN now stands. Some of the workers wore aprons covered with bloodstains, drying into darker colors, swatting at horseflies. In summer, the saloon doors were always open, for there was no air-conditioning then, and the joints all smelled of sour beer.

Briscoe described for Cynthia the brick facades of buildings permanently shadowed by the El, the boxy shadows on the cobblestones at high noon, hears the sound of screeching steel, almost painful when trains stopped at 53rd Street. Right there where the Lipstick Building is, his aunt Mary lived in one of the flats, his mother's sister, her sailor husband dead in the Pacific war, his body never found, and when they went visiting Aunt Mary on Sunday afternoons, for dinner and song and company, Briscoe loved peering at the trains from the front windows of the flat, the faces of the people within, who never looked at him, or even at each other. He wanted to know who they were, and would spend a tabloid lifetime finding out.

Briscoe remembers the day the nickel fare ended in 1948 and how everyone complained bitterly about the increase when he and his father stopped to chat on Saturday mornings. He remembers listening to the radio every day, no television then.

Music and serials and news. And baseball. He remembers Giant games playing from open windows, and how everyone hated the Yankees and the Dodgers. He remembers too the day the Briscoes packed up to leave, all they owned put in cartons, or wrapped in sheets of newspaper, then stacked in a truck that was leaving for Brooklyn, where his father had bought the house in Sunset Park. A house with a backyard and a tree and eventually a dog. Bought with a V.A. loan. A different world.

Enough. It's all gone now.

He crosses Third Avenue, walking quickly. Part of his past is under his feet and the future is right in front of him. He moves into the Lipstick Building, taking his press card from his jacket pocket. Thinking: Now Cynthia is part of the past too.


**8:20 a.m. Josh Thompson. The High Line, Manhattan.**


He is in the street but he can't see the sky. There is a man standing off to the side, with a wild gray beard, a heavy plaid shirt.

—Mornin', soldier, he says.

—Morning, Josh Thompson says, his throat cloggy with phlegm. He grips the MAC-10 under the blanket and poncho.

—Go ahead and hawk up the lunger, soldier.

Josh calls up a wad from his throat, makes a pulpy ball on his tongue, spits it three feet to the side.

—Where is this? he asks, looking around him.

—The High Line. Used to be a railroad spur. Then it was dead for fifty years. Now they planted it with stuff and made a park out of it. Right up above your head.

—A park?

—Yeah, a park in the sky. The High Line, they call it. There's an elevator down there, you wanna see it. Hey, you must need to piss.

—Yeah.

—Let the brake out and I'll walk you.

He rolls Josh into a shadowed area, filled with packing crates.

From the darkness, he wonders where the Aladdin is from here. As he does every time he has to piss, he thinks of payback.

—You need a paper to read, soldier?

—Sure.

He takes the newspaper. Two women on the front page. One blonde. One black. The headline says:

THE LAST DINNER PARTY

Who are these people? Josh thinks. Why isn't Iraq on the front page? Or Afghanistan? They just don't give a rat's ass, do they?

The bearded guy leaves him alone. Josh starts unzipping his jeans, unfastening his diaper.

### 8:35 a.m. Sandra Gordon. Lobby of Lipstick Building.

She walks across the crowded plaza, following others through the revolving doors. She is wearing high boots, a heavy coat, a warm wool hat. The *New York Times* is under her left arm, home-delivered but unread, and she grips a Mark Cross briefcase. She will open the paper when she reaches her desk. Not an electronic reader for the *Times*. The *Times* itself. To see if there is news about Myles Compton. And his co-conspirators. She wonders if Myles made his plane, if that's what he was taking to wherever he will hide for the rest of his miserable life. The poor son of a bitch.

Then she glances at the newsstand, the newspapers blocked by two men buying nuts or gum or even newspapers. One of the men moves and heads to the elevator banks. Sandra's eyes fall to the low shelf of newspapers.

She makes a sharp sound of pain, and falls to the polished stone floor.

### 8:40 a.m. Ali Watson. Office of Joint Terrorism Task Force, Manhattan.

He is still filled with the night, lying on a cot in the small dark back office. Nobody has tried to rouse him with knocks on the door. He knows they are out there in the office, absorbing information, thinking about chatter from many places. For now, they will get along without him. He's better off here than alone at home. They will let him grieve.

His mind is jagged, alive with crude scribbles he saw from his Mazda, which Malachy parked in front of his house. His brain jangles with the graffiti on the wet walls of empty Brooklyn streets, marks without verbs, just names, the narcissism of vandals. I am, they snarl. I exist, they brag. All the names invented, pseudonyms without warnings or declarations of love. When Ali was young, and he saw the words "Bird Lives" on a subway wall, he knew the message was about Charlie Parker, and the words were saying that his music would live forever. And so it has. This is not like Bird. I want to buy a spray can and write *Mary Lou Lives* on all the unwashed walls of the city. State it. Shout it. Make the verb clear. Make it about her, not me. Refuse to join the legions of I. All those young fools declaring that they exist. Shouting: I am alone, as lonesome as God, and here is my mark. I exist, and fuck you.

*Mary Lou lives, you assholes.*

He sits up on the edge of the narrow bed, and remembers the drive at dawn to the mosque, where he spoke to the imam. He woke the man up, and was allowed inside. He said to the imam that if he heard from Malik, please tell him that his mother was dead. That he should call his father. The imam was gentle, trying to console Ali, but shrugged and said he had not seen Malik in a long time. Maybe years now. Ali said: What about Jamal? Yes, sometimes he comes, the imam said. Jamal is still a Muslim. He even made the *haj*. He has nothing to do now with jihad. Ali knew that, knew Jamal's address too. He said nothing more to the imam about Malik, but did give him a card.

–Call me, if you hear from my son.

–Yes, sir.

–I'm sorry for waking you up.

–I wasn't sleeping, the imam says. I was praying.

–Pray for me.

–I will.

–And above all, for my wife.

Ali walks blindly now to the wall of the tiny room in the JTTF, feels for the light switch. Flicks it on. He blinks in the hard blue light of the fluorescent ceiling bulbs. The pale green walls are blank. Then he steps to the sink, turns on the tap. Thinking: This is like a cell in a very good prison. I am sentenced to solitary.

Never thought I'd survive Mary Lou. Not because I'm older, because of this job. You race to a domestic dispute and a man and a woman stop beating the shit out of each other and turn on you. Both of them. A knife or a gun, that's part of the deal. Or there's a robbery of a jewelry store in Chinatown, and you see the guy running through the screaming crowd, and a truck blocks his way, and he turns and fires. Over and over again. Day by day, year by year. Life in this job is a goddamned lottery, with odds against. Ali Watson always thought she would bury him. Why *you*, Mary Lou? Why not *me?*

He dries his face, runs a comb through thinning hair. He sees that his eyes are rimmed with red. And turns away from the mirror. Now I have to do the clerical stuff. There's nobody else. Just me. Arrange a funeral. In Brooklyn. Pick the cemetery too. Dodge the press. Plead national security or some goddamned thing. Ask Ray Kelly to help. Call the lawyer about insurance.

First I gotta find someone else.

### 8:50 a.m. Sam Briscoe. Publisher's office, Lipstick Building, Manhattan.

He is sitting on a leather couch in the reception area, casually scanning the *New York Times.* His hat and coat are in the closet. He is warm in his suit jacket. Behind him on the wall are raised letters in Caslon bold, spelling out the name chosen long ago by Elizabeth Elwood: "World Enterprises, Inc." Simple and modest. There is a large portrait of her by Everett Raymond Kinstler on the right side of the lettering, placed there after her death. The portrait perfectly captures her intelligent, sympathetic eyes. It was commissioned by her husband long ago, and hung over the fireplace in the living room on Sutton Place until he died. Then she moved it into the library. Her son Richard moved it here, after the apartment was sold. He donated most of her books to the public library, but Briscoe is certain that he chose none of them for himself.

He has been waiting now for twenty minutes,

and the receptionist has explained with chilly vagueness that the publisher knows he is here. The door into his office remains shut and Briscoe knows why. He glances at *Forbes, New York* magazine, and the lone copy of the Friday edition of the *World,* with its wraparound and the faces of the two women. He wishes he could stretch out and sleep.

The door opens. And a man and a woman emerge, holding coats before them in laced fingers. They are obviously from Homicide, but too young for Briscoe to know them. Richard Elwood is behind them, his white shirt open, tieless, looking solemn.

–Thanks again, Sergeant, he says. It's a horrible, horrible tragedy, and I hope you catch whoever did it very soon.

–We will, the male cop says, while the woman nods. They shake hands with Elwood, glance at Briscoe, and go to the outer door leading to the elevators. Elwood gestures to Briscoe to come in. They shake hands briskly and Elwood closes the door behind them.

–Hello, Sam, Elwood says. Great paper today. You were right to do the wrap.

–Thanks, Richard.

–I just wish it had never happened.

–Me too.

The office has more square feet than the old apartment on East 49th Street. Briscoe glances around and sees that everything remains as it was a few months earlier, when he last came for a visit. The bar. A cork wall behind Elwood's desk, busy with a collage of index cards, newspaper clippings, Post-its, business cards. A wall with framed photographs of his mother with Ted Kennedy, Bill and Hillary, Mike Bloomberg, Bush the Father, and young Elwood himself. One of him as a little boy. Through a wide window Briscoe can see Queens. Elwood leads the way to the sitting area, with a couch, two wing chairs, and a low table. A Mark Rothko rises above the couch, all reds and yellows. The table is bare except for a single copy of the *World.* Elwood sits in a corner of the couch, and gestures for Briscoe to take the near chair.

–Cynthia Harding was a wonderful woman, Elwood says.

–She was. Did the cops tell you anything new?

Elwood stares at his hands.

–Not much, he says. They have two theories. One, a guy saw guests leaving the party, waited, took a chance on the door being open, and got lucky. He finds the Watson woman in the kitchen. She runs up the stairs, yelling. He stabs her. Then Cynthia comes out of the bedroom, and he stabs her too. Then starts a fire and runs.

Briscoe waits. Then:

–What's the other theory?

–It was somebody one of them knew. Maybe both of them knew.

Briscoe stares at Elwood.

–The Watsons have a son, Briscoe says. In his early twenties.

Elwood shakes his head slowly.

–They didn't mention that. I mean, would a son kill his mother? Like that? I guess, maybe. Like you told me once: It's a tabloid city. But, ah, hell, I know they never tell everything to people like us. Until they're, like, *sure.*

Elwood rises abruptly.

–You want coffee, Sam?

–Sure.

Elwood goes to the door, opens it, whispers to the receptionist. He comes back, but remains standing. He breathes in heavily.

–Sam, I hate to say this. But I'm closing the paper.

A pause.

–When?

–Now. Today.

He lifts the paper, holding each corner with thumb and forefinger.

–This is the last issue of the *New York World.* My mother's paper.

He bends and lays the newspaper on the low table. He turns his back and faces Queens. Briscoe rises, removes his jacket, and drapes it on the back of his chair.

—That's a mistake, Richard. We own this story. They'll want more.

Elwood turns, a smile on his face.

—On Saturday? Maybe snow coming tonight? Come on, Sam. Get real.

Briscoe comes up beside him. They can each see the dumb blank faces of high-rise apartment houses, a sliver of the East River, condos where there once were squat fuel tanks on the Queens side. A fragment of the 59th Street Bridge. A shard of distant Citi Field. Briscoe thinks: Where is the Pepsi sign?

—It's inevitable, Sam. Closing the paper.

The door opens behind them and the receptionist crosses the room holding a tray with two cups, a silver pot, some pastries.

—Just leave it on the table, please, Elwood says.

—Yes, sir, she says, and goes out.

Elwood is quiet for a beat. Then:

—Where was I?

—Inevitable.

—You know, the delivery system is changing, very fast. The ads have dried up. And eighty percent of our expenses go to paper, ink, and delivery. Eighty *percent*. Not to journalism.

—You need to—

—I need to close the thing, Sam. But that won't be the end of the *World*. I've been working for months on the plan.

—What plan? I haven't heard about any plan.

—Let me show you. We have a website already, as you know, so—

Briscoe has almost never looked at the website. Thinks: The kids who do the mechanics work right here, in this building. The three of them combined as old as I am. He has met them once but can't remember a single name. He wonders if they smoke. Elwood walks to his desk, Briscoe behind him, and sits before the computer to the side of his desk. Briscoe knows what's coming. Then it's before him, the home page, in handsome Caslon, bold and medium, a photo from Afghanistan, a local angle on health care.

*TheWorld.com.*

Elwood keeps talking fast, excited now, all about the changing business model, the market share, the younger audience, about availability on electronic readers, about the way the *Times* now has more hits on its website than it has daily sales, and how the *Wall Street Journal* is charging money for access and...Briscoe has heard it all before, from all sorts of people, and he flashes on Elizabeth Elwood all those years ago in Paris, her enthusiasm, her sense of possibility and purpose. She never once used the phrase "business model," although she surely had one. Elwood keeps talking, clicking on a traffic jam in color video, on the sports section, on style and gossip and how you could blow up the pictures of the stars and print them out.

Then both are silent. Elwood turns to Briscoe, who remains standing.

–So?

–It looks good.

Briscoe turns away, hands in his back pockets.

–That's all? Elwood says.

He rises now, the computer locked on the home page.

–We need the Saturday paper, Briscoe says. We need a chance to say good-bye.

–*Sam,* you don't get it, do you? It's not good-bye. On Monday morning, we say *hello.* There'll be no good-byes. We'll have ads starting Sunday morning on New York One, and every day next week. Right after the weather! Channels Two and Four too. It will be a media sensation. The first month will be free to everybody, then they pay six bucks a month. We'll be out in *front* of the pack. We'll—

Briscoe walks to his chair and lifts his coat.

–Good luck, Richard.

–What? I want you to be *part* of this, Sam.

—You mean, you want me to be the guy that lays off people?

—There have to be layoffs, Sam. But you *are* the *World*.

Briscoe buttons his jacket and smiles.

—Richard, I'm a newspaperman.

He walks to the door.

—Where are you going?

—I've got to make some calls. I don't want my people to hear about this from some fucking blog. And I have to get my lawyer to call your lawyer about severance and all that. Good luck with everything.

He salutes the photographs of Elizabeth Elwood and walks out.


*9:20 a.m. Consuelo Mendoza. Chelsea Hotel, Manhattan.*

She waits for the light to change, because she always obeys small laws, and when it's green, she crosses Seventh Avenue. In the distance, Consuelo sees the sign for the Chelsea Hotel, which looms large and brown and dark. It's on the south side of 23rd Street, but she stays on the north side. The cold wind blows hard from the river. Her breath makes small gray clouds.

She stops in front of a clothing shop but doesn't look into the window. She stands with gloved hands jammed in her coat pockets and stares at the hotel. This is surely the place whose name he wrote on that piece of paper long ago. That time when he went to New York and came back with his wife and broke her heart. Fifteen years ago, when she was still almost a girl. If you need anything, Señor Lewis said, call me. Three days after he returned with his wife, Consuelo fled to Huajuapan, eight hours on three different buses, full of anger and bruised pride.

On this cold New York morning, she doesn't know if he is here, and both the anger and the pride have long vanished. Who can insist on pride if the children will end up on the street in the rain? She called the hotel anyway and it was still the right number but the man who answered said that Mr. Forrest was still sleeping, try later. So he was there, and still alive. *Y pues, estoy aquí.* I'm here. He's here too, up in one of those rooms with their iron balconies.

Consuelo knows he must be very old now. *Un gringo muy viejo.* He was old back then too, but full of life. Staring at her nakedness in his studio, wearing shorts and sneakers behind his easel, drawing or painting her breasts, her waist, her buttocks. Her long hair. Her uncallused feet. Her

213

hands. Laughing about how hard it was to sleep now in his *cama de piedra*. His bed of stone. Singing songs by Don Cuco, singing about the *anillo de compromiso,* the engagement ring, and wailing, full of lonely hurt, *"A dónde estás?"* Oh, where are you?

*Si necesitas algo, llámeme,* he said. If you need anything, call me. Those were his words that time, when she thought he would come back alone, to her.

She thinks: I need help now, Señor Lewis.

A job.

Or a loan.

Now.

Fifteen years later.

She waits, as people go by in both directions, most hurrying, some strolling, more people in twenty minutes than she'd see in Huajuapan in a month of fiestas. Taxis honk and cars too, and the buses push hard, bullying the others. On the sidewalk, nobody bumps into anyone else. They turn sideways, or pause, or stop. But nobody challenges another to get through. A black man with one leg swings by on crutches. Two light-skinned Latinas go by giggling but Consuelo can't hear the jokes. They are walking quickly so Consuelo knows they have jobs that must start at ten. Nobody looks at her. *Ni modo,* Consuelo thinks. No matter: I want it that way. I am nothing to most people, to all but a few. Raymundo. The kids. My friends. But she doesn't move from her place in front of the clothing store, afraid now that if she sees Señor Lewis he too will not know who she is. For good reason. She is no longer the girl he painted long ago.

Then she gathers herself. She walks to the corner of Seventh Avenue, waits again for the light, crosses with a dozen other people, and moves right on the south side of 23rd Street. She goes past the main entrance of the hotel, which is flanked by brass plaques. She peers casually through the glass doors to the lobby. People talking. A desk at the far end. She walks on. Then stops, and turns and walks back, through the doors. Nobody turns to look at her. A young woman is talking to the balding man behind the desk. His beard is trimmed. He wears a necktie and a jacket. Behind his glasses, he has kind gray eyes. She removes her gloves and shoves them into her coat pocket.

—Thanks, Jerry, the young woman says, lifting mail and a newspaper. I'll see you later.

—Sure thing, he says, as the woman steps into a waiting elevator.

Then he looks at Consuelo.

—Can I help you, ma'am? he says.

Consuelo clears her throat. It's hot in the lobby.

–Yes, please, she says. I wan' to see Mr. Lewis Forrest.

The man behind the counter shrugs.

–I'm afraid he...

–Please, Consuelo says. I'm an old friend from Mexico. He painted me many times. I nee' to see him, please.

The man squints at her.

–Y'know, I think I've seen his paintings of you, señora.

–I was much younger then, she says, and smiles a thin smile.

–So was Mr. Forrest, the man says, and laughs. *Much* younger.

–But he's here?

–Yes. He just doesn't answer the telephone.

–Please, I—

The man squints harder.

–Tell ya what, he says. Just go up there and knock on the door. What the hell? It's eight-oh-two.

–Thank you very much.

She turns to the elevator, presses the button, her heart beating faster now. The doors open. She steps in. The doors close. She presses 8. The elevator jerks, and starts up, rising slowly. Consuelo thinks of getting off at 8, waiting for a moment, then leaving again. The doors open. She steps out.

The hall of the landing is wide and high and badly lit. There is brown wood everywhere, with doors all shut. In the center of the hall, she can see the railing of a staircase. She steps to the railing and looks down. It seems to be descending into hell, or at least purgatory. There are paintings on the walls as far as she can see. She turns away, fighting off a shiver of dizziness. She hears footsteps on stone, from another floor. Then she walks to the first door on her right, sees the number, sees the next, and starts walking toward the bright rectangle of window light at the far end. The numbers must start down there with 802. She can hear talk from the rooms, the sound of a television set, classical music, laughter.

She stops at the last door, within a small dark alcove. Here it is. Eight-oh-two. There is no bell. She knocks. The old knock, from the house in Cuernavaca. *En clave.* Bop-bop. Bop-bop-bop. Nothing. She knocks again. She hears the low *ruff* of a dog, the sound of a dog's nails on wood. Then a shuffling sound. Slippers, perhaps. Or callused feet.

Then from beyond the door:

—Yes? Who is it?

–It's me, Señor Lewis.

–Who?

–*Yo.*

She hears a chain falling against wood. Then a heavy lock turning.

The door opens. He's standing there, as old as the earth. She realizes that his eyes see nothing. *Un ciego. Hijole.*

–Consuelo? he whispers, disbelief in his low, trembling voice.

–*Sí,* señor.

He looks frozen.

–No. Is it *you?*

He reaches with both hands to her face. She takes his hands and places them on her cheekbones.

–It's you, he whispers. *Tú,* Consuelo. *Mi corazón.*

Tears begin leaking from his blind eyes.

He walks her into the apartment, holding her hand tightly, the dog clearly knowing that she is friend, not foe. He helps her off with her coat, and she stuffs her hat in one of the sleeves. The odor of the place seeps into her: dried sweat, socks, stale air, the large black dog. They pass the huge easel, with its wild angry painting on the crossbar, move around chairs, ease past a stained couch. Then Lew Forrest pauses. He points with his right hand, his painting hand, up to the wall, to the portrait of

Consuelo as a girl. Beside it is a portrait of his wife. La Señora Gabriela. La Francesa. Both of them are young. Consuelo feels a pang of old hurt. He squeezes her warm bare hand. His hand is cold.

—*Eres tú, no?* he says. The one on the left. It's you, Consuelo.

She can see her own smooth younger flesh, her thinner neck, her more delicate shoulders, the green and orange shawl from Huajuapan draped over one shoulder and one breast, sees the hard dark nipple of the other, and remembers sitting for hours on the edge of the bed in the studio in Cuernavaca, while music played, and Señor Lewis stared hard at her, all of her, and made a feathery caressing sound with his brush on the canvas.

—*Sí,* Señor Lewis, she says. It's me.

—After my wife died, I could put you both together. First in the lobby. Then here. On that wall. For an audience of one. Me.

It is her turn to squeeze Forrest's hand. And then they are talking in a mixture of Spanish and English, as they did long ago. The hurt eases. She hopes her English is now better than his Spanish. She can see his lips making words that he does not say. Uncertain. Unable to remember. Then he clears his throat.

—How old were you then, Consuelo?

—Seventeen.

*–Diez y siete,* he whispers. Seventeen. *Hijole!*

*–Y tú?* she says.

–Old, he says, and laughs. *Un gringo viejo.* Even then.

She laughs too.

–I was madly in love with you, Consuelo. *Muy, muy loco.*

There's a beat of grave silence.

*–Yo también,* she says, her voice lower. Me too.

He must have heard the note of sadness in her voice.

–I...I don't know why I...

*–Ni modo,* Señor Lewis. *Como se dice,* it was a long time ago.

Forrest stands there for a long moment, as if seeing nothing at all. Not the old paintings. Not her. Not anything in the world.

Then he takes her elbow.

–Come, he says. Sit beside me on the couch. I'll call down for coffee.

–You have a coffeepot and all that? I can make it.

–No, no. I gave the damned thing away. You know, I can't see much, *mi vida,* and I keep making a mess. Pouring coffee on the floor instead of in the cup.

He chuckles and then goes on.

–Anyway, I gave the pot away, and kept the

cups. I'll call Jerry, down at the desk. What do you want, *querida?*

They talk it over. Just black coffee? *Sí.* A bagel? *Sí. Con mantequilla? Sí.* How about a cheese Danish too? *No, no,* Señor Lewis.

He picks up the old black telephone from a table and talks to Jerry downstairs, while Consuelo gazes around the long narrow apartment, at the shelves full of art books and volumes of poetry, at the paintings leaning against each other beside the walls, the long flat metal cabinet that she knows from Cuernavaca must be full of drawings and prints and watercolors. He hangs up the phone and walks her to the tan dirt-streaked couch, which is three cushions wide. The cushion on the far right is stacked with more drawings. Forrest grips the left arm of the couch, turns around to sit with a sigh, and points Consuelo to the center cushion. She sits straight up on the edge, hands clasped on her lap. The dog moves around to the side, and stretches his legs on the floor. There is a silent awkward moment.

—Well, Lew Forrest says, what brings you here, Consuelo?

She waits for a long beat, gathering words, and strength, and will. Telling herself: Just say it. Say it straight out.

–You said, that time, the last time, when you went to New York, you said to me, Consuelo, if you need help, call me. You wrote the name of this place for me. On a small piece of paper. I was so hurt I just went away. I kept the paper.

She shows him the folded sheet from a composition book, but then holds it, for he cannot see.

–I thought I was coming back, he whispers. Alone.

She lets those words grow cold in the stale air.

–*Pues*. Here I am, señor. I came back to see you again.

–You did. Why?

–I need help.

–What kind of help, Consuelo?

She starts to speak but the doorbell rings. Forrest grips her hand.

–Could you...?

-*Sí*, Señor Lewis.

–Here, he says, taking bills separately from each pocket.

He hands her four bills.

–That's a ten-dollar bill, and three singles, *verdad?*

–*Sí*, señor.

–Okay, that includes the tip.

She walks to the door, the dog first stretching, then padding after her. She opens the door. The delivery boy is Mexican, wearing a Mets cap. Well, maybe he's *un guatemalteco*. He squints at the dog, but seems relaxed. He is holding a gray corrugated cardboard tray with slots for the two coffee containers and the wrapped bagels. He seems surprised to see Consuelo's face in this doorway that he has come to in the past.

She takes the tray and hands him the bills.

—*Gracias, joven,* she says.

—*Por nada,* señora, he says. Then smiles and adds: *Y que viva México!*

She bows, holding the tray with both hands, and smiles, closing the door with her foot. She moves across the studio to the small kitchen.

—*Hay tazas,* señor? Cups?

—*Sí, sí,* Consuelita. On the shelves.

The sink is filthy. She takes two unmatched cups from the shelf, rinses them in the sink, dries them with paper towels from a roll lying on its side. She can hear Lew Forrest singing in a dry choked voice. A scrap from the past.

*A dónde estás,*
*A dónde estás...*

She is washing a grimy plate, blue designs on white, her eyes suddenly wet. A song from those days. Cuco Sánchez again. *A dónde estás.* Where are you? She dries the plate with a fresh paper towel and uses its dry edge to tamp the corners of her eyes. She unwraps the bagels and puts them on the plate. She moves to the couch, pulls over a chair, and lays the plate on the seat of the chair. She goes back quickly for the cups. Forrest stops singing. The aroma of coffee is winning against the sour odor of the room.

—*Aquí,* señor, she says, taking his painting hand and placing it on the handle of his cup.

—*Qué milagro,* he says, chuckling. What a miracle! Coffee in a cup! Not cardboard! A true miracle.

—*Sí,* señor, she says. *Y* bagels *también!*

—Watch out for that dog. He might think they're for *him.*

He feels for the plate, takes a bagel, and pulls it into halves. Then pauses.

—Okay, what kind of help, Consuelo?

—A job, Señor Lewis.

—Start from the beginning. When you went home to Oaxaca.

She tells him the short version of the long tale. Huajuapan. Raymundo. Marriage. The two of them slipping across the border west of Laredo. The long ride north in a bus. New York. Cleaning houses, then cleaning offices, studying English in the church, teaching English to Raymundo, who found work in a coffee shop, first delivering orders and washing dishes and cleaning grills. Then cooking. Getting paid more each year. Not a lot. But more. After little Eddie was born, they moved to a one-room studio apartment in Brooklyn, and after the second child, the girl Marcela, they found this house in Sunset Park. Two floors. Parlor floor and basement, the Irish woman called it. Pretty high rent, for a place that was a wreck, but with Consuelo and Raymundo both working, they managed. They fixed up the rooms. They made the little back garden bloom with flowers. Then, three years ago, the Irish lady died and they started sending the rent money to some company. Money orders. Then everything started to collapse two years ago, and now she had lost her job. Now they could be evicted. With three kids now. Eddie, Marcela, Timmie.

—I thought you might know about a job. Maybe I could even work here. Clean your place once a week, and the halls, and other apartments. Maybe you know other places, señor. That's what I thought. Businesses, offices. Anything. Well, not anything. Nothing with . . . *cómo se dice, vergüenza?*

—Shame? Never, Consuelo. Never with you.

He is quiet for almost a minute. Maybe longer. She hopes he can't hear her heart beating. He still holds the bagel. His face says nothing.

—Let me think, Consuelo. You know, this god-damned recession...

—*Sí, yo entiendo.* I understand, señor. That's why I lose, uh, *lost* my job.

He bites the end of his bagel, gnawing it, chewing intently, then swallowing. Thinking.

He says, Do you know the computer?

—*Sí.* My son, he—

—Good. I don't have a clue about it.

He leans back, staring at nothing he can see.

—The people I know, he says, the people who buy my paintings—they're all very quiet right now. *Como se dice,* laying low. Waiting. The very rich ones don't give a rat's ass. The money keeps rolling in. But others, they're cutting back. They're afraid. One of them just died. Yesterday. An awful death. A wonderful woman. I guess it's on television too.

She feels herself going limper, softer. He's trying to say that he can't help. *Pues. Ni modo, ni modo.* No surprise. And looking at the mess of the studio, she is certain that a loan is impossible.

—Even here at the Chelsea, they're cutting back. Some people, they lived here for years, they can't pay the rent. Painters give the hotel paintings instead of rent. Others, they just pray, even the atheists. None of them want to live in a homeless shelter.

Consuelo sees his eyebrows tense as he sips his coffee, both hands wrapped around the cup for warmth. She can't bring herself to press him, and begins to feel regret about coming to see him.

—I need to make some calls, he says.

—*Gracias,* señor. But don't, please don't, uh, go out of your way.

—No, no, it's no bother. It's just, you know, it should be a job with a *future.* You're young, *mi vida.* You're beautiful. You speak English real good, Consuelo. You know the computer. You're smart as hell...I don't know...You don't have to clean up after people. Maybe—

—I'm illegal, señor, she says, in a flat voice.

—What the hell? Half the guys I grew up with were illegal—and they were born here!

He laughs out loud.

—And those *malcriados* from Wall Street, that Bernie Madoff—what the hell are they? Legal?

Consuelo smiles. She knows three women who worked on Wall Street.

—*Sí, pero—*

His face is flushed now, the way it used to be in Cuernavaca when something on TV set him off about politicians and the *pendejos* of the world.

—Your kids are Americans, right?

—*Sí,* Señor Lewis.

—Well, they ain't going anywhere. And neither

227

are you. You *already* cleaned enough offices to make sure *they* never have to clean them. You need a job that helps you get them into *college*...I have a lawyer friend. Specializes in immigration cases, Irishmen, Chinese, Mexicans...Named O'Dwyer. I think he can help straighten this out, this illegal stuff...

He sips his coffee. She sips hers too. A slight bitterness lies in the dark liquid at the bottom of the cup. She looks at him, his knotting brow, his slackening jaw. Pity rises in her. A man who loves pictures and cannot even see his own work. A man who loves poetry and cannot read. A man who loves friends and company and women, and is here, in this place, alone.

She places the cup on the chair.

–I mus' be going, Señor Lewis. My children...

–Of course.

And then, almost urgently, he touches her forearm.

–Consuelo, *mi vida*. I want to say something. Just to you...I truly loved you...I did...I was way too old for you, even then, but you made me feel younger. More alive. It showed in my work. In my eyes...When you went away, I thought, I should have married her. I should have married *you*.

–You were married, señor, she says softly.

The sentence hangs there.

—Yes, I was. And the truth? I loved her too. I loved my wife, Gabrielle. *And* you. Most people don't understand how that's possible. Except in some goddamned telenovela...If I could have had both of you, I'd have been happy...In the same house. At the same table. But she would never go for that and neither would you. Pride is always stronger than love. Or maybe love is impossible without pride. I don't know...But there was another thing. She was sick. The doctors in New York, they said, she...Ah, *ni modo*. Never mind... I was too old to follow my heart. And all these years later, I still think of you. And here you are.

She tries breathing softly, relieved that he cannot see her face.

Forrest drains his cup, lays it down gently, feeling for the edge of the chair before him. Then he rises, pushing on the arm of the couch, and stands. The dog stands too. So does Consuelo. She wishes she could begin cleaning now. Send him to the lobby with the dog. Open the windows. Call her friends. Bring brooms and pails and soap and mops, bring Pledge and Windex, make everything shiny, make the air as sweet as the house in Mexico, give him a new clean life. Bring music. Bring Don Cuco with his harp. Bring José Alfredo with his cantina songs. Bring him joy.

—You gave me many gifts, Señor Lewis.

—And you... did that for me, Consuelita... After you, I did my best work.

—I'm sorry for coming here to bother you.

—No, no. It's been a delight. *Corazón*...

He turns his head to where her voice is.

—Now, *mi vida,* go to that desk. Write down your married name, your husband's name, the three children and the years they were born and where. Write your address and telephone number. And what do they call it? E-mail. I want to talk to this lawyer, O'Dwyer. And I want to start calling my friends about work.

—*Sí,* Señor Lewis.

She begins writing with the lead pencil. The point is blunt. Forrest is silent, but she can hear his dry breathing. He must have stopped smoking. There is no odor of nicotine in the dirty air. He can hear when she finishes writing.

—Now, listen to me, *muchacha.* When you go downstairs, see Jerry. Make sure you see him. The bald guy at the front desk.

—Señor, I...

—See him.

He embraces her. She kisses his leathery cheek.

—*Mil gracias,* Señor Lewis. *Para todo.*

She takes her coat, pulls it on, adds the hat. She feels as if she will never see him again.

–This is not good-bye, he says. *No es adios. Es hasta muy pronto.* Until very soon.

–*Sí,* señor, she says. And opens the door.

–*Mucha suerte,* she whispers.

He chuckles and says: Luck is what we both need.

And she's gone. Forrest can hear her steps receding on the tile of the hallway.

He picks up the telephone.


## 10:10 a.m. Malik Shahid. Sixth Street, Gowanus, Brooklyn.

Jamal sits at the kitchen table, his back to the bright garden, facing Malik. He is trying to look relaxed, dressed in a cashmere sweater, white J. Crew turtleneck, slacks, his left foot encased in a desert boot, perched on his right knee. He peers at Malik through slightly tinted yellowish glasses. His beard is neatly trimmed. Buppie of the month, Malik thinks, another infidel fuck. My friend Jamal. My jihadist comrade.

–What are you gonna do, Malik? he says.

–Whattaya think I'm gonna do?

–I don't know. I know what you *should* do.

–Yeah? What's that?

–Call your father. Go see him. Don't run.

—Shit, Malik says, dragging the word across three syllables.

—You know they're looking for you, Jamal says.

—Why me?

—Malik, your mother's been murdered by someone. Along with the woman she worked for. A rich, well-known woman. It's all over TV. It's on the radio. The cops want to talk to everyone who might know why. Or *who*.

—You know how I feel, Jamal. My mother's been dead for years.

—Stop shittin' yourself, brother.

Malik goes quiet, his eyes wandering to the sink, the dishwasher, the stove. Jamal has been a dark silhouette against the brightness of the garden. Now he flattens his foot on the kitchen floor, and leans forward.

—You can't stay here, man. You know how my wife—

—I came for our stuff, Jamal. The box. You know, with—

—It's not here, Malik. You think I'm nuts?

—Where is it?

Malik's face hardens. Jamal jerks a thumb to his left.

—Down there, a block and a half. Been there three years, at least. At the bottom of the Gowanus.

—What? You never asked me if—

—You were in the *wind,* man. How'm I suppose to find you? Facebook? Call information? Google?

—You coulda buried it in the yard.

—You think my wife wouldn't notice? Get real.

Silence. Jamal stands, folds his arms across his chest. The tree in the garden is skeletal, with an icy sheen.

—Can I sleep here a few hours?

Jamal turns. Without his beard, Malik looks younger, even forlorn, or lost.

—My wife is due back soon. She just dropped my daughter at nursery school, then went shopping. I mean, you said you seen her leave. The house is too small for you to sleep here without her seein' you.

He doesn't have to spell out the rest. Malik knows that Jamal's wife is the kind of infidel bitch would call the cops on a Muslim.

—Why would you want the stuff? Jamal says.

Malik doesn't answer. He rises, stands aimlessly, folding and unfolding his arms, then leans against the stove.

—I hope you're not planning some fucking show, Malik. Kill yourself, take a lotta people with you.

—Shut up.

—Like these dumb-ass white guys, all packing

heat, walk into a gym or a church or a campus, start shooting, kill a bunch a' people, then shoot themselves. Two-day wonders in the tabloids. Then nobody knows their names.

Malik whips around from the stove, slicing the air with a carving knife.

*—Shut the fuck up, Jamal!*

Silence.

Jamal's face trembles. He eyes the five-inch blade.

Then Malik lowers the knife.

—Sorry, he whispers.

He lays the knife on the stovetop, turns, and walks quickly down the hall to the gate under the stoop. He zippers his coat.

Jamal waits, hears the gate clang. He feels his body go rubbery and boneless. He struggles to breathe.

*10:15 a.m. Sam Briscoe. New York Luncheonette, 135 East 50th Street, Manhattan.*

The waiter takes the plates away, with their traces of scrambled eggs and crisp bacon and the crust of an English muffin. He puts the check beside Briscoe's cup and refills the cup with black decaf. Briscoe tries to remember what he has forgotten in his need to fill these coming hours with details. Clerking death. The process he first saw when he was ten and one of his Irish aunts had to arrange a wake for her dead husband. Don't grieve, or at least not now. Take care of details. Deal with the boring parts. Get too busy for weeping. The aunt said to Briscoe's mother: I'm too damned busy to feel sorry for anyone, even myself.

Using the hated cell phone, Briscoe had called Matt Logan first, waking him up, telling him what had happened. I don't want you to hear the news from the new media, Briscoe said.

Logan laughed: I already did. That CelineWire one. You know, Wheeler, the schmuck you fired a couple years ago.

Briscoe laughed, and said, Never fire a guy who can type. He explained that he would cash out, and recommend to the publisher that Matt run the new online version of the *World*.

—Am I being punished? Logan said.

—No, Briscoe said. But you'll be getting paid.

Then he called Janet, his secretary, and told her to call a staff meeting for five o'clock today. They'll all have the news already, he said. But there'll be forms to fill out, applying for the jobs that will be left. And we have to say good-bye. He told her to call each of them. To meet in the city room. Everybody who could make it. Sportswriters and photographers and advertising guys and pressmen included. Closed to outside press. He gave Janet the news too, of course, and told her not to worry, she'd still have a job.

–Yeah? she said. But I work for *you*.

In a way, that was true. She'd worked for him about a dozen years, a lifetime in newspapers. He told her everything would be okay. At least for now, he added. But he wanted her to start packing his office things, the books, and photographs, and files. The Hermes 3000. The pica rule. You know, he said. The stuff.

He told her that he would call Helen Loomis himself, later, since she had worked a double shift through the night.

–Let her sleep, he said. Janet started to get weepy, and said, This ain't right.

–No, it's not, Briscoe said. But you have to eat.

Then he called the publisher back, making sure that it was okay to name Matt Logan the new editor. Elwood said yes, but only if Briscoe agreed to become editor emeritus, serving as an adviser to TheWorld.com. Briscoe said he wanted to think it over but would have his lawyer call about details. Elwood said: Don't worry, Sam. Either way, you'll get everything that's due you.

Now Briscoe sits in the coffee shop. For the first time in years, he is in a coffee shop without a newspaper on the table. There is nothing else to read except the menu and the check. He thinks: I need a slim volume of Yeats to carry around with me.

He pays the check and walks out into the cold sunshine. The sidewalk is less crowded now. The people with jobs are all squatting above the street in front of their computers, trying to will a Big Score out of the bouncing numbers. But there are very few shoppers entering the stores, and no tourists at all. The sky is now darkening in the west. He starts assembling a list of other calls to make. His daughter, Nicole, first. In Paris. Haberman at the *Times.* Myron at the *Post* and Ng at the *News.* Or just call Mike Oreskes at the AP. Briscoe will call Susan Jones at the museum and ask her to send a crew to pack the cartoons and the old typewriters in the hall. To ask for Janet.

But who does he call about Cynthia Harding? She had no children. Except maybe Sandra Gordon. The girl Cynthia adopted, without papers. *That party in Montego Bay... what year was it? The tall blonde woman and the small black girl pulling books off shelves...* He pauses, takes a deep breath. Tells himself, Clerk this fucking thing. Now. Will there be a memorial? Surely yes. Probably at the library. Maybe Janet can find out. All of us can walk past the lions, past Patience and

Fortitude, and enter her cathedral. Is there a will? Call Cynthia's lawyer. First thing. Soon as I get home.

Jesus Christ. Stop. Go home.

He hurries down the steps to the 6 train but can't look at the offerings of the newsstand. He swipes his Senior Citizen MetroCard, the card he calls his New York passport. Moves along the waiting area, hands deep in his coat pockets. He fingers the card, then imagines sweat ruining its surface, and returns it to his wallet. Thinking: If only I'd gone to Cynthia's party at Patchin Place. Stayed over. Walked Mary Lou Watson to the car. But no. I had to work. Like so many other nights. Still, if I'd taken the night off, maybe none of this would have happened. Maybe I'd be calling Cynthia now, explaining about the *World,* and asking her out to a late dinner. Instead of snacks in bed. Or takeout. Or dim sum on Saturdays. Maybe...ah, fuck it.

At Grand Central, four graying black doo-woppers come into the car, in rough winter clothes, sneakers, men in their fifties or sixties. They begin to sing.

*Why, oh why, do I*
*Live in the dark?*
  *(day and night, babe)*

A woman in her fifties smiles, but won't make eye contact. A girl in her twenties looks amused in another way. Where she comes from, they never see such an act.

*Why, oh why, do I*
*Sleep in the park?*
*    (can't pay no rent, babe)*

The doo-woppers have the look of men who spent too many years rehearsing in the yard at Attica or Green Haven or Dannemora. They smile but their eyes are sad. One grips a blue plastic bucket. Briscoe drops a fiver into it, and the surprised man smiles brightly, showing yellowing teeth. They keep moving to the far end of the car.

*You were my woman*
*Round and sweet—*
*Then you took off*
*With a lowlife creep*

They step off at 33rd Street. Briscoe wonders when he first heard someone sing those lyrics. Summer of '55? No, '56.

*And here I am*
*A paper wrappin' my feet—*

Frankie Lymon? Didn't he finish badly? Dying of heroin. What year? Sometime in the sixties. Briscoe was working in Europe, so maybe it was 1964. Thinking: Gotta Google him. Frankie Lymon and the Teenagers. Or maybe the Platters. The flip side of some big hit. Who was I in love with then?

*Oh why, oh why, do I*
*Live in the dark?*

He remembers. Betty Haddad. Small, with lustrous black hair, a handsome hooked nose, oval face. Her parents were Syrian Christians. She loved dancing, which they did for a whole summer. Why did they fall in love? It was simple. She wasn't like all the Irish and Jews and Italians of Briscoe's tribes. Or more accurately, not like him. It took him another thirty years to realize that was one of the points of New York. Maybe the most important. It's the city of people who are not like you.

Same with Cynthia Harding. She wasn't like his people and Briscoe wasn't like hers.

*(day and night, babe)*
*Why, oh why, do I . . .*

He gets off the 6 train at Spring Street, and feels weariness eating his brain cells. At the top of the steps, he has to pause for breath, settling himself, breathing in the cold air. He walks west, slowly. On Broadway, there in the heart of SoHo, there are more people than he saw in midtown. The usual fat tourist ladies in wide threesomes are ambling down to Canal Street, to buy fake Prada and Gucci handbags. Nobody can get past them. Messengers on bicycles weave in and out of traffic. Horns honk in warning or exasperation. Four young tourists pause on the corner, speaking Italian, squinting at a map, and calling up something on a gadget. Presumably a GPS map. Briscoe considers asking them if they knew what had happened to Frankie Lymon. If not, maybe they could Google him, right there on the corner. Yeah.

He crosses Broadway, heading home. He will call his daughter in Paris and then Helen and then sleep.

**10:45 a.m. Sandra Gordon. Lipstick Building.**

Her door is open and she sits at her desk, glancing at proofs of the Cash for Clunkers ads. A very big client. Tottering now. Buy our cars, get cash back. Wondering: Did they do this for chariots in the last days of the Roman Empire?

Her right elbow aches. Her right hand trembles. She can't remember ever fainting before. Not in New York. Not at Columbia. Never in Jamaica. She remembers seeing the front page of the newspaper. Then looking up at the face of Kennedy, the young guy from media analysis, way down the hall, and he's whispering. "Are you okay, Miss Gordon? You want a doctor?" And she said, "Oh, thanks, Kennedy. I'm okay. I guess I fainted."

He helped her up and she saw about twenty people in the lobby, all looking at her. Men and women. She still hears Kennedy asking what happened, as he helps her stand. She remembers pointing at the newsstand. The stack of newspapers. The front page of the *World*. And saying: I knew that woman. The white woman. She gave me my life.

Kennedy went with her in the elevator, gently moving her away from the spectators, and into her office. She kept saying: No doctor, please, I'm okay, I fainted is all... Then the bosses were in her office, and one of them suggested she go home, take the day off, what the hell, it's Friday. And she smiled and said No, I have proofs to look at, and a lunch appointment and... They all looked uneasy, and the doctor was mentioned again, and Sandra Gordon smiled and shooed them away.

Now she rises from her desk, and looks out the window, south and east, toward where Cynthia Harding lived. The sky is darker than it was when she left home. She hasn't yet left her office, to walk among the other workers. No longer the mad men of the television series. No martinis at lunch. No smoking at their desks. They're tweeting, and texting on BlackBerrys, and checking Facebook or MySpace. Not for fun. For ideas. And to gossip.

She wonders if today, they're tweeting about her.

And out there in the city, Cynthia Harding...

She is thinking: I was gonna call her today. *Today.* To set up lunch and talk about the endless stupidity of the world, and the men who inhabit it. To make jokes about Myles Compton, wherever he might be. To laugh. To feel alive. And defiant. And let her know that I'm sad too and hurting.

She can't look over at the three crowded shelves of the office bookcase. Cynthia's photograph is there on top, along with two photos of Madda. Looking stern and serious in fierce Jamaican sunlight.

She can't look at the newspaper either, folded in the chair against the window. She can't go online

243

for breaking news. She doesn't want to know the details. At least not now. Maybe not ever.

Her secretary eases in without a word. Amanda Burroughs. A crisp British accent. She stands before the bookcase.

–Yes, Amanda.

–So far, no news about the burials, or services. Not at the *Times*. Not online. I called that Mr. Briscoe, as you asked. His secretary said he'd be available about five-thirty.

–I see.

–And here are three thank-you cards. Mr. Kennedy is out at a meeting, so you have time to choose one.

She lays the cards on Sandra Gordon's desk.

–Thanks, Amanda.

–Is there anything else, Ms. Gordon?

–Just one thing, she says, smiling wanly. Try to find me an Aleve. My elbow hurts like hell.

Amanda smiles in reply and leaves the office.

Now Sandra glimpses the photograph of Cynthia Harding. She averts her eyes, sees deep green foliage in Montego Bay, *Chitty Chitty Bang Bang*, rainy streets in Paris, that boat in the Greek isles. All with Cynthia. She turns to face her desk.

She feels breath rush out of her. Dry with anguish. But she does not faint.

## 11:15 a.m. Ali Watson. Brownsville, Brooklyn.

He is driving past the overgrown lots, where Jews lived for years, and then blacks, and now nobody lives at all. He has called Jamal and left his own cell number on Jamal's answering machine. He has told his partner to scan all chatter to see if Malik has been in New York. Hoping there's been a whisper from Oakland. Or Pakistan. Montreal or Yemen. Not here. Please God: not here.

But he needs to speak to the other one, the man who dragged them both deeper into the seventh century. Ali for a season. Malik forever.

He needs to speak to Muhammad Ahmad, who two hours earlier whispered the meeting place below the El at Saratoga Avenue. "Around the corner from Moorz Cutz, the barbershop," the man said. "Noon, okay?" Okay. If anyone knows whether Malik is in New York, and where he is, *if* he is—it's Muhammad Ahmad.

In his day, Ali Watson remembers, he was a great fraud, Muhammad was, but a fraud with charisma and savage humor. The most dangerous kind. Ali remembers his young eyes now, the blaze of certainty in them, the ferocity of his language when they met that time in Brownsville in a mosque that had once been a Baptist church and before that a synagogue. His legend was spreading as despair deepened. The year was 1969. Malcolm was dead. Martin was dead. Bobby was dead. Heroin was alive and Brownsville was burning. And there in the lots rose Muhammad Ahmad, aged eighteen, standing in flowing white robes on the roof of a burnt-out Chevy. Singing the early version of his siren song.

His slave name, as they said in those days, was Ben Jenkins, and he was born right here in B-ville. The résumé was the usual pile of clichés. His father took off before he was born. His mother kicked him out when he was fourteen. He was a junkie at fifteen and then sent to the reformatory called Warwick, after Ali, a patrolman then at the 7-3 on East New York Avenue, busted him for dealing heroin. In Warwick, he became a Muslim. Like thousands of other young jailhouse Muslims. Then his life started.

Now Ali pulls over to the curb. He turns off the engine, and sits there, watching, and remembering.

Ben Jenkins took the name of the man who became the Mahdi in the late nineteenth century, the star of a Muslim tale right out of Hollywood. As Muhammad Ahmad, he began preaching in the lots and then on street corners, the way the communists once did in B-ville, and the guys who recruited soldiers for the Lincoln Brigade, and the passionate socialists who wanted to create Israel. As always, the goal was utopia. The big time was a corner on Pitkin Avenue, up the block from the huge movie house. Ben Jenkins, now called Muhammad Ahmad, became a soapbox boy wonder, telling his audiences how the Mahdi built his army in the south of Egypt, gathering thousands of followers, preaching jihad, until he finally surrounded the British at Khartoum. The Mahdi's army captured the city and killed the British general, and militant Islam seemed clearly on the march. The Mahdi was now famous all over the world.

Listening to this passionate kid then, patrolman Ali Watson imagined the El as the walls of Khartoum, and fought off feelings he had when he first heard Malcolm preach. The song was a vision. He laughs, hearing Mary Lou's voice: *Are you nuts? You're a grown-up, Ali!* He gets out of the car now. Locks it. Shakes off Mary Lou's sharp, intelligent voice. Stands there trembling for a long minute, but not from the cold.

Still watching.

On all these street corners, now so empty, Ben Jenkins told the bitter crowds, seething with anger, that he had been chosen as the new Mahdi. He was chosen by the Messenger himself in a visitation on the roof of his building in the Marcus Garvey Houses. Then he moved on to his own divine message, his vision, his addition to the many Brownsville utopias. On that windy rooftop, the Messenger told him Allah wanted him to lead a black revolt, inspired and commanded by Muslims, and then to create an Islamic republic in the American South. Start with Mississippi, then get the white infidels out of Louisiana, Alabama, Georgia, northern Florida, and replace them with black believers. They could stay, whites and blacks, only if they accepted Allah, and agreed to *sharia* law. Otherwise, they must go, or die. Hearing all this, most blacks laughed. The way Mary Lou did. Some did not. Particularly if they were young. They saw a future.

He, the new Mahdi, would enlist all those Muslims whose faith died when Malcolm was killed. He would draw blacks to the Mahdi Army from all over the United States. The Panthers. The Five Percenters. America had enslaved them, crippled them, placed them out on the edge without power. America gave them the humiliation of welfare and forgot them. Now they would build the proud Black Zion. Gathering first in Mississippi, where blacks were already a majority. Where whites maintained power through the terrorist gang called the Ku Klux Klan. To meet white terror with black terror.

A kid from City College recorded a few of the Mahdi's street-corner sermons and, years later, turned the tapes into a very special bootleg. That audiotape, peddled on street corners and then in barbershops and at rallies at schools, attracted many young listeners. One was Malik. Father and son argued bitterly about the message before Malik went away for good. Now Ali has to find him.

Ali Watson begins to walk on streets where he was young too. He wanders to Legion Street and then Grafton Street, where he can hear the screeching of the El, passing over corners where the street gangs once ruled until heroin cut out their hearts. When he married Mary Lou, she insisted that they move. "This place is doomed," she said. On moving day, black smoke darkened the sky from a burning tenement two blocks away, and doom seemed certain.

Ali knew the B-ville story. He had seen it. The burning gashed every block and turned others into lots. Landlords paid twelve-year-old kids to torch the tenements so they could collect insurance money and buy condos in Fort Lauderdale. Some old dude dies in the building? Tough shit. Burntout automobiles were everywhere, stolen from other neighborhoods, driven until the gas ran out, then set on fire to become housing for rats. When Ali came over one time on the trail of a murder suspect, Brownsville looked like Stalingrad or Berlin in the old newsreels on the History Channel. When crack came, the neighborhood truly became a war zone. The infantry was made of young zombies with guns. Killing over ownership of a street corner. Killing old ladies. Killing their own mothers. At least the old junkies nodded out once in a while. The crackheads never did. They wanted more, and more, and more. Real Americans.

Ben Jenkins missed most of that. He was in Leavenworth. In 1980, the Feds nailed him and four others for possession of gelignite, four bag bombs made from boiled and dried horse shit, three AK-47s, fifteen Glocks, two MAC-10s, and plans to blow up the Statue of Liberty. One of the four associates was a rat. Off went the new Mahdi to serve twenty-one years of a thirty-year sentence. He came home in April 2001 to discover that the world he wanted to change as a kid was actually the good old days. Nobody he met remembered him, even those who had heard the audiotape. They were too young, even if, like Malik, they had learned the lyrics of his siren song.

After September 11, Ali tracked down Ben Jenkins. He was living in his sister's apartment, sleeping on a couch. Another middle-aged black man on welfare. Everything was out of him, including the gaudy illusion of the New Mahdi Army. His face was pouched and lined. White hairs sprouted from his nose and his stubbly beard. He had no woman, no kids, no job, no hope. His drug of choice was Marlboro Lights. Jenkins told Ali that he knew nothing about al-Qaeda or the men who smashed airplanes into the Trade Center, and Ali believed him. He was still in jail when the planning took place, and he had a solid alibi for the day itself.

After September 11, Jenkins became part of Ali's early warning system, which gave him a few extra dollars every month. Calling from pay phones. Meeting in odd parts of the city. He was still a Muslim, drifting from mosque to mosque, warding off loneliness in the company of other womenless men. But he was useful to Ali and the Joint Terrorism Task Force. He could recognize those young men who resembled his own younger self. And from the photographs Ali gave him, he could recognize Malik.

Now, in the distance, Ali Watson sees him, staring into the window of a hardware store, dressed in a heavy down jacket with a hood. Ali waits a minute, watching for anyone who might be watching Ben Jenkins. Then he hurries across the street. He walks casually past Jenkins, then turns his attention to a display of drill bits. He speaks without turning his head.

—I'm looking for my son, Ali says.

—I heard the other day he was out here a few weeks ago.

Ali feels his stomach moving.

—Why didn't you call me?

—I been sick, man. Some kind of a flu.

—You should've *called* me, Ben.

—Yeah. Sorry, man. I didn't actually see him. Some guy—

—Where was he? Malik, I mean?

—At that mosque on Georgia, near Livonia.

—The storefront?

—That's it.

Ali exhales.

—I'll take a look.

—I'll keep looking.

—If you *see* him, Ben, day or night, call me, hear?

—Yeah.

Ali turns to walk past him. Without turning his head.

—Hey, man, I'm sure sorry about your wife.

—Thank you.

**11:20 a.m. Freddie Wheeler. His apartment, Williamsburg.**

Freddie Wheeler feels like he's floating. Two feet above the floor. Ten stories above the street. He moves from bathroom to computer screen to window and back, and his brain is bursting with triumph. More than two hundred e-mails, and it isn't even lunchtime...The *Times* three times, looking for a comment...Not David Carr, though...Some reporter...The AP...The *Daily News*...Howard Kurtz from the *Washington Post* and CNN, he wants to know how CelineWire. com found out before everybody else that the *World* was folding as a newspaper and opening as a website...Calling me "Mr. Wheeler"...The *London Times* sent an e-mail, for fuck sake... Murdoch must be screaming about why the news wasn't broken in the *Wall Street Journal*...

He checks the BlackBerry.

Some bitter notes...Of course...Blaming the messenger...*Hope you're happy now, you little prick. McLeod*...An old fart from the *World* copy desk: *Ucksay my ickday you uckingfay astardbay.* Another hack from the copy desk...Pretty hip.

And, hey: CNN wants to send a crew!

And, holy shit, *Morning Joe* wants him Monday!

He jumps again...then reaches for jeans and starts dressing...He is starving now. Gotta eat... Gotta eat anything...Even eggs...Even just *toast*. Celebrate! He pulls a T-shirt over his head, and a heavy wool sweater...Céline would love this...A *victory* in a time when there are almost no victories...Hey, Briscoe: whattaya gonna do now, you half a Hebe? I'll tell you what you're gonna do... You're gonna *die,* baby...First the paper, then *you*.

He imagines his mother turning on *Morning Joe*...if they even get the show out there...And there he is! Her worthless son! On national television...A Pun-Dit!...Being asked for his opinions! Whattaya think now, Momma?

*Top of the world!*


### 11:40 a.m. Helen Loomis. Second Avenue and 9th Street, Manhattan.

She hangs up the phone, turns, and weeps in a surrendering way into the pillow.

—Oh, Sam, she whispers to herself. What's to become of you? And me? What's to become of us all?

She cries until she can cry no more and reaches

for a Kleenex. She blows her nose. Then sits up, and lights a cigarette. At least I got to smoke again in a city room, she thinks, even if it was for the last time. Not the last cigarette. The last city room.

Oh, God.

It's over.

She sits up on the edge of the bed, flicking ash into a saucer on the bed table, pulling her robe more tightly. What will I do now? she thinks. No more "Vics and Dicks," the long serial she has written for, what? Forty years now? Five dopes a day? Twenty-five a week. The dumbest knuckle-head criminals in the history of the city. Twenty-five a week means how many? Fifty thousand? Fifty-five? She thinks that she must do the math, with a pencil, on paper.

Thinking: Or was I Scheherazade?

Telling stories in order to live?

Even if they were not my stories. They weren't, but I owned them. They could have called the column "Knucklehead News." No Professor Moriarty among any of them. No Goldfinger. No Dr. Sivana, who called Captain Marvel a "Big Red Cheese." No Meyer Lansky. No Frank Costello. Absolutely no master criminals. My people were dumbbells all. The smart guys made page 3. But oh, how my guys made me laugh.

She tamps out the cigarette, stands, and

shuffles on slippered feet to the bathroom. The shower does not wash away her melancholy. She remembers the feelings that engulfed her after her husband died. Poor Willie. Cancer at fifty-eight. All through the weeks of mourning, she felt like a dot. The kind of period that ends a sentence. And then the newspaper saved her. Again. Sam saved her. Again. The guys on the copy desk saved her. The endless cast of "Vics and Dicks" saved her.

Now...

Drying herself, she is filled with gratitude for what they gave her. They still surround her in the apartment as she dresses in ski pants and wool sweater. Even the ones who got away. The white jerk in Sunnyside with the cape and the wild eyes, raving about killing Obama, and the cops lock him up for disorderly conduct and find eight Glocks and three automatics in his house. I had him for three hours and then they took him up to the front of the paper. She sees another white dumbbell, blond, handsome, in his twenties, a real Amurrican guy, and his real Amurrican blonde wife, with what used to be called an Ipana-tooth-paste smile, and how some black guy in a mask carjacked them, and forced them to drive to the Poconos, where the couple had a second home. The masked black dude tied him up, the husband says, then slashed his wife's throat and breasts while he was forced to watch. She bled to death. The cops listened to the tale for about eight minutes and then locked him up for murder. I lost him too.

Just last week, a knucklehead fresh out of Rikers sticks up an apartment where some woman deals heroin. He's got the Rikers Island jeans on, the belt taken away on Rikers to prevent suicide. The jeans sliding down toward the crack of his ass, always being yanked up. He runs out with the stash, hears people on the stairs, runs for the roof, the jeans fall to his knees, and he goes right off the roof. Four stories to the yard. Moral of the story: Always buy a belt before sticking up a smack dealer.

She sees them all as minor players in an endless demented version of *A Chorus Line*...One after the other. The game of Can You Top This? Saying that they didn't mean to do it. Saying it must have been some other guy. Saying that God told them to do it. A theater would be too small for all of them. They could fill stadiums. All of them proving the theory of original sin. Their tale without end better than anything by Saint Paul or Saint Augustine, John Wesley or Pascal. Like people in traffic court, all of them pleading Guilty, With an Explanation. The title of every human being's autobiography.

Cynthia Harding and Mary Lou Watson were not part of *A Chorus Line.*

They were page 1, for sure, and Helen had to write the story. Called in after going home, told she could smoke, with Sam walking around from his office to the news desk to the photo desk and then the news desk again, looking at photographs, or possible wood, or glancing at television sets. She knows that Sam was in love with Cynthia Harding for many years. He told her one night in the Lion's Head, when he was still drinking. He didn't have to tell her again tonight. She worked on the story.

Then, twenty minutes ago, he called to give her the news. The paper was being murdered too. His voice down, exhausted, telling her in a few words about the city-room meeting in the afternoon. Five o'clock. Telling her she didn't have to go. Someone there will be signing up people willing to work for the website. Sam said he would add her to the list if she wanted him to, but she told him she needed to think about it. That was a lie. She knew this was the end of all of it. For Sam. For her. For their whole goddamned regiment. And Sam has another task. Much more important than the paper. He will need time to mourn the woman he loved.

She knows that the gang is sure to go drinking

after the meeting in the city room. But where will they go? There is no Mutchie's anymore, down by the old Journal-American Building on South Street. There is no Lion's Head on Sheridan Square. There is no Bleeck's. There is no place left where they can bury their dead. Maybe they should rent a permanent suite at Frank E. Campbell's funeral parlor. Wherever the drinking spot is tonight, she is certain that Sam Briscoe will not be there.

What did Sam say to her once? Night is for solitaries. The day is for other people. That is why the night has music. Billie Holiday. "In My Solitude." There are no songs about lunch. Or shopping. Or meetings where everyone whips out laptops.

Today, for Helen Loomis, there can be no Billie Holiday songs. She tells herself, Get out of the house, girl. Maybe she can walk until she is exhausted. That's the cure. Maybe hike as far as the Metropolitan Museum, where she can look at the new Vermeer, in residence for a while. Maybe find Federico the mambo dancer, in daylight, and just talk. Surely find breakfast. No Second Avenue Deli anymore, not down here, but the stars of the Yiddish theater are still cemented to the sidewalk. Maybe go the other way. Down to the South Street Seaport. To where Sloppy Louie's was, the waterfront place where they all went after the shift ended at eight in the morning, ordering oysters for breakfast, and beer and whiskey, while the sanitation guys hauled huge garbage cans past their tables, reeking with fish heads and tails and bones. While everyone laughed or bitched or argued and then laughed again. Every one of them smoking.

Gone now.

The laughing boys too.

All of that was so long ago, her mother and father were still alive. Never comfortable with what she did for a living. Wishing she worked for the *Times,* not some low-life tabloid. Or better, taught literature in the Ivy League. *Jane Austen: Myth or Paradox?* She never did tell them what the boys in the city room called her column. "Vics and Dicks" they could never get. Mother and Dad. Nice people. And there were so many questions she never asked them, questions she never asked herself until after they were dead.

She gazes out the window at the busy avenue. Many Japanese students from NYU and Cooper Union, heading for the soba place on 9th Street, or the sushi joint, or the St. Mark's Bookshop on the corner. Delivery men. Lone men in long rough coats walking separately into the old Ottendorfer Branch of the public library. Others hurrying west to the methadone clinic on Cooper Square.

A traffic cop writing a ticket for a blue Toyota without a driver. Another old man with a plastic garbage bag slung over his shoulder. A young woman with her gloved hand in the crook of her boyfriend's elbow. Another woman, alone, middle-aged, walking on the splayed booted feet of an old dancer.

The sky gray.

Desolate.

She thinks: I'm alone now.

At last.

**11:50 a.m. Josh Thompson. Fourteenth Street, Manhattan.**

He wheels on sidewalks cracked and split, across potholed streets, up tapered corner curbs. He pauses. He watches. An older woman looks at him with pity in her eyes. He pushes past her, thinking, Don't pity me, woman. I'm here for payback. For me. For Whitey. For Langella. For . . . Most people move around him, with nothing in their eyes. They don't know what happened to him, and don't care. They definitely don't know what is under his tarp, under his cheap new blanket. Fuck it: they are not his targets. A man comes along with a seeing-eye dog. Wearing a long heavy coat.

A fat hat, shades turning his face to a masked blank. Is he a vet? From where? Desert Storm? No. Too old. Nam. Yeah. Gotta be Nam. He's got a limp too. Maybe a prosthetic. Left a leg in some fucking jungle. Join me, man. For some payback. The dog leads the man away.

He sees a young guy, with a big bubbly maroon coat and a Mets cap. Like mine. A large pin above the visor. SAY NO TO THE NEW VIETNAM. Too young to be a vet. Some college asshole. Doesn't give a rat's ass for anyone except himself. Definitely not me. Or Whitey. Langella. Alfredo...

Josh pauses near the curb. A Chinese guy sits in a car, smoking a cigarette. The motor is running. The fumes rise in the cold air, heading for the gray clouds. He can see vapor, but can't smell it. Now he sees a tall black woman, dressed like a boss, striding hard on high red heels. A thinner Michelle Obama. He sees her naked, except for the shoes, striding hard toward him, muscles tight in legs and belly, a triangle of black wiry pubic hair. She glances at him, her eyes cautious. He's thinking: Don't worry, woman. I got nothing to slide into you. I got nothing you can suck. I fought for my country, see?

He laughs a small bitter laugh.

The fumes are too strong now, making his throat sore. He starts again, moving on an angle to be closer to the wall. He sees a large concrete building, high, but not a skyscraper, full of contempt and power, like an officer. He looks up. Sees the sign. The Salvation Army. Two homeless women on the steps, one in flip-flops, her cold feet dirty as a sidewalk in this fucking city. The other one is toothless, talking to a third woman about four feet away on the sidewalk. This one is waving a bag of potato chips while she talks. Josh can't hear what they are saying, except for one word. Motherfucker. They use that word everywhere in New York. Kids use it. Girls. Just like Iraq. Pass the motherfuckin' salt, Private. Up the dozen steps behind the women, he can see a crumpled cardboard box with booted feet jutting out. The entrance to the building is sealed behind a huge gold-painted gate. There's a cross on the gate with two crossed swords and a huge S and a slogan: DOING THE MOST GOOD.

Doing good? The most good? Hey, in there, do *me* some good. Get me a new prick. Get me my wife back. Get me my daughter. Tell God to get on it, okay?

On the side, he sees scaffolding. A good place to crash, maybe? No, one side is open. Anyone can see me. And call a cop. Wanting to know what's under my tarp.

Josh sees words on the wall.

*... While there is a drunkard left, while there is
a poor lost girl upon the streets, while there
remains one dark soul without the light of
God, I'll fight — I'll fight to the very end!*

It's signed "General William Booth."

General of what?

Did he work with Petraeus on the surge? Does
he want to fight in Namistan? Or is he just a general in the Salvation Army? And if he is, why
doesn't God listen to him?

Josh wheels away, going back to where he came
from, down by the river. Down there, after breakfast on two slices of pizza, he asked a man to buy
him a blanket in some dump of a store. Told him he
would pay. Held out two twenty-dollar bills. The
man was maybe fifty, smooth face, overcoat with a
velvet collar. A black leather briefcase. Surely a Jew.

–How'd you get into that wheelchair, fella? he
said.

–Iraq.

–Wait here, he said and went into the store. He
came out with a blanket, thick and dark.

–Want me to do it for you, soldier?

–No, no. How much was it?

–Forget it, he said.

He laid the blanket on Thompson's lap. And
walked away without saying another word.

Don't go soft now, Josh Thompson thought. You ain't a charity case. Still...

He struggled to pull the blanket over his upper body without showing what else was there. Nobody seemed to notice. Not the blanket. Not the MAC-10. Just another loser in a wheelchair.

Now he moves through all the others, winners and losers, small kids and nannies, more old ladies, a security guard eating cake, another homeless woman with empty eyes. Then he sees a man in full Muslim gear. The little Muslim hat. The flowing robe with a jacket over it. Thick black beard. Holding a book. The only book. God's book. Remembered seeing guys like him on CNN at Walter Reed. Muslims in New York! He wants to ram the motherfucker. He wants to be challenged by him. His hands feel for the gun. For the trigger. But the man moves on without looking at him, and Josh does nothing. Telling himself: Wait. Wait until nightfall.

He crosses an avenue, cars and buses and trucks idling at a red light. His feet feel cold now, although he has no feet.

He passes a store for rent. Lots of stores for rent down here. An awning. Sees steps to a basement. Nobody inside or out. He thinks: Maybe I could crash here. Maybe I could get down the stairs to the basement. Six steps. Nah. He moves on, sees a place called Passion, selling adult videos for $1.99. Recession special for jerking off. And next door? Are they kidding? Village Kids Nursery. Next door to the jerk-off store! Josh laughs out loud. Then sees that little girl near Fallujah, the blood erupting from the hole in her chest, like a slow pump, her eyes very still, someone screaming. Maybe it was me shot her. I'll never know.

He hears a siren. An ambulance or a fire engine. And he stops, leans back, facing the dark sky. Josh Thompson starts to scream. No sound leaves his mouth.

*12:05 p.m. Sam Briscoe. His loft.*

He's in a gray sweat suit, white socks, slippers. He is fresher after the shower and has made some of the calls. Matt Logan again. Janet. Helen Loomis. But he doesn't want to call all of them, one by one. He doesn't want to call anyone. There is one more call he must make. The one he planned to make first, except that the newspaper, as always, got in the way. He goes to the desk, where the important numbers are written in large printed letters on a three-by-five index card. He lifts the phone and dials his daughter in Paris. A framed color photograph of her is beside the printer. Eighteen. The two of them in Monte Carlo that time. She's smiling, but her eyes, as always, are wary. A different photograph of that same scene is in his office at the newspaper. The photographer was Cynthia Harding.

Two rings. Three. Five. Then her recorded voice in fluent French, followed by English. Please leave a message. The voice cool and smooth in both languages.

–Nicole? Dad. It's almost noon in New York. I have some dreadful news...Cynthia Harding... and her secretary...were murdered last night. In the house on Patchin Place...And a separate matter, nowhere as terrible. The *World* is dead, as a newspaper. On Monday morning, it'll be a website...Without me. Which was my choice...I didn't want you to read either story in the *Herald-Tribune.* Or *Le Monde.* Call when you can and I'll explain. I'll be at the paper later in the day, to say good-bye to the troops...I don't know how to say good-bye to Cynthia. It's a bad day. Love you, baby.

He hangs up. Then walks to the window. No sounds penetrate the special double-thick glass. Some gulls circling. Gray sullen clouds. It feels like snow.

He goes to the couch. The morning papers lie on the low table. Delivered to the lobby each

morning. The television set is dark. He can't look
at the papers. Not even his own. And doesn't have
to anymore. From today he no longer is required
to pay attention. A kind of relief, maybe? No more
fucking deadlines.

He dozes but is too tired to sleep. He drifts to
that time in Monte Carlo. Cynthia Harding's idea.
Nicole a student at the Sorbonne. Cynthia arrived
by airplane from New York and went directly to
the hotel. Big place. Marble corridors. Black-tie
casino. He and Nicole took the train from Paris.
The girl was glum, either dozing or staring out the
window all the way south to the Mediterranean.
On her vacations in New York, Nicole had met
Cynthia at parties, fund-raisers, dinners, horseshit
events, one trapped weekend at a friend's house in
Southampton. She seemed to like Cynthia, and
Cynthia was sweet and smart and never treated
her like a child. Certainly not Sam's child. But in
Monte Carlo, Nicole was bitchy to Cynthia, play-
ing an adult, not a teenager. Cynthia smiled a lot,
in an amused, patient way, and her cool made
Nicole angrier. Finally, in bed in her room, Cyn-
thia said: Sam, don't you see? She's got a guy in
Paris. Why would she want to be here with *us*?

They all left in the morning. Briscoe didn't
own a black-tie costume, and Cynthia was never

fond of shooting craps. Nicole was clearly happy, so Cynthia was right. She usually was.

She ends up with her flesh pierced, her blood on the floor, not far from Mary Lou. Gotta find Ali Watson. We both need consolation.

Briscoe sits up abruptly, staring at the rows of books, the paintings. The Mexican girl by Lew Forrest. Her glistening black eyes, her luxurious golden flesh tell him again that the painter must have loved her. A gift from Cynthia. When I turned sixty-five. Cynthia's flesh was not this flesh. It was ivory. The sun could redden it, but she could never tan. And yet in the dark, with light seeping in from Greene Street or the hills of Tuscany, her flesh was golden too.

Nicole's guy in Paris was a Spaniard, from Barcelona. A medical student, who spoke Catalan, French, English, and some Italian. Cynthia said, Don't worry, Sam. She won't marry this guy, he's too pretty. She was right about that too.

The evening before he and Cynthia were to leave for New York, he went to a bistro with Nicole. They didn't sit on the terrace. Too cold. Instead, they found a table deep inside. The waiter brought the coffee. She was silent. And he can still hear what she asked when they were settled.

–Dad, why did Mom kill herself?

He squeezed her hand.

—I don't really know, Nicole.

She stared at him, while he stared at his own coffee. Seeing the troubled face of Joyce Miller. Mom. His wife. Nicole finally asking the question that she must have wanted to ask for years. Her silence demanding a reply.

—She didn't say anything to me, Briscoe said. She didn't leave a note.

—How did she do it?

The ice in her voice. Stabbing him still.

—Pills.

Now remembering Nicole's puzzled squint.

—That's all?

—No, there were plenty more things that happened. But that was the finale.

Wanting to be honest at last. Wanting to tell Nicole. To unload. To say the unspoken things. But giving her only a dreadful highlight film. Sitting there in the bistro while tweedy academic tourists looked for Jean-Paul Sartre or the ghost of Albert Camus. He told her about the reefer. Acid. Smack for a while. Freebasing cocaine mixed with ammonia. Then angel dust, which made her insane, even dangerous. With booze lacing it all together. He told her about his calls to Joyce's father in Ohio, pleading for help. Hearing indifference. Joyce in rehab. Then rehab again. Then rehab once more.

Then one afternoon she got a babysitter for Nicole, right here in the loft on Greene Street, and filled half a jelly jar with Del Monte fruit cocktail, put about forty pills in her pocket and a driver's license, and went off to join the skanks in Tompkins Square Park. The cops found her body hours later. Bent over on a bench with broken slats. No note. No farewell. Then cremation. Another sorry fucking tale that started in the 1960s and ended in the 1970s.

In the Paris bistro, Briscoe signaled to the waiter to bring fresh coffee.

—Where was *I?* Nicole said.

—After that night, you were at my mother's house in Sunset Park. In Brooklyn.

—And where were you?

—When your mother died? Covering the Democratic convention in Miami. I flew home as soon as the call reached me at the hotel.

—That's why we moved here to Paris?

—A few years later. Yes. After my mother died. Remember? She was helping take care of you.

Her jaw slack, Nicole stared out at the street in St.-Germain-des-Prés.

—It's so sad.

—It is, he said.

She turned and buried her head in his shoulder.

—Oh, Daddy.

—It's okay, baby, he whispered, while a few people stared at them. We get over almost everything.

We still do, he thinks. And gets up.


**12:40 p.m. Ali Watson. Castle Bar, Livonia Avenue, Brooklyn.**

He watches the street from a high plastic stool at the front end of the long bar, sipping a beer. Everyone is black. The bartender is large, young, mustached, his skin the color of coffee with lots of milk. His skull is shaved, and he talks with a small group at the far end of the bar. He is polite with Ali, but he knows a cop when he sees one. Ali slides off the stool and stands. The bartender walks toward him. The guys at the other end are silent.

—Take care, Ali says, and moves two singles toward the bartender. The tip.

—Yeah, the bartender says, and watches Ali leave.

Ali steps into the cold air, and turns right toward the far corner. Across the street when he was a boy there was a gymnasium on the second floor. All the Jewish gangsters went there to watch their properties in action. The last years of Jewish fighters. A guy named Bummy Davis was one of the fighters and he got killed going after some dumbbell who stuck up a bar. All of the players were gone by the time Ali was born, so Ali didn't know the location of the bar. But everybody knew the story. He talked with his partner about it once, but Malachy Devlin had never heard of Bummy Davis. Then, one morning at the JTTF, he arrived in a state of excitement.

–Ali, that Bummy Davis you told me about? Last night, there was a show about him on ESPN. Couldn't believe it.

–I wish I'd seen it, Ali said.

–I tried to call you, but—

The gym was a Baptist church when Ali was a teenager, and now it was a mosque. A very special mosque. Services were held in the wide-open space of the vanished second-floor gym. Young men moving on polished wooden floors, slamming heavy bags, turning speed bags into blurs, others boxing in a ring: the stuff of neighborhood legends, now replaced by prayer mats and submission to Allah. Mary Lou wondered why free men would bow to someone who wasn't there and he could never explain to her why even he had once done the same. It was like trying to explain the myth of Midnight Rose's, the candy store where the killers from Murder, Inc. met each night, down under the El at Saratoga and Livonia. The hit men loved egg creams and sharp clothes and killing people for a living. Laughing all the way. Or so the tale went.

When he took Mary Lou around Brownsville he told her about the place, and she asked, "What's an egg cream?" Like someone from Minnesota. He had to explain that it was a soft drink, but didn't have eggs in it, and she didn't get it until finally he took her to the Gem Spa on Second Avenue and St. Mark's Place in Manhattan and she sipped her first egg cream, thick with milk and chocolate syrup and seltzer water, and said, "I don't care what they call it. It's great."

Nobody has entered or left the mosque now in an hour. Drifters move along the avenue, passing the front door, lost in a fog of heroin or meth. For sure, not one of them longs for egg creams or for Allah.

Ali crosses the street quickly and walks to the door of the mosque. Blinds drawn within windows and the door. He rings a buzzer hard. Then again. Then knocks. It doesn't matter who is watching him now. They know he's a cop. Nobody comes to the door.

He walks to the corner and makes a right, heading for the lots behind the row of buildings. There are two rusting shells of automobiles in the space behind the mosque. And tire tracks in the mud, backing up, turning. He moves to the side, to avoid leaving his own footprints in the mud, and goes to the back door. Locked. He tries knocking again, sensing that nobody will answer. Thinking: Two mosques in one morning, without leaving Brooklyn. I should score some points with Allah. Inshallah.

He uses a Visa card to spring the lock, thinking: Too easy, then takes out his pistol, listens, and steps inside. The door has a wide, thick metal bar across it, but it's not wedged into its slot. Someone has left and couldn't close it from outside.

The lights are out, but he can see the large shapes in the leaking grayness of the rooms. He listens. There are the usual creaks from old buildings but no human sounds. No footsteps. No breathing. And yet he feels that someone is here. He moves forward on tiptoe. Pauses. Listens. Moves again, heading to where he knows the stairway is, and the living quarters where the imam named Aref seethes with daily bitterness. Ali has visited him over the years, as part of the job. To let him know he was being watched. Felt the anger that was never spoken. Put him on the master list.

He might actually be here. Hidden in a bathroom. Lying flat in the large room upstairs. Holding a pistol. Ready to repel infidels. Or more likely: he drove away in the automobile that left tracks in the mud. Or—

He peers into the living quarters and flicks on a tiny flashlight. Bedclothes unrumpled on the narrow cot. Nothing in the sink of the small kitchen. No water on the floor of the stall shower. Some newspapers in English and Arabic. No signs of a woman or children, no clothes, schoolbooks, or toys. Aref chose to live in purgatory.

Ali goes up the stairs. A few steps creak. Nothing creaks back. He steps into Allah's gymnasium.

There's a body on the floor against the far wall. Lying on its back. There are two toppled lockers to the right of the body, their doors open. Ali lets his pistol hang loose at his side and takes out his cell phone. He moves closer to the body while dialing Malachy Devlin. He looks down at the body. It's Aref, all right. His face has been battered, but it's him. Blood spreads beneath his head like spilled paint.

—Hey, partner, Malachy says. What's up?

—I'm in Aref's friendly neighborhood mosque. He's here on the floor, dead.

–Jesus.

–Call everybody, starting with the precinct. I'll let them in.

–Right.

–And in my files, there's a folder on my son, Malik. With photos. We have to put out a bulletin. Wanted for questioning. The whole Northeast. Use his photograph. Have an artist make a version without his beard or mustache. I think Malik might be driving the imam's car. And shit, maybe I'm nuts. It could be some other guy. But look in Aref's file. Get the make and license plate. Pass that on to everyone, starting with NYPD. Bridges. Tunnels. Arrest whoever the fuck is driving.

He glances at the toppled lockers.

–Ali, is this—

–I don't know anything for sure. It could be about my wife. And the Harding woman. Or just about this asshole Aref. But it could get even worse than a double homicide. We need the bomb-squad guys here. Technical guys. The whole enchilada.

–Right.

–Later.

Ali hangs up. He goes to a wall switch and turns on the lights. He glances down at Aref, whose eyes are wide in shock. He turns toward the shrouded windows. Malik, he says out loud. I'm coming for your ass.

### 1:05 p.m. Consuelo Mendoza. Sunset Park.

At last, Norma is gone. The babysitting is done, and the talking is over. The older boy will be home in an hour, and now it is only Consuelo and little Timoteo. The four-year-old is watching a cartoon on television, his face serious, his intelligent brown eyes taking in everything, but seeming to doubt what they are seeing. Consuelo is cooking lunch for herself and the little one. Beef patties from the market on La Quinta. Bought two days ago, when she still had a job. Carrots. Boiled potatoes. Avoiding grease. Trying to look normal.

But Consuelo is taut and jittery with confused emotions. She remembers the details of the morning with Señor Lewis and the images of the past that the visit called up in her, the bedroom in Cuernavaca, the girl she was then, the wild passion of her young flesh, the way she felt about this man who was even then *un gringo viejo*. She had told Raymundo about Señor Lewis long ago, but certainly not all of what had happened. She would never tell him any of that. Even if he asked, she would lie. Men never understand.

She remembers the one named Jerry, the bald one behind the desk at the Chelsea Hotel, and how he asked her to step around to the side, behind the desk, so that nobody in the lobby could see her. And he handed her the sealed envelope.

—Now you have to hide this, Jerry said. Under your clothes. Don't let anyone see it. Don't open it until you get home, okay? That's what Mr. Forrest says. Okay?

—Okay, she said, and turned away and stuffed the thick envelope under her belt. Then she went out into the dark morning and headed for the N train.

All the way to Brooklyn she worried that the envelope would slip. She clasped her hands on her waist, as if she had a tummyache, and tried even harder than usual to look ordinary, to look homely, to look unlikely to be carrying anything of value. The daytime crowd on the subway was less tense than the one at night. A dirty black man was sleeping in a corner seat, three lumpy plastic bags at his feet. Four standing schoolboys laughed and joked, joked and laughed. A uniformed cop leaned against a door. All the way to Sunset Park.

She let herself in with a key, and Norma called from the kitchen, where little Timoteo was staring into the yard. Smiles, laughs, a hug of her thighs from the boy. Consuelo took off her coat and stepped into the bathroom. Closed the door. She removed the envelope, laid it behind jars and small bottles inside the medicine cabinet. Later. Open it after Norma leaves.

Now she's gone, with *besos y abrazos,* and the boy is eating. Consuelo goes into the bathroom, takes the envelope, uses her forefinger to open it.

And sees bills.

Not dollar bills.

She slides one out. Crisp and new. It's a hundred-dollar bill. She has never held one before. She takes the others in thumb and forefinger. She begins to count. They are all hundred-dollar bills. Fifty of them.

*Ay, Dios mío.*

She holds the bills in her right hand and grips the bathroom sink with her left.

*Ay,* Señor Lewis.

*Ay . . .*


*1:15 p.m. Malik Shahid. FDR Drive, Manhattan.*

He is again playing a bored young man without cares, as he drives the Lexus uptown on the FDR. All the lanes are jammed, moving slowly uptown and down. The window open an inch. Hot in the car, with his coat. And the vest underneath. The holy vest.

To his right, the river is gray and dirty, with only a few small boats moving on its surface. In a narrow park, three flags are stiff with wind, blowing east toward Queens on the far side of the river. The gas gauge shows a quarter of a tank. Enough. No need to show his face at a gas station. The tire iron back there, in a Brownsville lot. The gun— He sees a police car in the middle lane on the downtown side, red lights turning, trying to push through to an exit. Lots of luck, assholes. Malik can't push through, so why should they?

He knows that by now someone may have found Aref. Someone else with a key. A wife. A member. Maybe a cop. So what? By the time they get going, he thinks, I'll be lost again. And I only need hours now to do what I have to do tonight.

He did look for a surveillance camera, out back of the mosque in Brownsville. But he realized a true search would take too much time. He jammed the tire iron in his waistband. Then got in easily: by knocking on the back door. He stared at the Lexus for a long moment, then knocked again. Aref answered. He didn't recognize Malik with a smooth hairless face. Malik smiled and talked and used Arabic, and Aref remembered and led him inside. Malik said he just wanted to pray. Aref seemed skeptical but they went up together to the big prayer room. It was empty. Malik confronted him.

—Where's the stuff? he said.

—What stuff?

—The stuff that goes bang.

Aref shook his head, speaking his own version of Jamal's speech.

—That's over, he said. We're Americans now. All of us, Malik.

—Yeah. Until they come to arrest you.

—Maybe you should leave now.

—Maybe not.

Malik took the tire iron from his belt, hefted it, placed it under Aref's nose.

—Is it in one of those lockers?

—Go look.

Malik shoved him toward the two tall lockers. With his free hand he opened the door of the one on the left. Prayer mats. Some clothes. No canvas bag with its precious contents.

He tried the second locker. Also unlocked. Same stuff. Then his rage took over. He grabbed each locker in turn and jerked it away from the wall. Both made metallic crushing sounds against the polished floor.

Fear rose on Aref's face. Which is what Malik

wanted to see. Aref glanced at the ceiling. Malik understood.

—Where's the ladder? he said.

Aref said nothing, and stepped past the fallen lockers and opened a closet door. There was a ladder, along with buckets, brooms, two mops. Malik stared at the ceiling, and saw a small ring in a depressed circle.

—Go up and get it, Malik said in a low voice.

Aref did what he was told. He climbed the ladder and pulled on the ceiling ring. A hinged panel opened. He reached in, swung around, and held a dark blue canvas bag.

—Now hand it down, Malik said. Gently.

Aref came down several steps and passed the bag to Malik, who grabbed it with his free hand. His eyes on Aref, Malik hugged the bag with the hand holding the tire iron, and pulled the zipper open with his other hand. Peered into the bag. Felt his blood pulse as he saw what he had hoped for. Closed the bag. And Aref began to run for the door.

Malik dropped the bag and went after him. Wrapped an arm around his neck. Turned Aref violently. And smashed the tire iron against the side of his head. The older man made an incoherent sound, full of shock and fatalism, and fell to the floor. Malik smashed the front of his face. Once, twice, then again. He waited. The older man did not move. Did not breathe.

–Stupid motherfucker! Why'd you *do* that?

There was no answer. Malik hurried to the blue bag. Unzipped it. Laid the tire iron on the floor. Then lifted out the black polyester object within. Opened it to its full width. Saw the hooks and cords, the small gray device with a white button. Saw the canvas slots snug with red bars. He glanced at Aref, who was not moving. Then he slipped off his coat and tied the vest across his chest and pulled his coat over it. Time to go.

He returned to Aref, and went through his trouser pockets until he found the car keys. And two twenty-dollar bills. He whipped off a scarf from Aref's neck and wrapped the tire iron in it and then headed down the stairs.

Thinking: Gotta be a gun here somewheres. Into the small bedroom. Feeling around. Lifted the mattress. There it was. A .38, like his so-called father used to have. Loaded.

And now he's in the Lexus on the FDR, East River Drive, heading to East Harlem, to a parking lot he used back in the day. The .38 under his ass. He sees people in other cars smoking cigarettes, using cell phones, texting on BlackBerrys. They're all going somewhere. To see wives and friends or friendly neighborhood pushers. Malik is heading for the night. For the finale. Thinking: It's just me now. Me and Allah. My woman Glorious is dead. My son is dead without ever breathing the air of the world. My infidel bitch of a mother is dead. Her rich blonde motherfucking slave owner is dead. Now Aref is dead, and I'm driving his Lexus. He was dead before I killed him. An imam with a Lexus: that's why he's dead.

Thinking: More people will be dead before the midnight hour. Including me. Around the world tomorrow, millions will celebrate when they hear the news. They will pray for me. They will call to me in Paradise.

Now I have my tools. All I need. Now I go on, alone.


**1:35 p.m. Helen Loomis. South Street Seaport.**


She is out at the end of the pier, in wool hat, long down coat, boots. Smoking a cigarette, her back to the wind. She is alone. Nobody else smokes anymore. Below her, the East River swirls and eddies, the water opaque. A lone gull flies a tour of inspection, searching for scraps to be shared by the sheltering flock. A tug moves north to pass under the bridges, heading for the Bronx. Off to her right, she can see the four masts of the *Peking*. She knows it was built in 1911 because she wrote about it for the *World* when two dopes dressed as pirates tried to rob it. There are no people on the wooden deck. Directly behind her is the three-story mall, full of shops, a kind of nautical theme park for people from out of town. Inside, she could have been in Des Moines. Some shops were closed for good. Others catered to the few customers. They were offering maps, New York souvenirs, cheap little versions of the Statue of Liberty or the World Trade Center or the skyline. Junk destined for garage sales in distant cities.

But back there, behind her, a short walk under the FDR Drive, into the square that is now perfectly cobblestoned and perfectly empty, was the place where every Friday was a good Friday: Sloppy Louie's. She sees them now, all of them, loud and laughing and cocking a hoot at the world. They ordered the freshest fish in New York, cod and fluke and halibut, still icy from the fish market up past the square. They made fun of everybody, including themselves. Newspapermen.

The whole thing is shuttered now. The fish market is gone to the Bronx. The aroma of fish replaced by the exhaust of stalled cars on the Drive.

She tamps out the cigarette on the rail, flicks the butt into the current. What the hell: Al Gore is nowhere in sight. She sees a helicopter rising out of the tumbling grayness over Brooklyn, sees it before she hears it, watches it cross high over the empty harbor, then descend into New Jersey. The ongoing search for terrorists. She turns with her back to the river and gazes at the tops of the buildings on Wall Street. They must be happy up there, she thinks. Then she sees a man slip out a door from the mall. White hair pokes out the sides of his hat, one of those Irish jobs that Sam always brought home from Dublin. The guy is wearing a long tweed coat, a dark scarf, polished shoes. He looks up at the Brooklyn Bridge, the cables like part of an immense harp. Then he peels off his gloves, takes out a pack of cigarettes, and lights up.

Helen looks south at the harbor and the distant Verrazano. She remembers a chilly night with her husband on the deck of the Staten Island Ferry, the two of them holding each other for warmth, and she spoke some of the words of Edna St. Vincent Millay. *"We were very tired, we were very merry—/ We had gone back and forth all night on the ferry..."* That night they tried again to make a baby, and once again it didn't happen. She wanted just that, just a tiny boy in a crib playing with his toes. They kept trying until a week before her husband died, and she never tried again. Not with anyone. Across more than thirty years. The little boy still plays with his toes in her dreams.

She turns away and the white-haired man is walking toward her. She hopes he veers away. He doesn't look like he wants a spare cigarette, or some change. For sure. But he doesn't veer away.

—Helen, he says. Helen Loomis?

Suddenly she knows him.

—Eddie Gaffney? she says. Is that you?

—I'll be goddamned, Gaffney says.

—What are *you* doing here?

He exhales, making a fluttering sound with his lips.

—My wife, she's in St. Vincent's, the downtown one, you know: a couple of blocks from here.

—Oh, Eddie. I'm so sorry.

—Yeah, well...

He shakes his head, takes a drag on the filtered Camel.

—And you, Helen? I heard the news about the paper on the TV at the hospital. You all right?

—Not really.

—Want some coffee?

—Sure.

He flips his butt into the river and they turn toward the mall. How long had it been since Eddie Gaffney walked away from newspapers? To become a flack, and then a lobbyist up in Albany? Thirty years, at least. How long since she'd seen him? Twelve years? Some funeral... He opens the door and she steps into the mall. Somewhere, Beatles music is playing. "Hey, Jude." Maybe the floor below.

–There's a place over in the corner, Gaffney says.

–Right.

She knows he will start talking about the days when the fish market was still here and they all filled the big table at Sloppy Louie's in the mornings. He won't tell Helen about his wife unless she pries. She won't. Over coffee, they can talk about the years when they each had the best of everything. Without much money. She thinks: The only way to fight nostalgia is to listen to somebody else's nostalgia.

*1:45 p.m. Josh Thompson. Fourteenth Street, Manhattan.*

More steps and he can't climb them. These lead into still another church. Dark faces, men and women, probably Mexicans. The sign says something in Spanish, ending with that word he can't say. Goo-add-a-luppy? Same as back home. All these Mexicans, it must be Catholic. Figures. But if you look at their faces long enough, they look like Arabs.

He moves the wheelchair closer to the iron spears of the fence, and locks the wheels. People move along the street in both directions, but none of them look at him. Across the street, past the buses and the taxis and the SUVs, he sees the King Food Chinese restaurant. Every kind of people here. Chinese too. This side of the street, they even got an Istanbul Café. Not just Jews and Catholics and blacks and Mexicans. Muslims too.

Then he sees an older woman looking at him. A Mexican. Or Arab. Short and dumpy, hair a little gray, the tan skin a little red from the cold. She has kind eyes. She comes over.

–Señor? *Necesita ayuda?* You need help?

–No, no, I'm all right.

–You wan' to go to chutch?

He smiles, shrugs. Then taps the arms of the wheelchair.

–No, no, lady. I can't. Not with this.

He waves at the high steps.

The woman leans forward.

–Wait a minute.

She turns and hurries to a side entrance, and

moves down the steps into a place Josh Thompson can't see. He thinks he should leave. Go away. Disappear. But he thinks of her eyes. There was no anger in her eyes. In Baghdad, all eyes were angry, even when people smiled.

Now she comes back, with two Mexican men, rough, dark, smiling.

—Mister, this is Joaquín, the woman says. He was in the war too.

The man smiles, salutes.

—You wan' to go to church, soldier? he says.

Josh hesitates, then shrugs his okay. He wants to be warm.

—Thanks, man.

The two men lift the wheelchair, and the woman goes forward, waving people out of the way. They go up the stairs, and gently place the chair on stone blocks, facing large doors. The woman is on point, the officer of the patrol, followed by Josh and the two Mexican men. The grunts. She speaks to them in a low, soft voice. They pause, while the woman opens one of the two large doors. Josh is wheeled into a long, high-ceilinged church, with rows of wooden pews, a Mass under way on a distant altar. The rear pews are mostly empty. Josh thinks: That figures, these people work in the day. The space is warm, with an aroma of food and incense and the sound of a hymn being sung by a chorus. He doesn't see a chorus. Must be a CD. Nice, though...

—Make yourself comfortable, soldier, the older man says, and both men walk away.

Josh sits on the aisle beside a pew. The woman touches his hand with her own warm bare fingers.

—Goo'bye, she says. You be okay here, okay? Warm. Safe. I go to work now. The guys, they'll check when you want to leave.

And she hurries away too, leaving Josh Thompson alone.

*2:35 p.m. Sandra Gordon. Her apartment.*

She comes around the corner, after leaving the office and grabbing a fast lunch. And sees two men in overcoats waiting at the door of her apartment house. Aw, shit. One in a trench coat, the other in tweed. Each is hatless, with neatly trimmed hair. She has never met an FBI man in her life but has seen plenty of movies. She wonders what took them so long.

—Miss Gordon? says the one in the trench coat.

—Yes?

—I'm Special Agent Roberts from the FBI and—

—Can we step inside? she says.

—Of course.

The agent in the tweed coat opens the door, Sandra follows him, and Roberts steps in behind her. The day doorman looks up from behind the desk, his eyes wary. Sandra goes directly to him.

—Anything for me, Andy?

—Yes, ma'am.

He places a package of magazines, junk mail, letters, on the counter before her. He smiles thinly, even protectively, and glances at the FBI men. Sandra lifts her mail, turns to the two men.

—Can we talk down here?

—We'd prefer your apartment, ma'am.

—Why not?

They go up in the elevator. No words are spoken. She knows the men are her own age, even younger, and must have seen the same movies she did. They follow her out of the elevator, all of them pausing as she unlocks her door. They follow her into the apartment and she flicks on a light switch. She puts the mail on a chair, then shrugs off her coat and places it over the mail.

—Well? she says. What do you want to know?

—We're looking for Myles Compton. Your friend. He was due in court this morning—a federal grand jury—and didn't show.

She shakes her head slowly, gestures for the men to sit on the couch. She eases into a chair facing them. Before them on a low table is a large volume of photographs by Annie Leibovitz. Sandra tells the FBI men about Myles's visit the night before, and how he said he had to go away, to Miami. And how he left. And how she hasn't heard from him since then. No, he didn't stay here for the night. No, she didn't know where in Miami, or any connection to another flight. He was always vague.

–Did you know about the grand jury?

–Of course. It was in the papers. He said it was all about people connecting dots that don't connect. I guess he meant you. Or the Justice Department.

–I see. Did he mention a certain Bulgarian?

–Not really, but it was in the papers. Yes. He said he was one of the investors. When I asked him about the newspaper story.

–Nothing else?

–We had a deal, Sandra says. He didn't talk about his business, I didn't talk about mine.

The silent man in the tweed coat makes notes, holding a small tape recorder against his pad with his thumb. Roberts says:

–Did you have a business relationship with him?

–Absolutely not. But look, if you think I'm involved somehow, I'd better get a lawyer, right?

She stands up, folds her arms as if she has noth-

ing more to say. Sandra thinks: This is as sponta-
neous as one of those goddamned reality shows.

–I understand, says Roberts, standing, then
taking a wallet from under his coat, and sliding
out a card. Just like all the movies. She takes it,
lays it on a small table, leads the two men to the
door, and closes it after them.

For a long moment, she leans her back against
the door. Her arm aches from the fall. She has a
headache. She will lie down, and read a book about
strangers, and take another Aleve, and hope the
pain goes away. Then she'll call Sam Briscoe to
find out about the funeral of Cynthia Harding.
Thinking: Oh, Myles, wherever you are, don't
drag me after you. And sees the face of the Bulgarian in the newspaper, his eyes full of ice.

### 3:15 p.m. Malik Shahid. Orpheum 7 Movie House, East 86th Street and Third Avenue, Manhattan.

He squirms in his aisle seat in an orchestra row
halfway from the entrance. The backpack is under
his seat. His back and shoulders are sore from
walking with the pack all the way from 104th
Street. Damned ticket cost twelve-fifty. Paid with
money for Glorious. Wanted just to borrow the

money. Took it instead. Oh. There are old people scattered around in the darkness, most of them white, but the theater is mainly empty. Malik is jellied with exhaustion. He sees glimpses on the screen of a white infidel whore unbuttoning her blouse, and closes his eyes. The music is loud. He sees Glorious in the darkness of the house in the Lots. Her breasts fat with pregnancy. Her skin. Always in the dark, because they could not use lights or some fucking cop might notice.

Glorious.

Dead.

Waiting for me.

He remembers in high school at Tech, reading about Lee Harvey Oswald, and how after shooting JFK he got away but then shot some cop and ran into a movie theater. What happened then? Can't remember. Malik's fingers touch the pistol in his belt. The tire iron down a sewer. The .38 is better. If I gotta use it, I use it.

Now he has to rest, and then go to visit Aladdin. To rub the magic lamp. To summon the djinni. To turn the lamp into that place in the Bronx he saw on television when he was three or four, sitting beside his mother on the family couch. First thing he can remember. Seeing all the fire engines and the hoses and hearing talk about ninety people dead, or something, and they were watching because his father was there. One of the cops. They even saw him once on TV, in his over-coat, a badge pinned to his chest. Badge of dis-honor. They were still his mother and father then. "This is mass murder," his mother said. "Mass murder!" And Malik didn't know what she meant by that, not then, didn't know the word "murder." Or, truth be told, the word "dead." Except that a lot of people were dead and nothing else, no weather, no sports, nothing was on TV except that. Dead. What were the words they kept say-ing? Over and over?

Happy Land.

Yeah, that was it:

*Happy Land.*

Tonight he will create some happiness in this land. For Allah.

He opens his eyes. The infidel white whore on the screen is weeping into a pillow. The guy is smoking. Never read a word of al-Quran. But he and the whore hate the Prophet, and Allah too. They never learn anything. Not in Iraq. Not at Fort Hood. They don't know that they will all die, unless they submit to Allah. They will die one at a time. Then fifty at a time. For now. Then more and more and more. Malik imagines a great white blinding light, a rumble that gets deeper and deeper, then the howl of a ferocious cleansing wind: and then nothing. *Allahu akbar!*

On-screen, the white guy is now driving alone through a place with palm trees. L.A.? No, no. Miami. Is that Don Johnson? No. Too fat. The sun bright. The sea blue. Miami. A town he's never seen except in the movies or TV. And will never see now.

### 3:45 p.m. Sam Briscoe. His loft, Manhattan.

A siren wakes him. An ambulance, for sure. The soprano sax of emergency. The sound fades but he does not return to sleep. He glances at the clock. Three forty-five. Day, not night. He is in bed in the dark bedroom, but doesn't remember getting there. He was on the couch. Now he is here, in a sweat suit under the covers. He turns, groping for the cool part of the sheets. As if he can find another half hour of warm darkness.

*Why, oh why, do I...*

He sees Cynthia Harding for the first time, when she was young and he was too. She is on the stage at the Village Gate on Bleecker Street, and

Art D'Lugoff is alive, the guy who ran that wonderful joint, and Charlie Mingus too, and the place is packed. Telling himself now: Write all that. Write her on the stage to make the case for books. Speaking for just a few minutes, too quickly, because she is not an actress. Speaking for the library, not herself. For all kids and all old people and everybody in between. For those who need books in order to live. She quotes Robert Louis Stevenson about how young writers must read like predators. And she says that all of us, not just writers, must read like predators too. For books are food, she says, for every single one of us.

Write how the rich crowd stood and cheered her words in a reserved uptown way, while the jazz crowd maintained its permanent cool, and she seemed embarrassed and made a small nervous steeple of her fingers, and bowed, and then smiled, and Mingus fingered his bass, and the group bounced into *If they asked me, I could write a book...* and Briscoe wanted to meet her. And then D'Lugoff waved him over.

He sits up now, wanting to write for the first time in years. Remembering more clearly that first meeting. When he was still married to Joyce. And Cynthia was married to her first husband, a professor at Columbia. When there was not yet a *New York World*. When his daughter was not yet born.

Cynthia at once shy and strong. A lifetime ago. He stares at his hands. He wants to take a yellow pad and a good fountain pen in his right hand and sit with a board in his lap and write. He knows that his hands have memory. But his hands now are blotched with age spots. They carried no spots when he met Cynthia Harding. Nor did hers. Time does the spattering. Later, she seldom complained about the way they lived in the world. She would sometimes erupt in exasperation, and go away, for as long as a year. She even married a guy she didn't love, and that was another two years. Briscoe would rush to the safety of covering a war. Or the troubles of others. When they were together again, there was never an accounting. Not from her. Not from him. She didn't speak about him to anyone else. He lived by the same rule. Once, when she mentioned marriage to him, he told her he didn't think he had the talent for it.

–Maybe I don't either, she said.

–Maybe nobody does, he said, and they both laughed.

–What's the line from Chekhov? she said. If you're afraid of loneliness, don't marry.

And they laughed again. She tried marriage anyway, that second time, and retained Briscoe as an option to ward off the loneliness. Briscoe—and books too. "With a book in my

hands, and a soft light," she said, "I'm never alone."
And she lived that way, with Briscoe, or without
him. She had her year of living dangerously, he
knew, but never went into details. He didn't
describe to her his own long series of episodes with
women after Joyce died, most of them enclosed in
parentheses as part of a longer story. The story that
was hers too...At first Briscoe thought she saw
him as a book she took down from the shelf,
savored, and then returned to a higher shelf. But it
lasted too long, like a serial by Dickens that had
great gaps and greater and greater richness as it
went on. He loved her more last week than he ever
had, the richness of her, the plenitude of her that
was part of his own consciousness, even when he
slept alone. Now, some son of a bitch has torn away
the last phase of that long narrative. We'll never
live those final chapters.

He must write it all, Briscoe thinks, good times
and bad, cataloging his sins of cowardice and eva-
sion and, yes, cruelty. And all the amazing good
times, the laughter, the surprises, the intelligence
with which she dissected the world. Write it all, to
get it out of his fucking head.

He leaves the bedroom in a heavy robe and
walks slowly past the books, wondering how many
of them were gifts from Cynthia Harding. Hundreds? Maybe more. She made him promise a few

years earlier that in his will he would put her in charge of his collection, and absolutely not allow them to end up on eBay or the shelves of the Strand. He told her that was a deal. He didn't ask about her collection and where it would go if she died first.

He leans against the bookcase. Fingering the bindings with his spotted hands. He knows that for as long as Cynthia was alive, he was never alone. She's gone. And now he no longer has the much less intimate comfort of the newspaper. The clock no longer moves without pity to the deadline. No more deadlines. But surely another chapter is beginning in this story without a last act. His story.

### 4:10 p.m. Bobby Fonseca. Victoria's apartment.

He wakes alone. The blue door is open, the toilet empty. Nobody sits at the round table, or the narrow desk holding the laptop and printer. Maybe she's playing games. From under the bed. He speaks her name. No answer. He pads to a chair, finds his cell phone, checks messages. Six of them. One matters. Big meeting in the city room at five o'clock. No guests. Staff only. Maybe that CelineWire prick is right. Maybe...

He returns to bed, lies there. Today's my day off. Sunday to Thursday. That's the gig. He closes his eyes. But what if it's really all over at the *World*? The *Times* is laying off people. Who knows what's up with the *Post* and the *News*? I see their reporters on stories, they're very worried. Except the old guys, the guys in their fifties. They figure it's all over. Playing out the string. Hoping to latch on as flacks somewhere, until Social Security kicks in, or Medicare. Worried about paying tuition for the kids' schools. Feeding the family. Paying the fucking mortgages. The *World* dies, my father will say, Hey, I warned you, Bobby. I couldn't explain to him why I loved it. Going to work where every single day it was something new, some new story, where I could learn about people, and sudden death, and human pain. Not reading about them. Seeing them. Then telling their stories. I tried to explain to him, Dad, I don't want to be rich, I don't want to be famous, I want to be *good*. And he said, Why can't you be good at something like *banking?*

Thinking: Dad doesn't get it. Maybe he never will. And maybe now I can never show him what it means to me. I'm a newspaperman. I've got the clips to prove it. I want to be a newspaperman for the rest of my fucking life. But maybe now, it will end. Just like that. At five o'clock this afternoon.

He thinks: What the hell time is it?

And hears a key turn twice in the door lock. There she is. Victoria Collins. Who just wants the chance that I got at the *World*. Her back is turned as she relocks the door. Shorter than I thought she was when she stood above me at a table, taking an order at Nighttown. A hard firm body. Small breasts. Short legs. Thighs that might get fat, but not for a while. She turns.

—Hey, Fonseca. I went for the papers. And some coffees.

Cheerful. She lays a paper bag on the table. Hefts about six newspapers.

—What time is it, anyway? he says, trying to smile.

She removes coat and hat, drops the newspapers on the foot of the bed. Glances at her watch, tells him it's four-fifteen.

—Jesus, Fonseca says. I gotta go.

—Oh, no ya don't, she says, in a cheeky growl.

She starts pulling her sweater over her head. Black bra showing. She picks up the *World*.

—Ya got the wood *twice,* Fonseca. The wraparound. The main paper. Gotta be a record! I bought the last five copies. And guess what? *They gave me a credit line!*

He sits up, blanket pulled to his shoulders.

—But—

She is slipping off her jeans, uses thumbs to remove her black panties. Then bounces onto the bed.

—We gotta celebrate, man.

She carries a copy of the *World* into bed, folded back to the second page of the wraparound, and slides it under her.

—Don't worry about making a mess. I'm gonna carry this paper to my grave.

She moves a hand under the covers.

—Oh, Fonseca, you're ready.

—I am, he says, and pulls her to him.

**4:15 p.m. Ali Watson. JTTF office, Manhattan.**

He is in his office with Malachy Devlin, Eddie Taylor, Frank Harris, and Mary Prescott. The squad. He feels that he has been given a part in some Off-Broadway play, or an episode of *Law & Order*. There is no script but everybody knows the lines. The meeting is a performance, even for Ali. The big shots told him he could excuse himself from all this, take a few weeks off. He insisted on being here. They are discussing, after all, his son.

Malachy has led the briefing. The city police have found the Lexus and are combing it for traces of Malik. That will take a while. There are hairs.

Prints. They are examining several different video cameras on the block, one in the parking lot itself, another above the doors of a small repair shop across the street. NYPD is looking at the images, trying to find Malik in them and see how he was dressed. There are advisories ready for release, drawings showing his face with and without a beard. A press release should be ready by five o'clock, after it's cleared in Washington. Then it will go out to the media.

—Once that happens, Malachy says, the shit will hit the fan.

—Yeah, Ali says. Thinking: What the fuck else can I say?

—The press will go nuts, Mary Prescott says, in her cool thirty-ish way. That would make three homicides and the possibility of a terrorist act.

—Yeah, Ali says. And we're looking for a cop's son.

They sit there for a silent moment.

—I'll have to disappear, Ali says.

The others look at him. His jacket hangs behind him on the back of his chair. His tie is unknotted. His cuffs are unbuttoned and folded above his wrists.

—Suppose it's not him? Mary says.

—It's him, Ali says.

He stands. Inhales. Breathes out.

—We have to figure out the target, he says.

Ali turns his back.

—The target will mean something...personal...to him. That's what Patchin Place was. Something personal.

He faces them again. Groping for a few more lines in a script that doesn't exist.

—Leave me alone for a while. Maybe I can remember something.

They all stand. Malachy clears his throat.

—If anyone calls for you...

—Lie. Tell them I'm mourning.


### 4:35 p.m. Sam Briscoe. City room.

He hears them when he is still in the hall, passing by the cartoons and the typewriters, hears the low rumble of many voices, meshed into one growling atonal baritone chorus, punctuated by stabs of high laughter and an occasional surprised yelp. Then he smells them: the odor of burnt tobacco, like a fog from the past. He turns into the corridor leading to the city room, and there they are: faces creating a blur, like a mural splashed and daubed in a fierce rush, from a palette of pink, ivory, black, brown.

From some distant part of the city room, Sinatra is singing "Come Fly With Me." *"If you can use some exotic booze, / There's a bar in far Bombay."*

Someone spots him.

*—Sam!*

And others yell his name, and they are coming forward to embrace him, blocking his passage. Then he hears applause. Sees some of them clapping soundlessly, with glasses in one hand, bumping their wrists, and more coming forward. He removes his coat, holds it. He sees steam on the windows overlooking West Street. A dark late afternoon.

*Hey, Sam...Hey, where's the Fucking Publisher?...Drink, Sam? What the hell!*

His sense of dread vanishes. They are all here. From the Queens and Brooklyn bureaus; from the police shack; Warren up from Washington; the old photographers and the young; Heidi and Albert from the library; four old printers from the days when the *World* had a composing room; the techies who tend the computers; the whole damned crew from advertising. Across the room he sees the tall balding man who designed the *World*. There's Scott Gellis, the sports editor, and what looks like his whole goddamned team, sitting on desks in the sports department, bottles on the desks. Gellis is smoking a plump cigar. Now Sinatra is singing "You Make Me Feel So Young."

Here comes Matt Logan, pushing through the crowd, flapping a hand at the pale blue nicotine fog. Briscoe remembers: Logan never smoked. One of the few. They embrace.

—It's all yours now, Matt, Briscoe says, and chuckles.

—Yeah. Goddamn it.

—It could be fun.

—That remains to be seen. Is the F.P. coming? Briscoe laughs.

—Never. He doesn't want to land on his back on West Street.

Logan smiles.

—Thank God. One hug from him and I'd never be forgiven.

Then he motions with his head.

—This lot here, Sam? Logan says. We could put out a hell of a paper.

—We already did, Briscoe says.

One of the older photographers, Barney Weiss, is moving around with his Nikon. Some of the younger reporters are using cell phones as cameras. Others reach over to tap Briscoe on the shoulder or exchange fist bumps.

—Whatever you do, Matt, don't pick your nose. You'll end up on YouTube.

Logan laughs, and angles away, and Briscoe sees Janet, making a secretarial face that demands his attention. He nods to her. Slowly he pushes through, smiling, explaining that he has to get rid of his coat, hears an outburst of laughter, sees a Mexican pizza delivery man looking baffled, holding at least five stacked pies. No sign of the Fonseca kid. *I hope he's getting laid. He sure earned it.* Here comes Dorfman, the city hall guy, smoking a pipe left to him by Murray Kempton. He says something that is lost in the general chaos of words. *Sam, hey, Sam, let's... No deadline tonight, baby... Who's got a bottle opener?... I'm not shittin' ya. The Iverson deal is... Where's Helen? Anybody seen Helen?*

Briscoe knows Helen isn't coming. Or said she wasn't. *She'd love the aroma of this version of a city room. Christ, fourteen years since I stopped cigarettes,* he thinks, *and I want one now. A whiskey too. Cynthia helped me stop both.* There's a clear spot now and he eases toward his office, where Janet is at the door. He shrugs off his jacket while he moves. Now another voice is playing on the CD player, wherever it is. *"Well, since my baby left me, / I found a new place to dwell..."*

And here coming into the city room is Billygoat, followed by a brigade of pressmen. They are all carrying bundles of newspapers. Briscoe stops, turns back into the city room. They plop the papers on desks, cut the cords, and start handing them out. Everybody is laughing. Briscoe sees the wood, and laughs out loud too, reaching for a copy.

WORLD ENDS!

And the subhead: *Jews, Irish Suffer Most.*
A photo from some apocalyptic movie shows floods, toppling skyscrapers.
Briscoe scans smaller headlines in a stack on the left, with page numbers, shaking his head, chuckling at them all, guffawing at a few.

*Mexicans Demand New Day of Dead p. 9*
*Sharpton: Proves God Is Black p. 3*
*Taliban, al-Qaeda Thrilled p. 28*
*Health Care Plan Dead p. 11*
*Glenn Beck, GOP Blame Obama p. 2*
*Palin Applauds 'Rapture' p. 5*
*Albany Gang Dies in Vegas Debut p. 10*
*Two-State Solution in Middle East: All Die p. 14*

In the lower-right-hand corner there's a box:

*Tomorrow: INSIDE HELL by Richard Elwood, F.P.*

The complete back page shows a slack-jawed Jared Jeffries with a basketball bouncing off his chest and the headline:

UConn Women
Beat Knicks by 23

Here Briscoe guffaws. Then Billygoat has him by the elbow, pushing him toward the pressmen, and the rest of the crowd, and both face the cameras, holding up the front pages with everyone else, the photographers clicking away. Even the photographers are laughing. Barney Weiss photographs the photographers, from the front and from behind. They will all soon have prints, to hang on walls for the rest of their lives.

Janet is now beside Briscoe, grabbing his sleeve with a free hand. She has his coat and jacket under her arm.

–There's a shitload of messages, she says. But you better call Dick Amory first.

–Yeah, okay.

She grabs his arm, waving off people, guiding him to the office. They both know that Amory is Cynthia Harding's lawyer. In the office, Janet hangs the coat and jacket on the clothes tree, sits down, starts dialing. Then Janet nods to Briscoe as he slides behind his desk, making a phone sign with her hand. He picks up the phone, gestures to her to close the door.

–Hello, Dick.

–I'm sorry for your trouble, Sam. For *our* trouble. Our loss.

He's a decent guy, Amory. And a terrific lawyer. Not a Court Street ambulance chaser. That's why Cynthia chose him.

–Thanks, Dick. So what do we do?

–For a service, there's different possibilities. The Ethical Culture place on Central Park West. They can do it late next week.

–Nah. It's a nice place, but it's not Cynthia.

–What about a Catholic place? She talked about it a lot. She said she wasn't religious but she liked the art and the music. Maybe St. Patrick's—

–Too grand. Maybe *Old* St. Patrick's, down by Little Italy. She sent them money once for a library.

–Yeah, Amory says.

–They can have a bigger memorial a month from now, at the library on Forty-second Street.

–Perfect. You got the name of a guy at Old St. Patrick's?

–Hold on...Janet, go find Farrell and ask him if he has a contact at Old St. Patrick's, downtown, not the cathedral.

She gets up and moves into the crowded city room.

—I'll have it for you in a few minutes, Dick. What else?

He hears Amory exhale.

—Big trouble. For you. In her will, she names you as executor. She left you some money too. And some paintings...

—Fuck. I don't know a goddamned thing about that kind of stuff. I'm a newspaperman, Dick. Or was.

—I'll help.

—I just want to get the fuck out of town.

There's a beat of silence. Then Amory speaks.

—Look, Sam, none of this has to be done on a newspaper deadline. Go away. Take a break for a month. When you come back—

Janet returns, hands Briscoe a paper with a name on it.

—Dick, I have the name of a priest at Old St. Patrick's.

They talk for another minute and agree to meet on Monday. Briscoe hangs up. He sits there gazing into the city room, which is full of rowdy laughter, people slapping fives, shaking their heads, telling lies and war stories and doing anything to hold back tears. A few are wearing the fake page 1 on their chests, held by tape or pins. Briscoe knows what he is seeing. A wake. He notices now that some of them are wearing black armbands. Matt Logan is one of them.

He turns and stands, his reverie over. Janet waves the messages.

–There's others, she says. Including the F.P.

–If he calls, tell him I've caught a boat for Morocco or something.

–You want the others?

He takes the cluster of notes and leafs through them. Imus. The mayor's office. David Carr. Howard Kurtz. Oreskes at the AP. Liz Smith. Matt Frei at BBC America. Howard Rubenstein. NPR. The *Columbia Journalism Review*. NYU. *Morning Joe*. To talk about the future of newspapers. Or any news about services for Cynthia Harding. And there: Sandra Gordon.

Wanting to know about services. About a memorial.

*Sandra Gordon*. Remembering again that party in Jamaica when she was a child. Cynthia helping her to education and life. A pretty girl. A proud beautiful woman. He folds the note and slips it into his shirt pocket.

He gazes out and sees dozens of them eating pizza. A truly New York wake.

–I guess I have to make a farewell address, he says.

—You'd better, Janet says.

—What are they all going to do? he says.

—Far as I know, every one of them signed up to work on the website. Including me. You gotta reapply, you know. And the F.P. isn't gonna hire us all. That's the point. Right?

—I'm afraid it is.

Janet is in her forties. No husband. No kids. Maybe no fella. He never asked.

—What are you going to do, Janet? If the worst...

—If Matt doesn't need me, maybe I'll move to Florida. My sister's there. Who the hell knows? First things first. I gotta get the stuff in this office packed, and then shipped. To your house or storage or—

—My house. I can sort it out later. Some stuff goes up to the museum, the stuff in the hall...

—I know. I got your memo from three years ago somewhere. But we need to seal the office too, so nobody steals anything.

—Perish the thought.

—You better get out there. Or they'll make a citizen's arrest.

Briscoe dreads going out to make a speech, but he has to say something. He remembers a guy at the old *Journal-American,* an editor who used to stand on his desk and wave a pica ruler like a sword, urging his wards to charge the barbed wire. The paper died anyway. But while they lasted, his speeches caused great laughter in Mutchie's. He thinks: Above all, I will not stand on a desk. Or wave my last pica ruler.

—Let's go, he says.

Janet follows him into the city room, which now gets quieter. Heads turn to Briscoe. A new song is on the CD player.

*Why, oh why, do I*
*Live in the dark?*

And is abruptly clicked off. Briscoe goes to the city desk. Logan is there, wearing his black armband. Briscoe glances at the windows and sees a light snow falling through the purple darkness of West Street.

Then he faces the dense circle of people that has formed around the city desk, more than two hundred of them, many sipping drinks, chewing pizza, some with arms folded, others with hands jammed in pockets. Men, women, some in the rear standing on desks, photographers making pictures, some old reporters taking notes from the habit of a lifetime. Briscoe clears his throat and begins to speak.

—As most of you know, oratory is not my thing. So in the tabloid spirit, I'll try to be short and, uh, sweet. I want to thank every one of you for giving me the best years of my newspaper life. You also gave New York a newspaper that added to this city's knowledge and intelligence and—for want of a better word—its genius. Not one of us who worked here ever had to apologize for being part of the *New York World*. And that was not because of me. It was because of you. Journalism is a team sport. And you were the team.

They applaud. Briscoe hopes they are applauding themselves, not him.

—Now everything has changed. I don't have to tell you why. Don't have to explain that the delivery system is changing by the hour. That the recession has killed too much advertising revenue. You know all that. But I hope every one of you gives everything to the *World* online—everything that you gave to the newspaper. Make it real journalism, reported, edited, where the facts are beyond dispute.

He pauses and turns to Logan.

—In Matt Logan, you have one of the greatest editors I ever worked with, and he'll make sure that happens.

They applaud some more.

—Wherever the hell I am, I'll be reading you. And remember to kick ass, and take names. Thank you—every single one of you.

Logan nods to the left, where Fonseca is paused

before the CD player. Briscoe thinks: Good, the kid made it. Then, from out of the past, from the vanished beery walls of the Lion's Head, from other saloons now gone, from many snowy nights when nobody went home, come the Clancy Brothers. A ballad. A lament.

*Of all the money that e'er I had*
*I spent it in good company*
*And all the harm I've ever done*
*Alas 'twas done to none but me . . .*

Logan is singing hard, and so is Briscoe, and so are others who were formed by those nights on Sheridan Square when all of the Clancys were still alive. Fonseca is not singing. Too young to know the words. Briscoe sees Sheila McKibbon from the dayside copy desk off near the windows, singing, her face dark with melancholy. Another graduate of the Lion's Head. And there, taller than some of the men, wearing a down coat that is wet on the shoulders, newly arrived, is Helen Loomis. She is smoking. And singing.

*And all I've done for want of wit*
*To memory now I can't recall*
*So fill to me the parting glass*
*Good night and joy be with you all . . .*

Briscoe starts moving through the crowd, hugging every one of them, whispering his thanks. The singing goes on. He makes his way to Helen. Her eyes are mildly glassy, from cold, or sadness, or whiskey. It doesn't matter to Briscoe. Or to her.

–Thank you for coming, Helen, he whispers.

–Thanks for everything, Sam.

–You okay?

–No.

–Neither am I.

–Yeah. I can see.

–We'll have lunch next week.

–That would be great, Sam.

–Sloppy Louie's, okay?

–We'll have to settle for dim sum, Sam.

Briscoe hugs her again, and feels her loneliness pushing into his own lonesome heart. He kisses her cheek, and then starts walking to his office to retrieve his jacket and coat. Still singing. The wake still building.

*But since it falls unto my lot*
*That I should go and you should not*
*I'll gently rise and softly call*
*Good night and joy be with you all...*

Logan is outside the office as Briscoe leaves. Briscoe hugs him.

—Sam, see ya, man, he says. May the wind be always at your back.

### 5:20 p.m. Bobby Fonseca. City room.

Leaning on the edge of a desk in the city room, music playing, everyone milling around, he wants to cry, but knows he won't. Reporters don't cry. Someone told him that the song at the end, "The Parting Glass," was out of the Lion's Head and he wishes he had known such a place. He wasn't even born when they had all those nights of song and argument. Neither was Victoria Collins. She wanted so much to come here today, but the message said no outsiders, and even with her credit line, she was an outsider. He'll see her tonight. Maybe take her to his place in Brooklyn. Where will Mr. Briscoe go? He wonders what kind of sickness leads someone to slash a woman's flesh. Any woman's flesh. Cynthia Harding's flesh. Mary Lou Watson's flesh. Or Victoria's flesh. So that all the passion and desire and laughter flow to the floor.

—Don't be glum, Bobby.

Matt Logan. A consoling hand on Fonseca's shoulder.

—I need you, kid. I need you to kick ass. I need you to help make this a great, professional website.

321

—Thanks, Matt.

—Call the desk Sunday at nine. I'll be here. I want you to do a follow on the Patchin Place murders. Unless something else is breaking.

—Will do. And Matt? I'll try hard to kick some ass.

A fist bump on the shoulder, and Matt Logan moves to a knot of the others. Fonseca thinking: We're not orphans yet. So why do I want to cry?

And here comes Barney Weiss, Nikon hanging from a strap.

—Hey, kid, we're going drinking and you're invited.

—Where?

—We're tryin' to figure that out. There's some kind of benefit someplace near the High Line... Remember what Bernie Bard once said: If it ain't catered, it ain't journalism.

Fonseca chuckles. He doesn't know who Bernie Bard was, but he loves the tabloid attitude. He moves across the city room, in search of a Coke.

**5:50 p.m. Lew Forrest. Chelsea Hotel, Manhattan.**

He signed the papers without being able to see them clearly. Jerry from the front desk guided his hand to the place where he must sign. Jerry, my personal banker. The lawyer said, Yes, that's it, Lew, and Forrest scribbled the name. He did this on three more copies. Then Jerry stamped each copy with his notary machine, signed his own name, and it was done.

He had called the lawyer around one o'clock, told him he wanted to change his will, fast, because who knew at his age? He dictated the changes, and the lawyer came to the Chelsea around five. He took the elevator with Jerry. They sat at the big table. The lawyer filled in the names and addresses of the people, and the phone numbers. Lew Forrest signed. They left. As simple as that.

And now, sitting in the room, longing for the aroma of oil and turpentine in a time of acrylics, he is filled with a sense of relief. Everything is now settled. There are clear instructions to the gallery that handles his work. The lawyer knows his role, which is to defend Forrest's intentions. Even Lucy from *ARTnews* and Jerry from the front desk will have their shares. Of what's in the bank. Of what might come into the bank from future sales. Forrest knows there's always a bump in sales when an artist dies. He has nobody else on the planet to take care of. And most important, Consuelo Mendoza will be safe for the rest of her life.

The growing silence tells him that snow is

falling. He hears an iron shutter banging gently somewhere, so there must be wind. For me, he thinks, snow is the most treacherous condition, even with Camus taking me for my walk. Maybe Lucy can take him, and I can wait in the lobby. I wish I could see the snow.

Then in his mind he sees Consuelo's kids heading for Sunset Park, lugging a sled. And he knows she will call. She has to explain the money to her husband. He might think there was something shameful that brought this windfall. He thinks: I will have to come up with a consoling lie. That I failed to pay her when I left Mexico. Something like that. Like a book that's overdue at the library for fifteen years. And tell Consuelo to bring her husband and the kids to visit me. Once the husband sees me, his jealousy will die. I'm a fucking wreck. Maybe the kids could take home some of the books. Maybe, if I die first, and they have a yard, they can take Camus home too. Like all Labs, he loves kids.

Then thinks: If she comes here with her husband, I'll have to take the painting of Consuelo off the wall. Hide Consuelo when she was young and in my bed, with her golden skin, her hard dark nipples, her silky pubic hair, the hair beneath her arms, the hair on the back of her neck, the delicate calligraphy of hair. Her heat seeping into me. Warming me. Heating my heart and my blood.

Hide all that, he thinks. Save it here in my head, in the cave of memory, like a secret pulse. To die when I die.

### 6:15 p.m. Consuelo Mendoza. Sunset Park.

The lock clicks. Raymundo is home. The girl starts shouting, *Papi, Papi, Papi,* and the two boys leave the television set to greet him. Raymundo is smiling, and hugs each kid, then turns to Consuelo, and hugs her too.

–Ah, *mi amor, cómo estamos?* he says.

She whispers in his ear: Good news, *mi amor.*

She pulls away, while the kids race around, and Raymundo removes his coat and looks at her. He makes a move with his head, raising it an inch to say, What's wrong?

She takes his coat and says, *Ven.*

They go to the bedroom together. She hangs the coat, then opens the top drawer of the bureau, her drawer, and removes the envelope.

–There's a story here, she says, holding the envelope.

He looks puzzled. And she tells the story of the

old *gringo* she worked for in Cuernavaca, a sweet man, old then, older now, blind, a painter. Señor Lewis. She does not say what they did in bed. She never will. But she tells Raymundo that she reached out to the *gringo viejo* today. For help, finding a new job. The first time she had seen him in fifteen years. Then she hands him the envelope.

–Open it, she says in Spanish. He takes it, a wary look on his face. Then opens it.

–*Hijole,* he says, holding the thick wad of hundred-dollar bills in thumb and forefinger. Then he falls back on the bed. He looks up at her.

–This is true? he says in a soft doubting voice. Not a lie?

–You know me better than anyone in the world, Raymundo.

–I just, I mean, who *does* such a thing?

–A good man. Old now. With no children. We can go over to see him tomorrow. Bring the kids. You can meet him. We can bring him flowers. Help him clean up. Make him eat.

She sits beside Raymundo on the bed. There are tears in his eyes.

–How much money is it? he whispers.

–Five thousand dollars.

He grabs a pillow and sobs into its soft thickness.

Then Marcela pushes into the bedroom.

–Papi, let's go to the snow!

He pulls the pillow away.

–*Sí, mi querida, pero primero la comida,* he says. Yes! But food first!

He starts to laugh then, and sits up, and hands the envelope back to Consuelo, and hugs the little girl, and says in English, Food first! And then the snow.

Consuelo thinks, Yes, the snow. All of them. And thinks: Then we can return exhausted to sleep in our own beds.


**6:20 p.m. Bobby Fonseca. The A train.**


He holds the pole in his gloved right hand, the other *World* guys close around him. They are packed together in the rush-hour train, maybe eight of them, including Helen Loomis. Murmuring jokes. Chuckling. Fonseca is silent. Thinking: I get a double wood and the paper folds. Fuck. He flashes on the faces of the night: Harding, Watson, the woman whose son had been killed. Remembers a professor at NYU, an old reporter, telling him: Ya gotta learn to forget. Ya gotta leave all the pain in the city room. Report it, write it, and go home.

Not that easy. Maybe if I had Victoria Collins with me every night. Maybe then it would be a home, instead of a place to sleep. Now it's a fixed-up Brooklyn tenement full of college kids, with a view of a red-brick factory turned into condos. Growing up in New Jersey, Fonseca imagined Brooklyn before he saw it. From movies. From photographs. Saw its light. Its beautiful brownstones. He found his pad in his last year at NYU, paid $350 a month for a chopped-off slice of a railroad flat. Too much, for a place the size of a small attic in Montclair. Still, it's bigger than Victoria's place. The bathroom has a sink, for fuck's sake.

His father and mother came once to visit and his father said, "For this, I spent all that money?" And never came again. But it was Brooklyn, in a neighborhood renamed the South Slope by the real estate guys, with the subway three blocks away and places to eat on all the corners. It just never became a home, even after I got hired at the *World*. Where I wanted to work fifteen hours a day. For the rest of my fucking life.

He hears Barney Weiss mention CelineWire and that nasty shit Wheeler who writes it. That asshole probably even thinks he brought us down. Not the recession and the loss of ads. Not the delivery system. Him. Well, at least I had it for a while. He remembers what Mr. Briscoe told him when he handed Fonseca his first working press card. When I got mine, Briscoe said, I wore it to bed for a month, like it was a dog tag. Fonseca did the same thing. And that first week his father called, after seeing Fonseca's byline in the paper, and said, "Damn, Bobby, I am so goddamned proud of you." He could hear a tremor in his father's voice, and then heard him say, "Maybe now you can get a decent place to live." And Bobby Fonseca laughed.

The train slows. The *World* crowd faces the doors as the 14th Street station appears. Fonseca sees the sign: IF YOU SEE SOMETHING, SAY SOMETHING. Nah, if I see something, I write something. I'm a reporter, man.

# NIGHT

## 6:45 p.m. Sam Briscoe. Patchin Place.

A S THE SNOW FALLS SOFTLY, he stands with his back to the Jefferson Market Branch of the public library. There are still lights burning in the tall former courthouse, rising still out of the nineteenth century. How Cynthia loved having a house a block from a library! On his head is a woven wool cap he found in the office, made years ago by Kevin & Howlin in Dublin. He was in Dublin with Cynthia on a day of sun, showing her the sights. Where Yeats lived on Merrion Square and Shaw not far away and the monument in St. Patrick's to Jonathan Swift. The bookstores on Dawson Street. The National Library. She said: Sam, I could *live* here. And he laughed. So could he. *"Of all the money that e'er I had…"*

He is facing Patchin Place, where two bundled uniformed cops remain on guard and the gates are draped with yellow crime-scene tape. A patrol car is parked on the Sixth Avenue side of the entrance, its windows opaque with steam.

He is not much of a believer but he tries to pray. No words come. Except "sorry." Cynthia was not much of a believer either, but told him once that she tried to read a poem each night as if it were a prayer. Maybe, Briscoe thinks, memory is a prayer. And he remembers fragments of snowy nights when he walked with her from the Lion's Head, one long block away, and came here with her and she made tea and they snuggled before a movie on the couch in the den. The snow is now general all over New York. Softly falling into the dark mutinous Atlantic waves. He thinks: No, not Atlantic. It has to be Shannon, two syllables. Joyce was right.

He has entered from the Sixth Avenue end of West 10th Street. He notices that a woman is now standing in the snow-flecked shadows at the Greenwich Avenue end. A heavy fur hat on her head. Long down coat. Heavy boots. Very still. Alone. She is staring into Patchin Place too, where the snow is now gathering on Cynthia Harding's stoop, tamped down in the center by the feet of cops.

Briscoe moves slightly to the left, stamping his feet as the uniformed cops did. The lights are still burning on every floor. He can see shadowy figures moving in the windows. Technicians. Crime-scene guys. Examining every hair. Down the block the light from street lamps seems spectral. Trucks moan up Greenwich. Buses on Sixth Avenue. The woman is still there. He can't see her face.

Then a door of the police car opens. A detective steps out. In civilian clothes. With a hat over his black face. He stares at Briscoe. And walks over. The snow pelting him. Briscoe knows him.

—You waitin' on something, man?

—I'm not, Lieutenant Watson.

Ali Watson brushes snow off his eyelashes and squints. Then smiles thinly in recognition.

—Hello, Sam.

—Ali. I'm so sorry about what happened. Mary Lou was a wonderful human being.

Ali sighs.

—The same with Cynthia. I know, uh, that you and her . . .

—Yeah. A lot of years.

—What are you doing here, Sam?

—Trying to pray.

A pause.

—That's not easy, is it?

–Not anymore.

They are both silent for a long moment. The snow is blowing east.

–I heard about you and the newspaper, Sam. It was on the radio.

–What the hell. I had a long run.

–So did me and Mary Lou.

They stand in silence.

–You got a suspect?

–Yeah. But I can't talk about it. Not yet.

–Of course.

Briscoe removes a glove, takes a card from his wallet, writes his home number on the back and hands it to Ali.

–When this is over, Ali, you want to talk, we'll have dinner somewhere.

–That's a deal.

Ali walks slowly back to the police car. He did not produce a card and Briscoe knows why. Briscoe turns. The woman who was waiting down the block is gone.

He moves to Greenwich, passes the small garden, and turns left onto Sixth Avenue. She's on the corner, trying to flag a taxi. And then he sees her face. He hurries to her side.

–Sandra Gordon...

She looks startled. Then relaxes.

—Oh, Sam. I thought that was you, but—

—Were you praying too?

—Sort of... Really just telling her how, as long as I'm alive, she's alive.

She has the same vocal rhythm she had when she came to New York, at once clipped and melodic. The sound of the islands. He remembers her going with Cynthia to buy clothes for interviews at colleges, and later for job interviews. He remembers her at Cynthia's old place uptown, and then in Patchin Place. For lunches. For parties. Never for fund-raisers, even after Sandra started making good money. Polite, but never servile. Able to speak when asked questions, but not a performer. A listener.

—Want some dinner? he says.

—Of course, she says.

They cross Sixth Avenue and walk east on 8th Street. She hooks a gloved hand to his arm. The snow falls heavier. Driven by a wind off the North River. Coming from Jersey. The Great Lakes. Canada. They pass shops for rent, and a pair of middle-aged women, their heads lowered as the snow blows in their faces, and three drunk college boys, one of whom looks at Sandra, shouts a sentence as he passes that ends with "Obama."

—It's comforting, Briscoe says, to know that young guys are still assholes.

Sandra Gordon laughs.

–They get worse, Sandra says, as they get older.

They cross Fifth Avenue. To the right through the snow, the lights make the Washington Square Arch lovelier than ever. A man stands at the corner, staring into the whitening park, holding skis. They move on to the east, passing more empty shops, and others that are closing early because of the storm. A scrawny man in a camouflage jacket and worn jeans stands huddled in a doorway, holding a cardboard cup. He says nothing. His eyes are dead. Briscoe has no change. They move on. Briscoe thinks: How many times have I walked this street? Five thousand? Ten? More? How many times with Cynthia Harding?

Here at last is University Place. Across the street was where the Cookery stood for so long, with Barney Josephson running it.

–Didn't Alberta Hunter sing there? Sandra says. I was too young to ever see her. But I heard she was great, here in the Cookery.

–You're right. It was full of life, that place.

–She's gone too.

–She is.

Sandra squeezes his arm a bit harder. He doesn't mention the Cedars, doesn't try to explain that it stood right here, where this ugly fucking white-brick building is now, that Pollock used to come here, shit-faced, and Franz Kline, with his grace and good manners, and how Briscoe was infatuated one winter with Helen Frankenthaler, and her big swashbuckling paintings, and her beautiful face, and how Frankenthaler was in love with a critic. A critic, for Chrissakes!

At the corner of 9th Street they cross University Place. Sandra releases her grip. Briscoe takes her elbow and opens the door to the Knickerbocker. They go in. To the right, in the bar, five or six people are watching New York One and images of the storm. He turns away. He doesn't want to see the rest of the news, and he's sure Sandra doesn't either. The large dining room is half empty. Sandra unzips her coat and smiles as the maitre d' comes to greet them. Sandra has a beautiful smile.

They are led to a booth for four, lots of room for coats and hats and a handbag, and out of the sight line to the TV. Sandra is wearing a black sweater, black slacks, no jewelry, no lipstick. He doesn't stare at her. But when she speaks, he can see her full lips, her cheekbones, the many variations of ebony. He flashes on the ebony pencils that copy editors used for marking stories written on paper by typewriters.

—For the first time in my life, Sandra says, I fainted this morning.

She tells him about seeing the front page of the *World* in the lobby of the Lipstick Building, and coming to with men leaning over her.

—It was like someone had punched me in the heart, she says.

—Yes. I know.

—Oh, Sam, I'm sorry. I didn't mean to say this is about me. Above all, it's about Cynthia. That means it's about you too. In a different way, a larger sense, it's about a lot of people who never met her.

—That's the truth, Sandra. But it *is* about you too.

—We have to make sure that her...work goes on.

—It will.

A waiter comes and takes a drink order. White wine for Sandra. Diet Pepsi for Sam.

—How long since you stopped drinking? she says, smiling.

—I don't know. Years. Maybe thirteen?

—So you were drinking still, that time in Jamaica, when I got my first job as a waitress?

Sam smiles.

—I was. You did a hell of a job.

She smiles again.

–Thanks. That's when I first met Cynthia too. That same party. And she got me to talk about books. Above all, about the pictures in *Chitty Chitty Bang Bang*. I couldn't even read yet.

–Books were her favorite subject.

The past tense again. Drinks arrive. She stares into her wine.

–Oh, Sam, what are we going to do?

The question hangs there. The waiter returns and takes their food orders. Shrimp for Sam, arugula salad for Sandra. Lentil soup for both. Then he remembers the slip of paper with her number, plucks it from his shirt pocket, shows it to her.

–I was going to call you when I got home.

–To tell me what?

He recites the clerical details. About the possible Mass at Old St. Patrick's, and the burial up in Woodlawn in the Bronx, as close as possible to Herman Melville. He tells her that the library on 42nd Street would surely have a memorial service too. There'll be a scholarship at NYU in Cynthia's name, he says, for students of library science. This while they sip on soup.

–What about the house on Patchin Place?

He pauses.

–She told me once that she wanted it to be used by poets, from all over the world. Maybe four or five at a time. Poets who need time off, just to brood. Now—

He shrugs. Now the house is one of the most notorious murder scenes in the city. He doesn't need to tell her that. Or that some poets might actually be inspired by the ghosts.

–And you? he says, changing the subject. How are things, otherwise?

She tells him about Myles Compton, how he left, how the FBI came to visit, how she had to get a lawyer, and how she has not heard from the man, not yet. She doesn't know if he's in America or Europe or Peru, doesn't know if he's dead or alive. He feels an unstated sadness in her voice, but says nothing.

–And you? she says.

He tells her about the death of the *World,* and the wake in the city room, and the website that starts Monday. She squeezes his forearm.

–Oh, Sam, what a day for you.

–You too.

From the bar he hears a burst of whiskey laughter, rising above some music. Lady Day. *"Moonlight and love songs / Never out of date..."* He thinks: I need to call my daughter again. I need to sleep.

**6:50 p.m. Beverly Starr. Belleville restaurant, Park Slope, Brooklyn.**

Almost time, she thinks. Check paid. Coffee still hot. She is at a corner table on the side of the long bistro, sitting alone on the banquette, with a view of the restaurant from one wood-paneled end to the windows on Fifth Avenue. Snow is falling. Chester Gould snow. Big fat flakes falling on Shoulders or Flattop or Mumbles. She is drawing in a small notebook, making notes. And enjoying the comforts of the familiar. The bar stacked with bottles and a few high stools. Mirrors on both sides of the long room, for tracking waiters or prospects.

She often comes here in summer, when the doors are open to the air, walking up the hill from her house, then three blocks to the left. It's always packed with young mothers who park their Hummer-sized strollers outside and hold kids on their laps. On this night of snow, only a half dozen other tables are occupied, three of them by couples. The snow falls steadily on the parked cars.

To the right of her table, four young women from the Like Brigade are drinking margaritas. The dreaded four-letter word is fired in tremulous salvos. She wishes she could call on the

343

exterminating angel of her graphic novel. She blinks. Blinks again.

She dials the car service on her cell.

—Hey, it's Beverly. How about ten minutes? In front of the Belleville.

—Sure t'ing, Bev.

She slides out from behind her table, walks to the coat rack, grabs her coat and hat, and heads for the door. Then goes out into 5th Street. And stands there. The snow is clean. The snow is odorless. The snow doesn't lie.

Under a lamp, she pauses and looks up at the snowflakes as they fall. She focuses on one, about fifteen feet above her. Separating from the others. Blinks. The flake has just been born. It sways from side to side, as if hearing soothing music. She blinks again. Then the flake hurries down to the cement of the city. She counts, and at the number two, the snowflake is gone forever.

A car horn beeps on the corner. She turns.

**6:55 p.m. Josh Thompson. Fourteenth Street, Manhattan.**

That Old Guy with the white beard had warned him about the snow. The Old Guy in his own wheelchair. He was outside the church when the Mexicans carried Josh down the steps. Josh looked up at the sky, which resembled water in a glass when you pour some ink in it. The Old Guy pulled up beside him. He told Josh it was coming. The snow. He said, Don't even *think* about being out in the snow, soldier.

Then the Old Guy started giving Josh a short course in living in a wheelchair in New York. Those grades at the corner? the Old Guy said. We call them "cuts." They are suppose to be one-eighth of an inch at the bottom. Surprise, surprise! Some of them are a full inch! Try to get up one! You need to use your weight! Lean forward, then move the fucking wheels like your life depends on them, which it does. Going down the cuts, lean back and lie low, go slow, don't let your weight topple you face-first into the fucking street. For sure, some asshole driving a sanitation truck will back up and run over your head and turn the chair into an ashtray!

—When you stop somewhere to admire the view or the ass of some broad, lock the chair. So it don't roll in any direction! Don't go near Sixteenth Street. It's the worst street in New York. And stay off Madison Avenue in the Sixties, where all the rich people live. They don't want cripples in the neighborhood, so they don't have cuts. Or they're at an angle. And late in the day and especially at night, don't let any young assholes offer to carry you anywheres. Or push you. They think it's funny to race you along a block or two, then let you roll...I'd like to shoot the fuckers!

—In the snow you can't even see the potholes so you're goin' along crossing the street and everything looks even and whoof! You go into a fucking hole full of snow and fall on the side and hit your head maybe, and break a fucking arm maybe, and the buses and trucks and cars, especially them Jersey drivers, are all honking and yelling, and you figure: Fuck it, I may as well die. And here in Fourteenth Street, especially with snow, don't go over past Ninth Avenue. There's cobblestones there and they get like glass from the snow and you slide all over the fucking place and there's Pakistani limo drivers don't know where they are, tryin' to fine some restaurant in the Meatpacking District, they call it now. And shplat! They kill you too. All right now, soldier, the Old Guy says, his beard as white as the snow. Enjoy New York.

And he was gone, moving in the other direction. And here is Josh Thompson alone, with fewer people on the sidewalks, fewer cars or buses or trucks. He is aimed at the river, facing the street of cobblestones leading to the old mosque, leading to Aladdin's Lamp.

He begins pushing the wheels, slowly. Heading west. To the minarets. He looks back for the old Mexican woman who was so nice to him. She's nowhere in sight.

### 7:10 p.m. Malik Shahid. Muhlenberg Branch of New York Public Library, West 23rd Street, Manhattan.

Malik is alone at a small table near the windows, the snow falling on the street behind him. Again, he is trying hard to look normal. A solitary man among seven or eight other solitaries. Wearing his coat as if permanently cold. His cheap black beret stuffed in a pocket. Far from the radiator on the far end of the room. He is making marks on a ruled yellow pad with a new ballpoint pen. Both letters have been written and he wants to read the long one again. The envelope is addressed to Michael Daly at the *Daily News.* The columnist. They'll put it on the front page, with big fat head-lines. The envelope already carries a stamp. It is not yet sealed.

Malik has a large book open in front of him, and is trying to look as if he is studying it and making notes. The book is *The Thousand and One Nights*. The heathen book that tells the story of Ala'ad-din, meaning "nobility of the faith." What faith? Not Islam. He looks intensely at a page, holds a finger to a sentence, then writes on the yellow pad. Like a scholar doing research. Pressing angrily with his ballpoint pen. If the heavy white bitch behind the desk even bothers to look at him, she will see a young black man, doing work toward a degree, maybe. The words written on his yellow pad say something different from the words he fingers in the book. He does not see the words in the book.

*Aladdin's Lamp.*
*Aladdin's Lamp.*
*Aladdin's Lamp.*
*Aladdin's Lamp.*

In his head, the words are like a chant. From a madrassa. Or like Sirhan Sirhan in his journal, the words used as the name of a book Malik once read.

*RFK must die.*
*RFK must die.*

Malik glances at the clock. Thinks: Almost time to leave. He removes the longer letter and reads:

*To Everybody:*

*If you read this, I am in Paradise. I have obeyed the commands of Allah to do my best to cleanse the world of sin and corruption. I have chosen to obey the Quran. In the filthy corrupt West, all sin is per-mitted. I have chosen to follow the command of Allah. To erase. To purge. To cleanse.*

*I have purged my own mother, as commanded. I have purged her slave owner. I have purged the sinful imam who defied his faith by collaborating with enemies. I wish I could have purged my so-called father, who is a policeman for the oppres-sors, and dared to use the name Ali. That will be the duty of some future servant of Allah, some other sol-dier in jihad. In another few hours I will purge many other sinners who defile what was once a holy mosque.*

*In Paradise, I shall live forever in the company of those I love and those who loved me. I shall live with the blessed ones. I shall live with Allah's heroes and servants. I hope my example will inspire others.*

*Allahu akbar!*

His signature is boldly written at the bottom. With the date.

He folds the letter, slips it into the stamped envelope, licks the gummed edges of the flap, and seals it. He does not need to read the stamped and sealed letter to his so-called father. It's very short. Addressed to him at the house in Brooklyn.

> *All I wanted was to borrow some money to take my woman to a doctor. Your wife sneered at me, told me to leave, threatened to call the police. She is dead now, along with her slave owner, and so is my woman and our child. And the fake imam.*
> *I didn't kill them.*
> *You did.*

> *M.*

Time to go. He pulls on his beret and closes the book, tears off the top page of the yellow pad, and slips the pad beneath the book. He folds the page and pushes it into his back pocket. Thinking: I don't care if they find out I did it. After I do it. But some cop stops me on the way, he might wonder what this nigger is doing with a yellow pad. Malik stretches in a feigned sleepy way, zippers his coat, pulls the beret more snugly on top of his head. Then he nods and smiles like a young Uncle Tom at the white woman behind the counter, and goes out into the snow.

Across the street, Malik sees a young woman leave the Chelsea Hotel with a large black dog on a leash. A Lab. Thinking: Just like the Lab we had at home when I was what? Ten? His name was Sarge. My so-called father trained him. Had a guy come over from the bomb squad to help. Taught Sarge to wait. Taught him to sit. Teaching me at the same time. Telling *me* to sit. Like it was a joke. Doing that to me all my life, even after Sarge died, only four years old. Blamed me for the dog's death too. I was walking him down by Myrtle Avenue, and some bitch crossed his path, some bitch in heat most likely, and Sarge lunged for her, I lost the leash, and a bus hit him and killed him. Allah surely had some reason. But I didn't know that then.

He walks to Eighth Avenue, drops the letters in a mailbox, crosses the street, heads downtown. Thinking: I better not take another bus. The bus I took to 23rd Street, that worked. A gamble I won. Thinking: They don't check the buses like they do the subways. They put a cop on every bus, they'd have to start a New York draft. Subways are different. He remembers the signs: IF YOU SEE SOMETHING, SAY SOMETHING. Yeah. Be a snitch. God bless America.

He sees a black man in the doorway of a

shuttered store. Cardboard cup loose in his right hand. His eyes closed. No hat. No gloves. One leg under his ass, the other stretched out, snow gathering on his jeans and his unlaced sneaker. Malik thinks: How you like that fucking Obama now, baby?

He walks to the next block, steps into a deep doorway of a store with metal shutters covering the windows. Stamps his feet. Flexes his hands. Stands there watching the snow fall. And remembers that meeting he went to, out past Brownsville in East New York. Two years ago? Three? Less? Set up by Aref. Four other believers showed up. No names, please, said Aref. Malik didn't know one of them. Most of them Malik's age. Two guys with Paki accents, but all of them arriving separately. Nothing in the room but a table, folding chairs, and couches. A safe house. For believers on the run.

Then an older guy arrived, maybe sixty, clean-shaven, a little fat, losing his hair. Gray suit and tie. Carrying a briefcase. He looked like a professor Malik had during his first semester at CUNY. Teaching some course in literature. He laid the briefcase on the table, nodded at Aref, who locked the door. Then he snapped open the top of the briefcase and took out a vest. Spread it wide. Said, "You all know what this is, right?"

They all knew. They'd seen the vests on all the filthy anti-Muslim TV shows and the pages of tabloid newspapers. Yeah, they knew. Holding the vest, the older guy gave a brief lecture. Explained that Semtex was a plastic explosive, made in the Czech Republic. That it had no smell, he explained, but even *one* of those red bars had tremendous explosive power. The vest held six. They could only be ignited by one of these. At which point he held up a small detonator. "You slide the wire inside one of the pouches, attach it to a wire wrapped around a Semtex bar, and then press the button. That's all." And if the wearer is shot at, one bullet hitting a Semtex bar would do the same thing. Ka-boom.

The older man paused, then explained that Semtex was used by various groups around the world. The most famous case, he said in his flat voice, happened in 1988, when a small amount was used to blow up a Pan Am plane over Lockerbie, Scotland. *This* model, he said, was developed by Hamas. Malik saw two of the other students nodding in approval. Then the man was finished. He folded the vest, laid it back in the briefcase, closed the top. He paused, and said: *"Allahu akbar."* And walked to the door.

Standing in this doorway on Eighth Avenue,

staring at the snow, Malik wonders where that man is right now. And the four others who were his audience that night. He knows where Aref is. Tomorrow, all of them, except Aref, will remember that night. No matter where they are. The South Bronx or Somalia. They will see Malik's face in the papers or on the TV, and know him. And pray for him. And praise him. For rubbing the magic lamp.

### 7:20 p.m. Beverly Starr. Washington Street, Manhattan.

They are making good time. The driver took the Brooklyn-Battery Tunnel, then West Street, where she saw snow falling through the emptiness of the place where the twin towers once stood. Then side streets. The driver explaining in the rhythms of old Brooklyn: *Figget Fourteen' Street. Cobblestones there, in this weather we'd slide right inta a furniture store...* Then here, with the High Line rising to the left. Straight out of Gotham. Bob Kane would have loved it. Jerry Robinson would've drawn it. The wind blowing snow from the west.

The car stops on the corner of 14th Street. She looks across the street and sees the whirls and curves and minarets of Aladdin's Lamp. She blinks. Records it. Then laughs out loud. Who says comic books make things up? She sees the palace as part Aubrey Beardsley, part Prince Valiant on a trip to the Orient, part Cecil B. DeMille. She hears Tony Curtis of the Bronx saying his famous line from some fifties desert flick: *Yonda lies da castle of my fodda, da Caliph.* If he ever said it.

—I'll call you when I'm ready, Harry.

—Take ya time, the driver says. I'm goin' to a diner an' eat.

Beverly Starr gets out of the car, her back to the High Line. Sees a crowd of about twenty people standing below a platform that must have once been a loading dock. Flashbulbs. Snow-muffled shouts. Stairs, a railing, the platform, then the doors. A black man in an Arabian Nights costume checking invites. Then to her right sees four homeless men in long overcoats and caps. Standing under an overhang from the days when they actually packed meat around here. Way past them in the snow, a guy in a wheelchair. Not moving. Beverly thinks: You can't make some things up.

She walks cautiously across the glistening cobblestones to the crowd, moves around the edge, starts up the stairs, hears shouts. *Hey, lady, lady, look this way. Hey, lady. Smile. Lady, say "bellybutton."* She hears the last word and smiles. Then

355

crosses the platform to the door. Hearing: *Hey, lady, what's your name?* The black bouncer smiles at her, and starts to say something, maybe an apology for his silly costume, when one of the double doors opens and a man in a gray suit steps out, smiling.

—Beverly! he says. Beverly Starr. How good of you to come.

Stan Seifert. The advertising guy who asked her to do the painting and invited her here.

He takes her elbow and leads her inside, saying: Your painting is just awesome.

She thinks: Please don't say "like."


### 7:28 p.m. Bobby Fonseca. Aladdin's Lamp.

He walks four feet into the loud, thumping room, the others behind him, and he wants to turn around. It's music for shouting, not talking. Tonight, of all nights, is for talking. For us, anyway. Or singing. He looks up the stairs, sees a dark painting on an easel, people pulling coats off suits and dresses, a tall guy smiling in welcome. That must be the benefit. Maybe they'll let us in. Gotta be quieter than this.

—I'll go up and check it out, he says to Helen

Loomis, who looks pained and lost. She nods. The others are squeezing a path to the bar, all except Barney Weiss. No cameras allowed inside. He'll take some shots outside, he said, while they find out the deal.

Fonseca goes up the stairs. A white bouncer in an Arabic costume stops him at the top. Built like a safe. Fonseca takes his press card from his jacket pocket, attached to the cheap chain around his neck.

—Press, he says.

—No press yet, the bouncer says. Fonseca thinks he looks like a guy from one of those ultimate-fighting shows.

—We'll let yiz know, the bouncer says. They got stuff to do first in there. Hit the bar, we'll find you.

Fonseca turns to go back. He leaves the press card dangling.

**8:05 p.m. Sandra Gordon. Her apartment, Manhattan.**

She undresses in the bedroom. The lights are out but the drapes are open to the falling snow and the room is filled with a luminous blackness. She sees herself in the mirror. Thinks: My kind of blackness. The same blackness that drew so many white men to me. Including Myles. The blackness of night and all its secret promises. Or so they think. Blackness can be banal too, baby. Ask a black woman.

In the living room, the telephone rings. She pulls on a robe and goes out into the large chilly space. On the fifth ring, the answering machine takes over. Then she hears her friend Janice. Fired five months ago. Self-medicating ever since. Booze and pills. They were supposed to have lunch that day but Sandra called her to cancel, got the machine, left a message. Her voice is clear.

–Hi, Sandra, it's me. Janice. I just got your message. I was suicidal in the morning, went to the shrink, and she prescribed some goddamned pill. I slept for ten hours. I'm okay, I hope. But hey, there's some kind of gig in the Meatpacking District. I'm inside now. For the homeless. Lots of dancing and some hot guys. I got an extra ticket, you want to come here. Call me on the cell and I'll bring the ticket outside to the smoking shed.

She clicks off. Sandra stares at the phone. Thinking: Thank God I didn't pick it up.

Thank God I can be here alone, while the snow falls silently and sleep comes quick.

**8:10 p.m. Ali Watson. Muhlenberg Branch of New York Public Library.**

Malachy Devlin pulls up in front of the library. The lights are turned off. Ali opens the door, turns to Malachy.

—She said she'd wait in the Chelsea, right?

—Yeah. I'll stay here, watch your back.

Ali closes the door and starts across the street in the falling snow. He pauses in the center lane while an empty bus goes by, heading east. A taxi follows the bus. Then he hurries to the entrance. He brushes the snow off his shoulders and slams his hat against his thigh. He goes in.

Against the wall on the left, an old man sits on a banquette with a large black dog at his feet. The dog looks up, but doesn't growl. At the desk, a fifty-ish black man leans on the counter, reading a newspaper. To Ali's left, beside a fireplace, is a middle-aged white woman, her large handbag on her lap. Ali goes to her, peeling off his gloves.

—Mrs. McNiff?

—Miss McNiff, she says.

—Nice to meet you. I'm Detective Watson. May I sit down?

—Of course.

She takes a manila envelope from her bag and lays it on the low table before Ali.

—I used gloves when I picked it up, Officer, so it—

—Thank you.

He puts his gloves on again and slides the yellow pad out of the envelope. The top page is blank. He holds it up to the light. And sees indents in the paper. Thinking: You dumb son of a bitch.

—Excuse me, ma'am.

He rises again. The dog's eyes follow him. The old man doesn't turn his head. Ali walks to the desk at the rear of the lobby. The night clerk looks up.

—Excuse me, brother, Ali says. Do you have a pencil?

—Sure thing.

The clerk fumbles under the counter, comes up with a yellow Eberhard Faber pencil.

—Thank you, Ali says.

He moves a few feet away and starts lightly rubbing the side of the lead point across the paper. Words emerge. Repeated four times. Like a chant. He shakes his head, turns back to the night clerk, and hands him the pencil.

—Thank you, Ali says.

He walks back to the woman.

—Thank you very much, Miss McNiff. This might be very helpful.

—Hey, you never know.

—Can I help you get home?

—Oh, I live way out in Bay Ridge.

—Wait here, if you can. We'll have a squad car take you home.

—Oh, that's okay. Not necessary. This weather, the subway's faster.

She stands as Ali writes down her name, address, and phone number, away out there in area code 718. He thanks her again and rushes out the hotel door.

## 8:15 p.m. Beverly Starr. VIP Room, Aladdin's Lamp.

She thought she'd be gone by now. But here she is in this soundproofed room up a flight of stairs from the main floor. The only evidence of the place outside the door is the physical thumping of a bass line. They had waited for a while to start the night until all the invited guests could arrive in the awful weather. Beverly went up the stairs with them, glancing at her painting of the homeless to the left of the door. Inside, the door finally closed, Stan Seifert had them all take ten seconds to remember a woman he said had done so much for this city and its less fortunate people. Cynthia

Harding. Many seemed to know her, and bowed their heads. A few even looked teary. Beverly used the shutters of her eyes to record them. And stood through a politely furious speech by an advocate for the homeless. Someone must have warned the speaker: Don't mention Goldman Sachs or AIG or Lehman Brothers. And Beverly thought: They must be hoping for contributions fueled by guilt.

Then Stan Seifert made one of those eloquent pleas for the homeless fund. He mentioned the homeless men right across the street from where they all were gathered. He reminded the group that there were far more in the outer boroughs. He applauded the gathering for their decency and for braving the fierce weather. They applauded themselves. Seifert gave special thanks to Beverly Starr for the gift of her painting. The crowd clapped with what she chose to believe was enthusiasm. Finally, he reminded them that the result of the silent auction of Beverly's painting would be announced in fifteen or twenty minutes.

A few people began moving to the door. Those who had made no bid. Each time the door opened they could hear the pounding music. Beverly wanted to leave too, but Seifert said, Please, no, we want a photograph of you with the winner.

So she waits. Looks for great faces. Blinks.

*8:20 p.m. Josh Thompson. Across the street from Aladdin's Lamp.*

He's against a wall, out of the falling snow, looking at the gathering crowd outside Aladdin's Lamp. Cold. Thinking: That Old Guy was right. Told me to stay away from here. The cobblestones making cars skid and women slip and the goddamned chair go every which way. But I'm an asshole. This ain't no mosque. It's a disco or something. Kind of place they'd never let me in.

He has watched the place for an hour, has seen limousines arriving, and chauffeurs holding umbrellas over the heads of the passengers. The long black cars then moving around the corner, to wait for a call when their owners are ready to leave. Watched people bowing. Smiling. Even laughing. He sees guys with cameras. Snow on their shoulders. Thinks: Must be press. He sees guys dressed like characters from old movies about Arabs. Not real Arabs. Not Arabs in Baghdad or Fallujah.

He looks to his left, down to what he knows now is called the High Line. Nobody up there. Snow blowing hard. Like that storm when he was eleven, coming home from school in Norman, the wind lifting him, the snow blinding him, afraid he'd never make it home. Confused and lost. No cars. No houses. Just snow. Howling. He started to cry that afternoon.

Until his father came in the pickup and found him. And he tried to hide his tears.

And Josh was ashamed. Of his fear. Of his panic.

The way he felt after they all got hit. Together in Iraq. The explosion. Two seconds of blinding panic.

And waking up in Germany.

Now thinking: Never woulda happened they didn't knock down the World Trade Center. Never woulda happened if we didn't invade Iraq. Never. I'd still have Wendy. The little girl. Maybe a son too. One I'd never let get lost in a blizzard.

Under his poncho, and his blanket, he caresses the MAC-10 with a gloved hand.

Thinking: Wait.

**8:31 p.m. Sam Briscoe. His loft.**

He keeps searching for a book that will help him sleep. Something he has already read and therefore doesn't engage that part of his brain that argues. Or won't demand that he get to the end. What always happens at the end is death.

Parts of his conversation with his daughter return. Her words were cool despite her late-night anguish. Nicole was now old enough to console him, the way he had consoled her during her own nights of terrible times.

—Put all of her pictures away, Dad, she said. Wrap them up. Put them in storage. For a year, at least. But don't leave them where you can see them.

Yes. That was smart. But not tonight. I'm too exhausted.

—Go off somewhere, she said. So your friends can't call. Where the papers — or worse, television reporters — don't run follow-ups and ask for your reactions. Go someplace where you once were young. Mexico. Rome. Or better, a place you never visited with Cynthia. Turkey. Ecuador.

She was right, of course. Get out of town. Now. Nothing beats murder at a good address. So they will follow this thing for at least three days. Maybe more.

—And hey: you can come here, Dad. Come to Paris. Stay with us in the guest bedroom. Go to museums. Eat in bistros. Buy books along the river. The weather is cold, but not dismal. And there are no tourists.

Paris.

Briscoe didn't care much for Nicole's husband. But he loved his smart, feisty daughter, Nicole.

And loved too their wonderful apartment on the Avenue Émile Acollas, with its high trees and wide sidewalks. At the foot of the Champ de Mars. The fifth floor front. The tiny elevator. The entrance hall, with the youthful painting by Lew Forrest of the Seine at dawn. A wedding gift from Cynthia Harding. The three rooms along the balcony, like an elegant railroad flat. Public rooms, they called them. Living room, petit salon, dining room. Each with a door opening to the balcony and a view that included the Eiffel Tower. Like a cornball romantic movie. Or cornball majesty. Didn't every example of the romantic include death?

He could call the airline now. He could leave tomorrow. Leave the clerical duties to others. Let someone else execute the wishes of the dead. Or put the whole thing off for a month. Paris. Call Mary Blume and Alan Riding and the remaining veterans of the Brigade Rue de Berri of the *Paris Herald.* Sit together in the Deux Magots. Make remarks. Laugh. Paris. Yes. Then he remembers Nicole's other words of advice. Go to a place where Cynthia Harding had not shared the bed. Caracas. Istanbul. Maybe—

The phone rings. He hopes it's not Sandra Gordon. But knows instantly that it's not. She would never call him at home, after dark. He picks up the phone. Static and word gaps.

—That you, Helen?

—Yeah.

—What's up?

—I'm in a joint with, uh, some of the gang from the paper and I hate it, and uh, shit, I want to go home.

—So go home, Helen.

—I can't...I mean, I tried. No cabs in this goddamned snow. Nothing over here...I'm way over near the High Line, Sam. Uh. On Fourteen' Shtreet. If I try to walk home...I die in a snowdrift, Sam. Christ, I'm a year older than *you* are, Sam.

Her voice is blurred with drink, exhaustion, age. He can hear mocking laughter behind her. Drunks. The early shift. He can see the snow falling.

—Where are you?

—Fourteen' Shtreet. Over near the High—

—No. You told me that. The name of the *joint*.

—The, uh, Ali Baba, something like that...No, no...the Aladdin Lamp. A pretty scary dump.

—They have a bouncer? he says.

—Uh, yeah, I guess.

—You know my rule, Helen. Never go in a joint that needs a bouncer.

He remembers doing a column about the mosque that once stood there. Thirty-odd years ago. When Muslims were a curiosity in New York.

—Can you, uh, come pick me up, Sam? Drop me home, uh, keep going to your house.

Briscoe pauses. He thinks: What the hell, the last act in an endless day. A kind of penance. And this is special: across all the years, Helen Loomis never asked me for anything.

—Sure, Helen. What's your cell number?

—I don't have a cell, Sam. I left it somewhere. The paper, I think... This nice girl... Janice. She dialed you for me on her own cell.

—Let me talk to her.

A younger voice gets on.

—Hello? This is Janice.

Briscoe talks quickly.

—Okay, listen, Janice. I'm in SoHo and I'll try to get a cab. Could you take Helen to the corner of Fourteenth Street and the High Line? Washington Street, I think it is... You know, where those wooden overhangs stick out? Give me fifteen, twenty minutes. I'll come by cab and hold the cab until she's in it.

—Uh, I—

—Please, Janice. She's one of the best journalists this town ever had, and her paper folded today.

Janice says, with annoyed reluctance in her voice: Okay.

He scribbles her cell number and starts

dressing. Thinking: Au revoir, Paris. Farewell, Istanbul. I'm heading into a blizzard, to a place with a bouncer.

### 8:40 p.m. Freddie Wheeler. Aladdin's Lamp.

On the dance floor, Wheeler thinks, *He made me*...That kid reporter...That Fonseca. Across the room, past the dancers, past this blond jerk dancing with me like a Gulfport shitkicker... Fonseca...His press card hanging from his neck. The others too. That tall broad from the *World*. Helen Loomis. Fonseca says something to the guy next to him, turns behind him and talks to another guy...Looking this way...A fucking posse.,.Is there a back door to this place? I don't think so... If there is, it's locked...Keep the crashers out or the check beaters in...Hey, Fonseca, he thinks. I don't want any trouble, man. I was just doing my job, man...Fuck with me, you end up in the can...Never get a job at the *Times* that way.

He turns his back on the dancing blond guy and goes left, under the stairs. Harder to see... Into a knot of necktie assholes...Nobody here I know or care about...Nobody...Just me.

### 8:45 p.m. Malik Shahid. Fourteenth Street.

He stands a bit apart from the homeless guys, hands jammed in the pockets of his coat, beret pulled low on his brow. The homeless guys are joking and laughing, all growls. Malik can't hear their words. Just the hoarse laughter. Glimpses the sudden red glow of cigarettes. Turns his head. Malik is watching the door across the street. Up on the platform. Over the heads of the gawkers and the photographers. Past the ropes. Three weeks earlier, when he first saw this obscenity of a building on a morning bright with sun, Glorious was still alive. The infidel bitch was still slaving for her white mistress.

That day he wandered through Chinatown to Cooper Union to Washington Square, avoiding Patchin Place, wandered alone, still bearded, everything a jumble, looking for money, looking for a dropped wallet, an old fool counting his cash at an ATM, a woman with an open purse, any kind of money for Glorious, money for the coming of the baby, money for food. Heading west on 14th Street. Walking, planning, then seeing a Muslim on a prayer mat at five o'clock. Removing his own shoes. Kneeling beside him. On the bare concrete of the sidewalk. Praying. Speaking the words of the Quran. The man gave him ten dollars.

Then walking again.

Toward the river. A cheap market down there someplace. Buy more food for the money.

Until he saw this obscene place.

The next day in a library, he Googled "Aladdin's Lamp." Read that it was once a mosque. One of the first in New York! Now a corrupt temple of sins of the flesh! Faggots and whores. He stood for an hour before it, walked to the side, around the back, looking for access, trying to shape a plan. The next day, the plan forming, Allah's plan, he went up the stairs to the High Line and saw the place from other angles, saw *into* it when some skinny Mexican was washing the upper windows. Malik tried looking like just another tourist. From Abu Dhabi, maybe. Or Nigeria. Thinking at the time: If I ever need a target, this is it. In other parts of the city, there were cops everywhere, and concrete barriers, and surveillance cameras, and men on high floors with field glasses. Men like his so-called father. Men who had found Islam, and then renounced the Prophet, renounced Allah. Fought jihad. Men who must die.

He looks carefully now through the falling snow at Aladdin's Lamp. Imagine if a mosque in Kandahar had been transformed into a palace for whores! What would the Taliban do? Make it vanish, that's what. The corrupted building is set back a good twenty feet from the curb, with a wide space that must have provided for eight or ten cars carrying faithful Muslims, and now serves by day as parking space for beer and drink trucks making deliveries. It's filled on this night of destiny with photographers and drifters and those who have substituted celebrities for God. They have money. They have homes. They even have umbrellas. I have nothing. Not anymore. No woman, no son, no father, no mother, no friends. I have only my own body. To give you, Allah.

He thinks: I must get through them, and up the three stairs to the platform with the velvet rope held on poles with minarets at the top. Past the bouncer in his costume. Get through the door with my holy container, dash inside, fast. Surprise is everything. He knows from his daytime observations that there is a stairway inside, leading to an upper floor, secret rooms. I am God's martyr. He thinks: It should be simple. Inshallah. The vest is ready. The detonator is hooked up and ready. I'm ready. He waits for the moment that says *now*.

### 8:47 p.m. Josh Thompson. Fourteenth Street.

He flexes and unflexes his hands, trying to give them warmth. He feels something ebbing away in him, like a tide going out on a seashore. He gathers himself. Soon all the shithead rich guys will come out. Then...

Across the street, off on the right, a short dark woman eases out of a side door next to some kind of clothing store. Head down. Hat. Walking fast on short legs. And he knows who she is. The Mexican woman who got the guys to carry him into that church. Goo-add-a-luppy. Where it was warm. Her God was a warm God. Not like some of the others. The goddamned Christians back home that want everybody to suffer, except themselves.

For a moment, he thinks about going after her. To that church.

But tells himself: Stay here. This is where it's at. Where the payback comes.

Over on the left of the front door, there's an open shed, with people smoking and bullshitting while the snow falls. Christ: There's even an old lady there, tall and skinny and smoking. Beside her, talking on a cell phone, he sees one young woman who looks like Wendy before she got fat.

Could she be his lost wife? Nah. Never. Maybe I should track Wendy down. He wonders where she is and whether little Flora is with her and whether it's snowing there too. He loved her once. Now he has trouble remembering her face. That fat broad smoking over there? Maybe she's Wendy.

Nah, he thinks. She couldn't find her way to New York with a tour guide. She's somewhere in the sun. Thinking about the guy she's meeting later. The guy whose joint she'll cop before the night's over.

He removes a glove and caresses the MAC-10. Cold. Very cold.

Go, he whispers. To the warmth.

Go.

He doesn't move.

**8:48 p.m. Helen Loomis. Outside Aladdin's Lamp.**

She hasn't been this cold in years. Where was it? In Gstaad that time, with Willie? He was skiing. She stayed in the bar. The Rolling Stones were on TV. Black-and-white. Some big European music contest. They sang "Satisfaction." That long ago. And where is Sam? The snow must have the streets screwed up. Can't feel my feet. I'm still here, Sam.

Watching the corner, like you said. Looking at the High Line, which I've never visited. The young guys from the paper all inside. Why'd I listen to them? Why'd I come here? An old bag like me?

Across the street, she sees homeless guys. Faceless. Bulky. Carved from black ice. Like the figures in the painting at the top of the stairs inside. Nobody can tell them to go home. What home? Some shelter that smells like piss? She thinks: At least I got whiskey in me. Too much. One more, I'm legless.

Where's Sam? He always keeps his word. Why'd I call him? To say a proper good-bye, I guess. He'll be gone in a day or two. Somewhere. Yeah. Wind coming hard now. From New Jersey. Of course. Or Siberia. Blowing snow off the High Line.

She takes out her cigarette pack. Pops one loose. Two left. Lights it with the one she's smoking. Thinks she hears sirens. Fire engines, maybe. Christ, I'm cold.

*8:49 p.m. Bobby Fonseca. Aladdin's Lamp.*

His back is to the bar. He sips a beer. Thinking: Still here. Woozy. The guys coming on to different women, using their dangling blue press cards as conversation pieces. Helen out for a smoke or something. Or maybe gone, the way Barney Weiss split after fifteen minutes in the snow. My brain mushed from the music, the deejay dressed like Ali Baba, waving his hands from the balcony. Where's his scimitar? No scimitars in Brownsville. The deejay's to the left of the VIP party. Some are leaving now, in coats, hats, and scarves. Their limos must have a foot of snow on the rooftops. Shit: here's that small broad again. Too much lipstick. Chewing gum.

—Sure you don't wanna dance, big boy?

—Not tonight. I'm in mourning, babe.

—In *this* joint?

She laughs and moves into the thick crowd. Tall women made taller by high spiked heels. Women with impossible breasts. Women giggling, bursting into tequila laughter. The guys all in heat. Some of them sweating. Others talking into female ears. Fonseca thinks: I can almost reach out and grab the lies out of the air. He hopes he can see Victoria Collins before the night is over. Flashes on her thighs. Her wet hair. The feel of her skin.

And across the room, beyond the dancers, he sees Freddie Wheeler again.

Makes Wheeler from some story he read

months ago in *Wired.* His ferrety face. Coat under his arm. Wheeler has seen Fonseca too. He starts pushing through the crowd. Heading to the left door.

Fonseca sets down his beer bottle and goes after Wheeler.

—Hey, you! he shouts in the din. *Wheeler!*

Wheeler stops as Fonseca reaches him. The two of them moving out the left door to the platform. The snow heavy. Wheeler looking at the photographers and beyond.

—What's your problem, man? Wheeler says, turning to face Fonseca. Making a sliver of his mouth.

—You, Fonseca says. And the evil crap you print each day, all of it wrong.

—I'm a reporter.

He lifts Fonseca's blue press card with thumb and forefinger. Tugs it. Face full of contempt.

—And this? This tells the world you are a fucking loser, kid. You and Briscoe and all the other—

Then Fonseca clocks him. Wheeler goes down on his back, his eyes blinking, his jaw moving.

—*Get up, you asshole!*

Fonseca's over him.

And then the black bouncer is there.

—Hey, hey, none of that shit now, he yells.

He shoves Fonseca toward the smoking deck. Flashes from cameras. Shouts. And here comes the upstairs bouncer. The fat white guy. He lifts Wheeler, swings him in a half circle, and hurls him into the crowd of camera people. Hitting bodies and heads. Umbrellas go airborne. Shouts of protest and shock. The black bouncer tries to intervene, but the white bouncer moves around him, shoves Fonseca, then grabs him by collar and ass and heaves him toward the smoking shed. Fonseca slams into Helen Loomis and she falls. The ashtray goes over too, spilling butts and sand across the deck. The snow is almost horizontal.

### 8:51 p.m. Malik Shahid. Fourteenth Street.

*Now.* He runs, slipping on the cobblestones, but not falling. A wave of photographers surges left to photograph the white dude in the crowd in the street. Still down. Trying to get up through the mass of legs. Off on the side of the platform another white guy, younger, stunned and rubbery.

Nobody pays attention to Malik.

*End* run, he thinks. *Go.*

He is up the steps, feeling stronger now than he

has ever been before. He rips away the velvet rope, toppling the minaret poles, and he reaches the doors. The right door is ajar about a foot. Leading to the dark sinful rooms. From the snowy distance, the muffled sound of a siren.

Then Malik is into the devil's workshop, into the whoring crowd, stopping, drawing the pistol from his trouser belt. Turns behind him. Kicks the door shut.

—*Stop!* Every fuckin' *one* of you! he shouts.

Malik's right arm is straight out. He rotates the .38 with a circular wrist movement, left, to the dance floor, right to the bar, then up the stairs. People at the top. Fancy clothes. Wide eyes. Turns behind him again. Seven or eight people at the doors. None of them move. All eyes on the gun. The room suddenly resembles a still photograph.

—You *move*, I *shoot* you!

He starts up the stairs. Three steps. Four. Then he opens his jacket.

In small awkward motions, he starts to unbutton his coat with his free hand, pistol still in his right. Now people are moving again. On the main floor, a tall blonde woman breaks from the frozen pack of dancers, starts across the floor, buckles, and falls hard on her hip. A shriek, cutting through the hip-hop soundtrack. Malik's coat is open.

And now they see the vest.

Taut across Malik's chest. The six red slabs of Semtex resembling soldiers at attention. The hip-hop rant keeps pounding. Punctuated by groans and weeping and another woman's shriek.

Malik thinks: I have them now. They must look at me. They must listen. I'm the last man they will hear in their filthy lives.

**8:51 p.m. Beverly Starr. The balcony of Aladdin's Lamp.**

She has her coat on, leaving with others, gloveless. Five steps down the stairs. Hears the screams. Looks down. Blinks. Sees a young black man waving a gun. Words lost in the pounding music. Turning. Gesturing. His eyes wide with rage and doom. Jesus Christ. She eases down the stairs, gripping the banister on her left. Freezes as he waves the pistol at her. Sees a jam at the door.

The young man turns so all can see what he's wearing under the coat.

Now she sees the vest across his chest. Familiar to all of them from bad television shows. A suicide vest.

The music scrapes into silence. The deejay tearing off his costume. One voice is piercing the air. The man with the vest.

—*Whores! Degenerates!* Listen *up!*

He shoves the gun in his belt. Now he's addressing the people on the dance floor. Maybe sixty of them. Men. Women. All of them frozen. As if blood and sweat are both coagulating. Some cowering, trying to make themselves smaller.

—*You have filled this world with filth and sin!* You have sent soldiers to Muslim countries, and killed Muslim *men,* and Muslim *women,* and Muslim *children!*

Beverly moves. Passes behind the man as he addresses the dance-floor people. She eases past a heavyset older man. A guest from the benefit. Heads for the crowd jammed against the doors. The doors open in, not out. Pushes into the crowd. Looks back at the stairs. Sees the enraged eyes of the gunman. His audience is not giving him what he has demanded: their attention. He's talking but she hears no words. She's shoved by the deejay, then turned sideways by a guy in a business suit. Smells sweat and perfume. Rush hour in hell. A chorus of shrieks. Jesus Christ: I could die here.

She takes a ballpoint pen from her pocket. Thinking: Not much of a weapon, but I could hurt somebody.

Beverly looks back. The young man on the stairs is holding a small object in his hand. A wire runs into the suicide vest. She knows what that is too. A detonator. Right out of *24*. Out of fucking comic books.

*—You have been offered Paradise, and refused it!*

Beverly sees a long-haired blond guy vault over the banister of the staircase, fall hard on one leg, pause and grimace in pain, then limp forward. To join the pack at the doors. A blink.

*—Allah has given you life and he will soon give you death!*

The jam tighter now, all breathing hard, panting, cursing. Shouts of *move, move* and *step back, let it fuckin' open!* The doors forced shut by the pressing weight of the panicky group. To Beverly's right, a small young woman leaps onto the shoulders of a shouting man, trying to claw her way over people's shoulders, heading to escape. Then slips. Falls facedown, wedged between a fat woman and a beefy man. Beverly blinks again. Record this. So if you get out...The goal for all of them is the twin vertical rectangles of the glass-paneled doors. And the snow falling beyond. She looks back. At the top of the stairs, her painting stands on its easel, abandoned, alone.

Thinking: I am about to die.

### 8:51 p.m. Sam Briscoe. Fourteenth Street.

Briscoe's taxi turns into the street and suddenly stops. Twenty feet ahead of them, four police cars have skidded on the cobblestones, then braked, red domes now turning. Cops out. Some fumbling under overcoats for sidearms. Briscoe asks the driver to wait, and the driver says, No, no, *police!* Trouble! Briscoe hands him a twenty-dollar bill and gets out, slamming the door. In the distance, he sees a chaotic, panicky tide of women and men squeezing one at a time out of one of the doors of Aladdin's Lamp. Then down the steps in a kind of stampede. Night of the locust. None are dressed for snow. No time for coats. He sees the right door open a bit wider. Hears the word "bomb."

He hurries to them while some rush past him toward Ninth Avenue. A gray-haired hatless guy in a suit hauls his wife across cobblestones. The man glancing behind him. Fear in his eyes. The woman yelling: My coat, my *coat!*

All that Briscoe sees is happening at once. Women in filmy blouses, short skirts, high heels. Men in sweaters and shirts. A woman slips coming down the steps from the platform. Falls backward. A young man stomps on her to get by, and then he loses balance and pitches forward, facedown on the iced cobblestones, and another man stomps on his back and keeps going. One lone woman, about twenty, earrings large and bobbing, totters toward Briscoe, seeing nothing, weeping, holding a bleeding elbow. The others resemble terrified civilians after a bombardment. They slip, fall, pile up. Throats are stabbed by heels. A heavy boot lacerates a young man's lips. Upper and lower.

Briscoe sees blood on others, torn flesh. Discarded women's shoes on the wet stone street. A young woman grabs another's blouse from behind, tears it away, and the woman begins bawling as she covers her breasts. Naked in a snowstorm. Then drops her hands to run. More piling up, nobody looking back. Dozens now. Screaming. Splayed, stomped, bleeding. One hopeless shriek. A bare-chested guy in Ali Baba trousers comes out the door, limping. Too thin to be a bouncer. Maybe a deejay? A waiter? Shaking both fists. In triumph? Or challenging the fallen. Photographers dart around, recording it all.

Helen, Briscoe thinks. Where are you, Helen?

Now four uniformed cops come running awkwardly from the police cars. No traction on the snowy cobblestones. Guns drawn. One goes up the steps to the doors, shoves the gun into his holster, raises one palm toward the people inside, ordering them to halt, to step back, to allow both doors to open. They don't obey. Looking over their shoulders. Below the platform, another cop points to the far side of the street, gesturing east. Briscoe hears the first cop shout: *Run. Run like hell!*

Briscoe drapes his press card around his neck and finally sees Helen Loomis over to the left, on the platform rising from the sidewalk. Standing there. Rigid, dazed, as the panicky young tide flows past her. She fumbles with a cigarette, looking toward the High Line. Briscoe calls her name but she can't hear him in the din. No way yet for him to get up the main stairs to her. Too many people coming down in terrified flight from whatever the hell is happening inside.

He goes to the left, trying to squeeze through the photographers, sees Fonseca making notes at the foot of the smoking shed, wiping with his coat sleeve at blood dripping from his nose. Briscoe calls his name. Fonseca hears nothing. And Briscoe can't reach him through the wall of cops and photographers. Moving now, like a quarterback, left, then right, then forward. Looking for an opening. He waves at Helen, calls her name, but she doesn't see or hear him. She is still staring toward the High Line. Washington Street. Briscoe thinks: She's waiting for me. I told her Washington Street, didn't I? The cabbie wouldn't go that way. A woman wearing pearls comes down the main stairs and someone grabs at the pearls and the string snaps. The woman looks down, pain on her face, starts to bend, then chooses to run. Briscoe shouts once more. Nobody can hear.

### 8:51 p.m. Ali Watson. Fourteenth Street.

Ali walks cautiously on the cobblestones, his eyes fixed on the doors. Alone. Wearing his badge. His gun hanging loose in his right hand. No time for vengeance, he thinks. This is my son. I loved him as a boy and I love him still. Done in by belief. The worst human disease. Only one goal right now: to stop horror. That's my fucking job. To prevent another Happy Land. Knowing that if he lives, this night will be with him for the rest of his days. And nights.

Behind him, Malachy and some uniformed cops are checking the people against the wall across the street. Homeless guys. Wanding them. Patting them down. Then, finding nothing, telling them to get the hell out of there, this thing could blow. Some move quickly. Others are slower, watching the show.

Ali goes up the steps two at a time, and the

uniformed cops greet him. The right-hand door is now fully open. He asks a sergeant where the SWAT team is. On the way. No time, Ali says. I'm going in. Cover my back.

Then Ali is inside. A dozen men and women are huddled against the far edge of the empty dance floor. Faces frozen. Others peering from behind the bar. Maybe more upstairs, hiding in bathrooms or lounges. Son of a bitch.

He looks up the stairs and sees his son near the top. Malik.

The only person who matters now.

Eyes wide. The suicide belt across his chest. Red Semtex. His lips are saying words, full of reverence and farewell.

*Salem al-Hazmi.*
*Hani Hanjour.*
*Satam al-Suqami* . . .

In his right hand, the detonator. Thumb on the button.

—Put that thing down. *Malik,* Ali says in a soft voice.

*Waleed al-Shehri.*
*Abdulaziz al-Omari.*

He is staring now at Ali, his voice rising in defiance as he recites the names of the September 11 hijackers.

—Malik, don't do this.

—Who are *you* to tell me what to do?

—I'm your father. I still love you, son.

—My *so-called* father.

—No, your only father.

Ali raises his .38 and aims it at his son. Thinking: Don't hit a Semtex charge.

*Hamza al-Ghamdi.*
*Mohand al-Shehri.*

Malik is breathing more heavily now, coming to the end of his private rosary. His eyes are calmer. Then he laughs.

—One more, Malik says. God's commander.

Before he can say "Mohamed Atta," Ali fires.

Malik looks frozen. There's a small hole in his forehead. His eyes are wide. Then he crumples, falling down the stairs like a mannequin. His head hits several steps. His hands are open and still and empty.

Ali Watson exhales. So does the room. Malik is not moving. His open eyes see nothing and Ali knows that he is dead.

He walks over to Malik, looks down at his face. No longer masked with a thick beard. The face of his son, whom he often had bounced on his knee. Bright blood is leaking from his brow, running to the side of his nose, down his cheeks. Ali sits on a step, and drapes an arm over Malik's shoulder, hugs him tightly, feeling his vanishing warmth. Tears fill Ali's eyes.

He whispers: Oh, Mary Lou. I am so goddamned sorry.

### 8:54 p.m. Sam Briscoe. Fourteenth Street.

At the foot of the whitening staircase to the smoking area, he raises a hand to Helen Loomis and she takes it, coming down one step at a time. She's unsteady. The side of her left cheek is scraped. Her eyes are blurry. He hugs her. She has heard the same sound. A single *blam*. Like a punctuation mark. Then silence. Then the uniformed cops relax. Opening both doors wide now.

–That's that, Sam whispers. The snow is finer now and icier, blowing harder.

Now firemen in full gear are at the scene. The SWAT team has arrived, looking frustrated in dark blue combat gear as the sergeant waves to them that it's over. Plainclothes cops are talking to the people now leaving, most wearing coats, witnesses now, showing identification. Some of them are weeping. Briscoe saw Ali Watson go in. He has not seen him come out. Most of the paparazzi have fled, to send out what they captured on their cameras, but a few remain, and reporters are arriving from other papers. Fonseca comes over to Briscoe, glancing at his watch, making notes in a spiral pad.

–Stick around, Briscoe says. This isn't over.

–I know, Mr. Briscoe. Did you see the guy who ran in?

–No.

–Neither did I. I was flat on my ass. But one of the cops told me he might have been wearing a suicide vest. I *did* see the cop that went in to get him. The cop that must've shot him. It was Ali Watson.

–The kid with the vest might be his son, Malik…

–Jesus Christ.

–Check it out. Even a website needs wood.

Briscoe taps Fonseca lightly on the shoulder, then leads Helen to the street. He sees three cops near the far wall. Four photographers are shooting in a kind of frenzy, leaning in, squatting, aiming at something on the wet sidewalk, while a young plainclothes cop tries to control them. Briscoe moves past them slowly, guiding Helen by the elbow. They are looking down at a gun. To Briscoe, it appears to be a MAC-10. The contras loved it in Nicaragua. So did the crack dealers here at home. Maybe there was an accomplice? Nobody touches the MAC-10, not even a cop. Briscoe looks back at the rubble of shoes, hats, torn or discarded clothes, a handbag. No sign of Fonseca. He should see this. Maybe they let him inside.

He and Helen start walking east. The snow is thicker now.

—Sam, we'll never get a cab around here.

—We gotta try.

—We could both end up in St. Vincent's.

—Eventually. Not tonight.

The snow keeps falling. Helen Loomis starts to shudder, then shake, as if ice has pierced her body. Briscoe hugs her, until the shaking stops. She grips his arm and they resume walking. Across the street, mannequins in bikinis pose in the bright window of a place called La Perla. They pass the dark shop of the Ground Zero Museum Workshop. Briscoe looks back and sees photographers and TV cameramen shooting from the rails of the High Line. Two different TV guys are doing stand-ups. He sees signs on the street now:

Lofts For Lease

And

Retail Space
Made To Measure

Lights still burn in clothing stores. Hugo Boss. Moschino. No customers are gazing at the clothes. At the corner of Ninth Avenue, there are some people in the Apple store. Briscoe thinks: I should be calling in notes to the city desk. Helen should be taking them for tomorrow's paper. Instead, we are here on a night of brutality, escaping like lost members of Napoleon's army, Moscow behind us. Looking for a taxi.

Two ambulances from St. Vincent's go by, making a slow throaty sound in the wet snow, followed by a vehicle from the fire department rescue squad. Each heading west. Into the snow. Briscoe and Helen cross Ninth Avenue to a small triangle of a park, the benches piling with snow. Across the street to the left is the Old Homestead Steakhouse, where there were usually cabs, even in snowstorms. But Briscoe can see whirling dome lights two blocks uptown, just past the Chelsea Market, sealing the avenue from any new traffic. There are no cabs arriving at the Old Homestead or waiting to depart. A car with NYP press plates turns into 14th Street, and the unseen driver taps the horn in greeting but keeps moving past them to Aladdin's Lamp.

—I wish I could write tonight, Helen Loomis says in a sad blurred voice.

—You will. In your memoirs.

She chuckles. Then from 15th Street, a car turns, and a uniformed cop wearing an orange vest uses his club to point it downtown. The car moves slowly past the Old Homestead, aimed at 14th Street and what becomes Hudson Street on the far side. Briscoe steps out of the park, Helen behind him. The car slows, then stops on the far curb, the engine still pumping exhaust fumes into the falling snow.

—Christ, Helen, I hope these aren't folks from "Vics and Dicks."

—My people.

A young woman steps out of the back door. There are other people in the car, which has snow gathered on its hood and roof.

—Helen! Hey, Helen, it's *me,* Janice!

Helen squints hard, then relaxes.

—It's the woman who loaned me the cell phone, she says.

The young woman shouts, Where you going?

–Second Avenue and Ninth Street, Briscoe shouts.

–Come on! Janice shouts. We have room for one more.

Janice waddles awkwardly across the snow in a lumpy way to Helen, takes her arm.

–Go, Briscoe says. I can walk to the subway.

–I can't leave you here alone, Sam.

–I'll be fine, Briscoe says. Go.

Helen allows herself to be pulled to the open door of the car, where he can see the heads and blurred faces of others, packed tightly. Helen is shoved in by Janice, who follows her, and slams the door.

–Go, Briscoe whispers.

He waits until the car pulls away, crossing 14th Street, moving into Hudson Street, becoming two more dirty red eyes in the snow. Briscoe stands there for a long moment.


*9:10 p.m. Beverly Starr. Pastis restaurant, Meatpacking District, Manhattan.*


She is at the bar in the crowded restaurant. Waiting for the guy from the car service. Some streets blocked. Sipping a tequila and tonic. Her heart still beating fast. Her right cheek is scraped, and she pats it with a cloth napkin soaked in peroxide that the maitre d' brought her. Other refugees from the benefit are at various tables, faces somber with a kind of blankness. She thinks: Post-traumatic stress disorder? They are whispering. Holding hands. Waiting for something that is not food.

She stares at her drink, closes her eyes. Sees her own slide show. A woman's snapped ankle flopping like a sock. A gaping older man who has lost his front teeth. A fat guy in an Ali Baba suit falling back under a high-heeled stampede. Opens her eyes. Snow still falling.

This is the kind of night when I need some guy to hold me. To whisper to me. To tell me that everything's gonna be all right.

Then smiles, and wonders who won the auction.

### 9:11 p.m. Sam Briscoe. Fourteenth Street.

He crosses the wide street to the downtown side, and begins to walk east, toward Eighth Avenue, where he can find a subway. The A or the C. He looks up at the buildings. Lights are burning in about half of them, with the shades drawn. Others are shadeless, windows on the storm. He sees one woman alone, watching the street, not moving. In another, there is diffused light from a television set. On the street, a lone woman walks a small dog. He steps around a Mega Millions sign, with a printed image of a man peering from behind the day's prize. His face is hidden, but his hairline recedes. Can it be Rudy Giuliani?

He slows now. His feet in their socks and boots are losing feeling. His gloved hands are numb. He imagines Helen Loomis in her apartment now. Or soon. Warming. Smoking a good-night cigarette. He wonders if her friend Federico the mambo dancer is across the street, moving to Tito Puente while the snow falls harder. He hopes so. He imagines Matt Logan, at home with his wife, wondering whether he can handle the brave new *World* of a website. Of course he can. News is news.

Maybe Fonseca will file for the site tomorrow. Maybe he can talk to Ali Watson before the snow stops falling. Or do a portrait of the guy he shot. Whoever the hell he was. The best story? It's his nutjob son. And he can be traced to Patchin Place. But maybe they don't connect. Maybe he's just a pissed-off former employee. Some neighbor says the music was too loud? An architecture critic?

Who the hell knows? Maybe Fonseca will discover the guy had a co-conspirator, a backup, the one who dropped that MAC-10. Or discover what was most likely: the guy was alone. The story now is that one night after his wife was murdered, Ali Watson killed a guy in the line of duty. Those are the known facts. So far. No theories, please.

The dead guy will soon be on a slab somewhere. Maybe even in the same freezing morgue as Mary Lou Watson. And Cynthia.

Cynthia.

I could not pray for her down at Patchin Place, Briscoe thinks. Backed up to the library fence twenty feet from Sandra Gordon, seeing the grief in Ali Watson's eyes. And here I am in front of Nuestra Señora de Guadalupe. When Briscoe was young, it was called St. Bernard's. The gate is open. He looks up the wet stone stairs at the red church doors. A light is burning above the arch. He starts up, then pauses. One door opens, and an older Mexican woman emerges, pulls her zipper to the top of her coat, buries her jaw in her scarf. He goes up a few more steps. She nods in a welcoming way. He goes to the top. He opens the red door and goes in.

### 9:15 p.m. Sandra Gordon. Her apartment.

The local news from New York 1 is on the set in her study. For possible news about Myles. The sound is off. She sits in an armchair, nibbling salted almonds, sipping a beer. Then she sees pictures of Aladdin's Lamp, police cars, panicky crowds, a woman reporter with a microphone. She turns on the sound.

*...possible terrorist attack. At least one alleged terrorist is dead. Scores were injured fleeing the scene, when the armed terrorist displayed a suicide vest in the crowded club. Police say...*

That's the place Janice wanted me to go to! Yes. Is she okay? Did she get hurt? Where the hell is she? A terrorist attack? On a disco? Makes no sense.

Then the anchorman is on. Making a clumsy segue. *Meanwhile, the investigation of the murders in Greenwich Village of...* She clicks off the sound and looks away, sips the beer, gets up, walks to a window to watch the driving snow. She counts to fifty and turns to the set. The anchorman again. Then a head shot of Myles! A kind of mug shot, without numbers underneath. Flicks on sound. *Police in Putnam County believe they have found the body of a Wall Street man who failed to show up at a*

*federal grand jury today. The man: Myles Compton.
The body was found by two snowboarders. The man
was shot twice in the head. Federal investigators had
no comment but—*

She turns off the set.

Sits there in silence.

Thinking: God, I'm too old for this.

Refusing to shed even one more tear.

### 9:16 p.m. Sam Briscoe. Our Lady of Guadalupe, 14th Street.

There is no Mass under way, but the lights are
shining. He has slipped into a pew in the rear. The
familiar image of the Lady of Guadalupe is high
on the altar, her dark Indian skin a sign of triumphant consolation, with some kind of painted blue
stream spreading beneath her. He has seen her in
many places. In Mexico, above all. In the old Mexico City cathedral where pilgrims come each
December to celebrate her goodness, hundreds
doing the last few miles on their knees, to leave
painted tin *retablos* asking for her intercession.
The lights in this church do not burn now at full
strength, except on the Virgin herself. Green-
painted pillars rise to the high dark ceiling. But
Briscoe can see people scattered through the pews.

Everyone is alone. No couples. No mothers and children. Few men at all. Up near the front on the right, there's someone in a wheelchair. Out in the aisle. To the right and left of the altar, candles burn in rows, and one older woman goes up and drops a coin in a slot and lights a fresh one.

Briscoe is certain he can smell the burning wax. Even here, far from the altar. He considers lighting some candles of his own. For Cynthia and Mary Lou. Of course. But for Ali Watson too. For Sandra. For her asshole boyfriend. For all the others, in those solitary rooms above the streets. For women scrubbing offices until the midnight hour. For baffled junkies in doorways. For my long-dead wife. For everyone at the paper. For the Fonseca kid, who thought he'd wear the same press card for years, and now... For all of them. People of the night.

He hears the elegance of Gregorian chant seeping into the dark places of the church, imposing grace and order out of the past. A CD, for sure. Briscoe thinks: Maybe we could bury Cynthia out of this place.

Maybe.

She would like that.

Briscoe tries again to pray. Once more, the words won't come. And he can't convince himself to walk up to the rack of guttering candles. He stands and hurries back to the doors. The cold hits him hard. He shudders, moves his hands like a prizefighter, snorts. Then goes down a shoveled path on the steps. He starts walking east, into the snow-drowned city. The wind is at his back.

**Pete Hamill** is a novelist, journalist, editor, and screenwriter. He is the author of twenty previous books, including the best selling novels *Forever* and *Snow in August* and the bestselling memoir *A Drinking Life*. He lives in New York City.